D1014679

THE SIGNAL FLAME

This Large Print Book carries the
Seal of Approval of N.A.V.H.

THE SIGNAL FLAME

ANDREW KRIVÁK

THORNDIKE PRESS
A part of Gale, Cengage Learning

GALE
CENGAGE Learning·

Farmington Hills, Mich • San Francisco • New York • Waterville, Maine
Meriden, Conn • Mason, Ohio • Chicago

GALE
CENGAGE Learning·

Copyright © 2017 by Andrew Krivák.
Thorndike Press, a part of Gale, Cengage Learning.

Thorndike Press® Large Print Bill's Bookshelf.
The text of this Large Print edition is unabridged.
Other aspects of the book may vary from the original edition.
Set in 16 pt. Plantin.

LIBRARY OF CONGRESS CATALOGING-IN-PUBLICATION DATA
Names: Krivák, Andrew, author. Title: The signal flame / Andrew Krivák. Description: Large print edition. | Waterville, Maine : Thorndike Press, a part of Gale, Cengage Learning, 2017. | Series: Thorndike Press large print Bill's bookshelf Identifiers: LCCN 2017004001| ISBN 9781410499288 (hardcover) | ISBN 1410499286 (hardcover) Subjects: LCSH: Large type books. | BISAC: FICTION / Literary. | FICTION / Historical. | HISTORY / United States / General. Classification: LCC PS3561.R569 S57 2017b | DDC 813/.54—dc23 LC record available at https://lccn.loc.gov/2017004001

Published in 2017 by arrangement with Scribner, an imprint of Simon & Schuster, Inc.

Printed in Mexico
1 2 3 4 5 6 7 21 20 19 18 17

For my father and my brothers

So now I am still awatch
for the signal-flame,
the gleaming fire that is to
harbinger news from Troy . . .
— AESCHYLUS, *Agamemnon*

For three generations they were drawn from water, made fatherless, or orphaned altogether, though there was no augury, blind prophet, or star that told of their fates. Each was raised to be disciplined and just. If there were books, they were well read. They passed down their own history by word of mouth. They were not inclined to speak of spiritual matters, but they believed that God had blessed them, for much had been made of what had been put into their hands, and not one would have said that it was his hands alone that had made it. What they shared were the wars. The wars of emperors, presidents, revolutionaries, fights to which men have always gone to fight, for an ideal, for a homeland, for a people. These were the truths that bound the family to each other and the land to which they returned when the fighting was done. But for one.

■ ■ ■ ■

PART 1
THE INHERITORS
OF LOSS

■ ■ ■ ■

CHAPTER ONE

A fire in the great stone fireplace was as constant in the house as the lengthening days when Easter was early and spring was late. But on the morning after his grandfather died, Bo Konar took the logs and the log rack in the living room out to the barn, swept the bricks clean of ash, and dusted the andirons so that they looked like thin faceless centaurs of black. Two days later, after supper, he and his mother, Hannah, greeted mourners at the door and led them from the foyer into the living room, where each knelt before the body of the man waked in a pine casket by the window, and said a prayer. Some lingered then in the kitchen and the wide hallway to talk about Jozef Vinich. How he had come to America after World War I with fifty dollars in his pocket, after the gold his father had left him paid for the train from Kassa to Hamburg and passage on the *Mount Clay*. How he had

13

risen from yard worker to co-owner of the Endless Roughing Mill. How he had acquired and managed two thousand acres of the most sought-after land in Dardan. How he had built the house where they all stood before he had turned thirty, something few men in that corner of northeastern Pennsylvania could have done.

No one stayed long. After Father Rovnávaha said the vigil prayers for the deceased, everyone in that room got up to leave, even the priest, and Bo sat alone in the lamplight on a straight-backed chair. Freezing rain rapped outside against the window glass. The old Lab they called Krasna snuffed and sighed on the floor. Bo hunched forward with his elbows on his knees and stared at his grandfather, dressed in a white shirt, blue suit, and a black tie Bo had never seen before. The face dull and wax-set. The misshapen right hand on top of the left at the breast. That one holding a string of wooden rosary beads. And he wondered why he and his great-aunt Sue would have to take turns sitting up all night with the body, because there was not a chance in hell that this man might just be asleep.

Where did you go? he whispered into the room.

He heard the sound of running water

coming from the kitchen and a sharp note of breaking glass, and the memory rose to him through the fatigue, a memory of the evening when his grandfather told him (a boy of ten then) to go on upstairs and get some sleep. It was spring. The cold spring that came after his father had died in what they said was a hunting accident, though his father was never a hunter. The meal over, light still hanging in the west outside, Bo asked why he had to go to bed so early.

Because we're going up to the high meadow with rifles in the morning, his grandfather said.

Bo's mother was rinsing dishes, and out of the corner of his eye he saw the glass she was holding slip from her hand, heard the sound of it shattering against the porcelain sink. Jozef looked over at his daughter, who shook her head as if to say, *Please, no.* Then back to Bo.

It's time you came with me, Jozef said.

They were up before dawn. There was toast and coffee set out, but his mother was not in the kitchen. His grandfather took the Marlin three-thirty-six and a Remington twenty-two out of the gun cabinet, and Bo thought of his father. His mother said that he had fought in the war in Europe, and the boy wondered if somewhere there might still be war, if it might have come to Dardan. His grandfather handed Bo the twenty-two. He held the rifle by the forestock, checked the safety, and said, Are we going to war?

Jozef stopped and stared at him. No, son, he said.

Bo looked down at the floor, and Jozef said, We're going into the woods to find a dog that has taken a liking to deer. That's all.

Outside they walked past the coop where they kept Duna, a Lab and collie mix, who pushed her nose into Bo's gloved hand. He wanted to ask if she was coming with them, but his grandfather did not slow, so he put his head down and followed. Through the orchard, past the horse paddock, into the woods, the fallen limbs and frozen, hard-packed leaves sounding like thunder beneath them, until they found the old trappers' path and walked along the hard dirt, Bo wondering if he would see anything else for the rest of his life but the creased and faded patterns of brown that tracked like roads on a map in the canvas coat on his grandfather's back.

They came through trees to the edge of the open field, where a silver horizon met silver grass bent down with frost and spread out flat before them. A farmhouse and barn stood at the distant edge of that field, and Bo wanted to ask who lived there, but he did not. His grandfather sat down on a large rock and levered a single round into the Marlin. Bo sat down next to him and moved his hands and feet to keep warm. They waited a long time, until the sun was bright and round above the horizon in the east, when his grandfather put a finger to his lips and pointed in the direction of where a doe had emerged from the trees. He slipped off his mittens, got down on one knee, and brought the rifle to his shoulder. Bo followed the sight line of the barrel and saw that it was aimed not at the doe but at the low-slung figure of a dog like no dog he had ever seen, sleek and hunched and twitching at the far end of the field. He looked at his grandfather, as frozen as the grass, then back at the dog just as it leaped. The rifle cracked and the animal arced back in one round motion, and Bo felt his bowels loosen, the warm spreading around him where he sat. He stood up fast, dropped the twenty-two, and ran.

He did not stop until he had gotten to the farm and collapsed by the dog coop. Duna wandered over on her rope and began to lick the back of his neck, and Bo heard someone coming out of the woods. *How could he move so fast,* he thought, and never thought that again. Bo turned and tried to get up but lay there on his back staring into the sky and sun. He blinked and the sun was eclipsed by a hat. He waited for his grandfather to kick him and tell him he would never touch one of his rifles again, but Jozef reached out his hand and said, C'mon. Let's get you cleaned up. Bo took it, stood, and walked with him through the orchard back to the house.

In the cold living room, remembering that day, Bo leaned forward in the chair and dug his palms into his eyes and rose. Krasna's ears pricked and she got to her feet, and they walked into the foyer and down the hall into the kitchen, where Bo could hear the muffled roar of flames beneath the iron top of the Pittston and feel the heat as he approached its verge. He took off the wool suit coat he had worn since supper and draped it over a coat rack by the door and sat down at a pale and simple table he had made with his grandfather out of beech felled on their land. He ran his hand across the surface of it as if to feel what he could of those days when he first brought the table into the kitchen and his grandfather touched the surface of it in the same way, and said,

Well, son, I do believe you have found your work.

Hannah shut off the faucet and dried her hands on an apron tied around her waist and walked over to the table. Her right forefinger was wrapped with tissue paper and tape and sticking up like a tiny flag post, and she stood not as though she was about to sit but as though she had just risen and stopped for a moment to listen to the unsyncopated ticks of the stove against the regular seconds of the wall clock. She lifted her head and pushed her hair out of her eyes with her left hand and took off the apron.

Are you hungry? she asked.

A little, he said.

She went over to the counter and returned with a plate of kielbasa and nut roll and placed it in front of him with a knife and fork, then reached into the refrigerator for a bottle of beer, pried off the cap with a church key, and put the bottle next to the plate.

Go on, she said, and sat down across from him.

She was nineteen when she became a mother for the first time in February '41, three days before her husband left for basic training. (He would see his son Bohumír as

19

a baby one more time, in April of that year, before he went overseas.) She looked no different at fifty. Round face set off by high cheekbones. Hair long and flax. Eyes a deep and pupil-less gray. The kind of eyes that make people either stare or look away.

Bo halved a round of the kielbasa and ate and followed it with a swig of beer. He took two more mouthfuls and laid the utensils on the side of the plate. He pointed to her finger. Is it bad?

Just some glass. I'll be fine.

He pulled the plate with the nut roll on it toward him and finished the slice in four bites, dusted his fingertips, and wiped his mouth on a napkin.

Is Aunt Sue going to want a turn at the casket tonight?

I don't know, Bo. She's asleep upstairs.

He watched her eyes move from the clock to the unlit hallway, then back to his plate. Have you had enough? she asked.

Yes, he said.

She stood and kept her hand flat on the table as she rose, her body bent toward it like she was listening still. She took the plate and placed it on the counter and turned back to her son.

Will you walk me past the living room?

He took her arm and pushed in the chair

and they moved down the hallway to the foyer. At the foot of the staircase she reached for the newel post, paused, and said, Let Aunt Sue rest. You stay with him. As long as you can, at least.

He nodded and she whispered, Thank you, and walked up the stairs with her hand leading along the banister.

He woke stiff and aching and stood up straight and stretched his legs. It was still dark, and he went into the kitchen and turned on the overhead light above the sink. He rinsed his face and mouth and toweled himself dry, then filled the percolator with water and coffee and plugged it into the wall. He opened the lid on the stove and put paper, kindling, and a quarter-split birch on the coals in the firebox of the Pittston, slid the draft, and waited for the wood to catch. Krasna was lying in her bed by the door. He took his hat and blanket-lined coat from a hook and called her. She looked in the direction of the living room and thumped her tail on the floor.

I told you, he said. He's not coming with us. Not anymore.

Outside, the rain and sleet had stopped and he could see the sky clearing in patches as the morning came on. He turned his collar up and they walked single file through the orchard, he and the dog, the branches of the trees bare but for the rime that covered them, and he shook his head at the fruit that would be lost if there was another night as cold as last night.

Inside the barn he flipped a light switch and moved in the direction of the stalls. Krasna circled and slumped onto a straw mat in the corner. They had always had goats. Two, sometimes three does they bred for the milk and to sell the kids. When he was a boy, Bo milked them twice a day. Then the job went to his brother, Sam. And then they were sold. Now only the cow was left, a small Jersey his grandfather used to call Miss Wayne. She had not given milk in a long time, but no one wanted to get rid of her. Bo patted her spine and dropped feed into a trough, and she lowed softly and set to eating. He looked around at the empty stalls and saw the window that had been broken in an ice storm that winter and boarded up, and he reminded himself to get to the hardware store for a new pane of glass. Then he whistled to Krasna and went into the chicken coop, where the Barred Rocks cackled and rose when they saw the dog, then settled and began to peck at the scratch he threw to them. He had made his own waterer the summer before, when they reduced the flock to five. It was a number ten plastic bucket with holes punched near the brim, placed upside down in a round cake pan. He turned it over and poured fresh water from a spigot into the bucket, then placed it back in the pan. He found four eggs in three of the nest boxes and put them gently in his pockets and went back outside.

Hannah was awake and cooking bacon in a skillet when he and Krasna came in by the back door.

Any of those hens lay? she asked.

All of them except Celeste and Renée.

Her eyes were streaked with red and she sniffed. Renée will come along. She's not spent yet.

Do you remember when there used to be a farm around here? he said, and placed the eggs on the sideboard.

I remember. I was thinking just the other day that we ought to bring that flock back up to twelve. Maybe I'll go out to see Virgil in May and get some new chicks.

She turned back to the skillet, and he hung up his coat and washed his hands in the sink, then walked over to the window and looked out and studied the orchard in the light.

The trees were always the first thing his grandfather spoke of in the morning, weaving a forecast for the day based on the curve of leaves or a bird he might see nesting in the branches. Or he would tell a story that began with the planting of a particular sapling, like the cherry he had bought from one of the truckers who brought timber to the mill and had its root pack bound in burlap and sitting on the front seat of his rig like a passenger, a gift bestowed on him by a crazy old hermit in Wellsboro in exchange for some cigarette tobacco. Jozef gave the man two dollars for it and planted the tree (he told Bo when the boy set to it with his Morseth knife and carved BK in the trunk) when the house was a bare frame of two-by-fours, the earth around it overturned and strewn with rocks and stumps and roots. He had painted in his mind a picture of that tree in bloom at the head of the drive, paving stones winding around it, right to the steps of the front porch. Then came some peach and pear, and soon an entire orchard of apple trees, so that the men who helped him finish the house (men who ferried inside the framing boards, pipes for the plumbing, brick for the chimney and fireplace, plaster and lath for the walls, and hauled up on scaffolding the roof slates and siding shingles) had to be careful not to damage the young trees as they passed, which became a growing design to the northeast and southwest of the terraced land on which the house rose. They would joke in his presence and say that Mr. Vinich had set out to grow an orchard, then decided to build a mansion on it. He never saw it as a mansion, though. Just a good house. The elevation that rose up out of the Salamander Creek Valley was called Rock Mountain for a reason, and had been since the town of Dardan was settled. Jozef Vinich, who grew up in the Carpathian Mountains, built his home in the manner of the nineteenth-century barons of lumber and coal in that part of Pennsylvania. He put what stones the forests and fields around him would give to the foundation, and brought in the rest. And when it was built, it was built so that it would not move, not for generations. Not for any reason other than time's inevitable decay.

Bo said, Just the other day I saw a hawk in the tree at the edge of the Cortlands'. Sitting up there like a weather vane.

I'll have to be careful to watch the chickens when I let them out, Hannah said.

I was thinking that ought to take care of the moles in the orchard, Bo said. But there won't be much fruit on those trees if we get another cold snap.

Hannah brought the skillet from the stove and plated the eggs. Those trees have gotten more care than the two of us put together, she said. They'll bear. Now sit down and eat.

Father Tomáš Rovnávaha arrived at the house on the mountain at a quarter to nine in his old International Scout. They met him at the door, and he hugged Hannah and took Bo's hand in both of his and asked if he had slept. Bo said that he had managed what he could.

Rovnávaha nodded slowly and looked down at the floor, then back up at Hannah, and said, Well, shall we?

He was tall and broad-shouldered, the priest, Like an oak, Jozef Vinich had said to him when they first met, and that was what he called the priest in moments when the older man thought it was appropriate. Oakes. His deep black widow's peak and well-trimmed beard had gone silver before his hair, so his face seemed framed by an argent glow. His parents had come to Pennsylvania when the Austro-Hungarian empire collapsed. Professor Rovnávaha taught Greek and Latin to students at the Jesuit

University in Scranton. Mrs. Rovnávaha taught piano at their home in the Hill Section. But there was a war on when young Tomáš graduated from high school in '43. He joined the First Infantry, landed at Normandy, and fought across France and into Germany and Czechoslovakia, frostbite in the left foot his only accountable wound. When he came home, he went to the University of Pennsylvania on the GI Bill to study philosophy, and in 1950 he entered the diocesan seminary. A late vocation, they called it. St. Michael's in Dardan was his first assignment as an assistant to the pastor, Father Blok. Tomáš Rovnávaha spoke Slovak to Jozef Vinich when they were introduced, because the man's voice reminded the young priest of his own father, and Jozef invited him to dinner at the house, where they talked into the night, and the friendship was sealed with an invitation for the priest to come trout fishing on the stretch of the Upper Salamander that ran through the northwestern corner of the Vinich land.

Bo sat in the kitchen while the priest and his mother and his great-aunt prayed in the living room, and he tried not to listen to the antiphonal drone of decades from the rosary as they drifted on the morning down the hall. He freshened his coffee and pulled a copy of *Time* magazine out from underneath a stack of mail that had come at the beginning of the week. On the cover was a photograph of an American serviceman (the magazine logo looking like it was caught inside the man's helmet band) and words to the lower right in yellow that read VIET NAM: THE BIG TEST. When Sam left on his first tour, Bo watched the news and read the magazine weekly, expecting to catch a glimpse of his brother through some photographer's eye. He told Sam this when he saw him thirteen months later, and Sam laughed and said, Not a chance, brother. Not a chance. And the night they drank their grandfather's good whiskey because Sam was going back for a second tour, he said to Bo, Don't look for me this time, all right? It's bad luck.

It was Rovnávaha's voice alone that rose up and out of the living room, the man sounding as though he could command the dead themselves to walk, and Bo remembered the day six months ago when the priest came to the house with the marine casualty assistance officer who told them that Corporal Samuel B. Konar had been reported missing in action in the province of Quang Tri. Bo watched his mother steel herself in the captain's presence, then break down when he left, wondering out loud how that news could feel worse than the news she had always feared the marine on her doorstep would bring. Rovnávaha stayed and prayed with her then, too, and when he began to read a passage from First Samuel (*You asked the Lord for him*), Jozef and Bo went out to the wood shop and closed the door and Jozef said, He's a good priest, Rovnávaha. You know that. Bo nodded and the two men sat there in their own silence among the tools and saws and scraps of wood.

The phone rang in the house and the praying ceased and Bo heard Hannah walk into the foyer to answer it.

It can't be late, she said after a pause. The funeral starts at ten. Her voice rose. Just get that car up to this house.

Bo heard the priest.

Stan. Rovnávaha here. What's the problem?

They were all moving now, and Bo knew that it was time.

Then send that one, Rovnávaha said. We're not going far.

They came back into the kitchen, Hannah shaking her head and saying, I've always hated that place. Used to be a movie theater. They ought to make it one again.

She went over to the counter and tried to pour her own coffee and spilled it. She cursed and apologized and reached for a towel. I should go sit with Aunt Sue, she said to the window.

No, Mom, Bo said. Listen. We'll put him in the back of the truck if we have to.

She slammed her coffee cup down on the counter and it sloshed out onto her hand and dress sleeve. Show some respect, Bo, she said, her back still turned to him, and Bo watched her hunch her shoulders and bury her face in her hands. He stood and went to her, hugged her from behind, and told her that he was sorry and that everything was going to be fine.

She lifted her head and wiped her eyes and sleeve with the towel, then nodded and tried to steady her breathing. Bo walked her back to the table, and she sat down and Rovnávaha came and knelt in front of her, took her hand and spoke softly to her, not like a child but like a daughter, grown but still in need of a father's love.

Bo is only trying to help, he said. It will be like this, Hannah, the memories of him. Whole swaths of them — things he told you, places you've been, people who'll remind you of him — will seem to rise out of nothing until there they are. Let them come.

They're painful now, but you'll be grateful. In time.

She stared at the floor so they would not see her eyes, and when she looked up again there was a fifties-model Cadillac hearse idling in the driveway, and Aunt Sue was standing in the kitchen. The old woman had on a black veil and wore a black dress with a brown cardigan over it. An airless scent of mothballs seemed to wrap around her like a gown, and she spoke to her niece in Slovak, as though these women were the only two in the room.

Hana, she said. *Je čas. Musíme ísť'.*

The mourners who gathered at the church of St. Michael the Archangel filled the front half of the nave. The pallbearers were men from the roughing mill, and they carried the casket down the aisle to the front as the spare congregation sang *The king of love my shepherd is.*

Bo, Hannah, and Aunt Sue sat in the front pew. Hannah read the First Reading and the Psalm, and Bo was surprised to hear his mother summon a voice so solitary and unwavering. *It's just the two of us now,* he thought, and then remembered Sam.

When she sat back down, Father Rovnávaha rose from his presider's chair and went to the pulpit, read from John's Gospel on the raising of Lazarus, and closed the book. His head was bowed as if his face might betray his struggle to be a priest when he wanted only to mourn the loss of his friend, and he pulled on the sleeve of his alb. Then he looked out at those waiting to hear him speak and began to tell a story of the time when he and Jozef had gone fishing on the Upper Salamander on a beautiful day in late October, the trees having lost most of their leaves but the warmth of the air and the hatch of blue duns reminding him of days in June on that same stretch of creek. At midday the water was in full sun and he reeled in his line, broke down his rod, and sat on a log to watch Jozef fish.

He said, Father Blok told me when I was new here at St. Michael's that the saddest day of his priesthood was when he buried Jozef's wife, Helen, for Jozef said what Martha said: *If the Lord had been here, she would not have died.* And so Jozef Vinich took his own sorrow to the place from where I watched him that day, watched him work his way across and downstream into the shade of a stand of willows, where trout were rising to a Royal Wulff pattern he had used and caught fish on ever since I had known him. And I realized, resting on that log in my shirt and waders, that the man of sorrow was still a man of faith, for he believed that what God had created had a beauty that would withstand all loss. Then, as if to prove me right, a fish rose and took the fly with a smack so loud that I sat up to see.

It was a big fish, the priest told them, and Jozef played it with a touch surprising for the man's toughness, until slowly, letting the fish run when it put on a burst of speed against the line and reeling in that line as it tired in the wider section of the creek, he eased his catch to the shore. Rovnávaha watched him as he sat the butt end of his rod into his vest, bent down to remove the hook from the fish's mouth, then held it up with two hands under its side like he might hold a newborn to the moon. It was a brown trout, almost two feet long, big for that stretch of water, for any stretch of water in Pennsylvania, and Jozef yelled from thirty yards downstream, Oakes! *Krásny, hej?*

The priest smiled, leaned over, and reached behind the log for the walking stick he had used to come down the escarpment so that he could ford the rapids in front of him and see for himself the beautiful fish that had come out of the waters at that place they called the bend.

Whether it was the warm fall, the exposed position of whatever den the snake returned to and emerged from year after year, or some fluke of estivation and age that kept it outside and roaming the woods, the timber rattler had found the hide from which to hunt beneath the fallen oak, and it remained there motionless and unperturbed. But the hand had come too close, and there was nowhere else for the snake to go, nothing else for it to do but strike.

The priest could not even be sure that the quick and deep cracked-parchment sound that had frozen him was a snake's rattle, but he felt the thud and the sting, and he yanked his hand up and out from behind the log and saw the sulfurous body and black chevron marks stretched and fat and clinging to the muscle behind his thumb, and he dropped.

Jozef released the fish and threw his rod on the bank all in one motion, ran along the stream, and waded across where the water was the shallowest.

Rovnávaha said to the congregation, I was sitting up and holding my hand as the bite began to swell. Jozef poured creek water over the wound with his hat, and I wondered, knowing that on my own I would not be able to get out of the woods fast enough, if this was the man before whom I would die.

Then the priest's voice rose there in the church, above the pipes that had begun to clang like dull bells against the walls as the heat within them stirred.

But if Jozef Vinich weighed options, he said, it was in a place where, if you knew him, knew where he was from, not one of us would likely have gone, let alone survived. He spoke to me gently in that voice of his, as though he knew I needed comfort, told me not to worry or to move, pulled my waders off as though I was getting ready for sleep, then knelt down in front of me and said, *Tomáš, I'm going to carry you out of here, up the escarpment, and to my truck. Say nothing and do nothing.* I said, Are you sure you can carry me? He held a finger to his lips and said, *Shhh.* Already his voice sounded hollow. My head was swimming and my hand throbbed. He leaned in, grabbed me by the waist, and threw me over his shoulder in one move.

Rovnávaha paused at the pulpit, then stood to his full height and shouted, Look at me! It was as though I was no more than a child to him, and he bore me straight up and along the rock path, and we rose out of those woods to the old logging road where he had parked that morning, and only then do I remember the sound of his voice talking to someone about the mountains, as though there was a third person in that truck with us.

They all watched then as the priest hid his right hand in the sleeve of his vestment and walked down to the altar steps, where he stood in front of the casket.

This is not a time for eulogies, he said, his voice tired-sounding. Although perhaps you will tell some among yourselves in days to come, for Jozef Vinich — the *vine,* you know, that means in Slovak — is a man we would do well to remember. No, I've told you this story because we live in Bethany, because we are a family, too, in which, as Saint Augustine says, one is sick and the other two are sad, and when the Lord says to His disciples, *Let us go there,* I know that this man, for whom I have wept often in the past two days, will live as sure as you, he said, and pointed to Hannah. And you, he said, and pointed to Bo. And each of you who has come here. For now, though, it is time we let him sleep.

Then Father Tomáš Rovnávaha reached out his hand and touched the head of the casket and whispered so that it was barely

audible from where Bo sat in the front pew.
Goodbye, my friend. I'll miss you.

CHAPTER TWO

Dardan, Pennsylvania, sits in the yawning cut of three mountains that long ago pushed away rather than collide as they rose, so that they came to resemble, in the topographic lines drawn later by the mapmakers, an unattached letter K. Hardwood forests surround it, and a ridgeline of the Appalachian range cuts off all but a few feeder streams from the broadening valley of the Susquehanna as that river, flat and silted and slow, broadens and sidewinds down into the Chesapeake Bay. The town's position behind this divide is no shortcoming of her founders — the hunters, trappers, and woodsmen who saw that the plainlike valley floor was positioned well for a town — not a blindness or ignorance of how or where one ought to settle in mountains rife with stone and rattlesnakes. The arm and leg of the K approach but never touch the back of the letter, which rests wide enough apart and at

38

such an angle that the sun rises and sets from late spring to early autumn on the exposed dip of its back, and the cold waters of Salamander Creek (before they drop into Troy Pass) leave their own rich silt of humate and the remnants of dead tree stoneground and rained upon like the blessed and dendritic valley of a promised land.

It was this land to which Jozef Vinich came to live in 1919. And it was this land in which he was buried fifty-three years later next to his wife. On a hillside at Our Lady of Sorrows cemetery in town. Father Rovnávaha commended the man's soul to God and committed the body to the ground. Those who were left at the grave drove back into Dardan Center to a place called Ruby's, where they had a repast around a table set for twelve.

The men from the roughing mill ate and did not linger, saying they had to get in at least a half day's work. Hannah and Bo were the last to leave. They stood outside in the parking lot of the restaurant in the wind and cold, under a sky of unsettled blue. Bo hugged his mother and gave her a kiss on the cheek and told her he had to go over to Dardan Hardware to pick up a pane of glass and a new gouge. She asked if it could wait, and he said no, there would be work to do when he got back to the mill, with no break for a while. I'm here, he said. I might as well.

He watched her drive away and he opened the door of his pickup, called Krasna, and walked across the street into the hardware store.

He went in by the loading bays and asked Jim Lavendusky, the store manager, if he could cut Bo a ten-by-ten pane of glass. The man said sure and measured the glass, dipped a cutter into a small cup of kerosene, and scored the pane along a straightedge. While he worked, he told Bo he was sorry to hear about his grandfather, that it was a loss for the whole town. Then he broke out the score, smoothed the edge with a sharpening stone, and wrapped the pane in brown paper. He wrote $1 on it with a carpenter's pencil and handed it to Bo. Bo thanked him and walked over to wood and lumber and told Phil Knapp he needed a new roughing gouge for some legs he was turning for a hutch he wanted to start working on now that it was spring.

You wouldn't know it, Phil said, and shook his head. No, sir, I can't help you with that.

He had an inventory sheet in front of him, and he stood by a rack of bins for lag bolts, carriage bolts, and large fasteners. He kept his head moving back and forth from the sheet to the bins, and he spoke to Bo without looking up.

I just got a new set of Sorby's in, he said, and pointed in their general direction. You'll see them over there with the others.

Bo walked past the walls of saws and shelves of mitres and planes, past an old green and yellow sign for Stanley Rule & Level Co., and kept moving in the direction of the woodworking tools, down the aisle of worn linoleum that Phil swept clean every day. He stopped in front of the display of the new Robert Sorbys, then walked to the end of the aisle, picked up a Buck Brothers carbon steel gouge, and untied the cloth bag to check that it was the size he wanted.

Phil yelled, Gettin' old up here, Bo! You got what you need?

Bo took his time walking back.

Sorry, buddy, Phil said to him when Bo appeared next to the rack. I'm late for lunch. Phil threw the last of a handful of lag bolts into the bin, looked at the cloth bag in Bo's hand, and sucked his teeth. You don't need to sharpen them Sorby's, you know. High-speed steel.

He shook a cigarette from a soft pack of Luckys and wrestled a butane lighter from the front pocket of his jeans. He scratched the flint wheel and lit his cigarette with a flame so high Bo thought the man's hog-bristled mustache was going to catch fire.

I like the feel of these, Bo said.

Phil took a long drag and blew a thin trail of smoke from his nose, put on a ball cap, and nodded. It's your wood, not mine, he said.

Bo knew that Ruth Younger worked the register at Dardan Hardware on weekdays and had since Sam left for the war, but he was still surprised when he walked to the front of the store with Krasna and saw her there, ringing up a woman for a birthday card and a clutch of stick candy. She wore a red apron that covered the curve of her belly, and under that she had on a red-checked flannel shirt open to the third button. Her black hair was pulled away from her face and tied back in a ponytail so that all you could see were her eyes, deep wells of green above the white-rose cast of her cheeks, and Bo noticed that she still wore the tiny diamond engagement ring his brother had given to her in Honolulu. She saw the dog, then looked at Bo and turned back to the woman. She slid the card and candy into a thin white paper bag, counted out the change, and said, I'll tell my father you were asking about him, Mrs. Sands.

Bo stepped up, put the glass and the gouge on the counter, and handed Ruth a twenty. She took the bill and gave him change and said, I'm sorry to hear about your grandfather. I really am.

Her ring hand touched her ear, and Bo could see a small mole above her collarbone and smell the perfume she wore.

Thanks, he said, and stuffed the change into his pocket. Died in his sleep. Doctor said he wasn't sick, just ready.

She reached into a box of Milk-Bones beneath the register and tossed one to Krasna. The dog sat down on the floor and gnawed the treat with her teeth.

I'd have come to the funeral, she said, but Mr. L. had no one else to work this morning.

That's all right.

How's your mom? she asked.

He tucked the glass under his arm as if it were a book. Hard to tell, he said.

It was Hannah who had told Bo, when they had gotten the news about Sam in November, that he had better find Ruth Younger and tell her before someone in Dardan spilled it to her out of meanness. Bo asked his mother what she cared about the girl, and Hannah brought her fist down

43

hard on the dinner table. I care, goddammit! she said. Jozef was there. Hannah stood to go, and he held her arm and said to Bo, Your mother's right. Whatever happened in the past and will happen now, it's still her grandchild.

And so Bo wrote what he had to say in a short note, telling Ruth only what they already knew. The next day he got in the truck and went to the hardware store, where she stood at the same register, handed her the note, and said, This is for later, when you're sitting down.

If he saw her around town, it was from a distance. Once across the long counter at Ruby's. Another time at a traffic light in the beat-up old Country Squire wagon she drove. Neither acknowledged the other. Not even a nod. Distance seemed to be their unspoken agreement, except when Hannah received a letter from the Navy Department in reply to her biweekly queries about her son. Their response was always the same, informing her that Sam was *still carried in a missing status.*

Like he's in a box somewhere, she would say, and the marines just haven't gotten around to opening it yet. And Bo would take that letter down to the hardware store.

If it were my dad, Ruth said, and shook

her head. I don't know what I'd do.

Bo shifted his weight and pinched the brim of the hat in his hand. He looked down at the dog and back at Ruth and felt his gut twist when it occurred to him that this was how his brother saw his fiancée when they stepped out of their embrace and she got on the plane that took her back to Dardan from Hawaii. She had gone to be with him on leave, one month before his second tour in Vietnam was over.

How far along are you? he asked.

Seven months. Due in June.

Well, if I can help at all, Bo said. With anything. You let me know.

She closed her eyes and opened them. All the troops are pulling out, she said, as though he had asked another question altogether. Just last night I heard Cronkite say on the news that Nixon wants everyone home by September.

They'll find him, Ruth, he said. You know my brother. He's going to be waiting on your doorstep the day you bring that baby home.

She wiped her cheek with the sleeve of her shirt and said, You're right.

Bo put his hat on and called Krasna. You let me know, he said again, and turned and walked back in the direction of the loading bay doors.

Wind rocked the truck on the road up to the farm, and Bo thought of the day Sam first mentioned Ruth Younger's name. Bo was working at the mill and paying rent to his grandfather to live at home. Sam came down the hall to his room one evening after supper and said, Hey, Bo, you'll never believe who talked to me at school today. Ruth Younger. What kind of hell do you think the old man would give me if I started saying more than hello back to her?

Sam stood in the doorway, leaning against the jamb, after saying this all in a rush. Bo told him not to worry about the old man. It was Hannah he would have to answer to. Sam made a noise like a blown tire and walked back down the hall. Then it was spring, followed by a long hot summer.

At the start of a new school year, he came into Bo's room again, his lip swollen and his eye bruised.

What happened to you? Bo asked.

Football practice, Sam said. It's nothing. I've got to talk to you about something else.

Bo closed the book he was reading and Sam sat down on his brother's bed. He was squeezing a rubber ball in his hand.

It's this Ruth Younger thing. I've got it

46

bad, brother. I need to be with her. I just need you to be on my side. Will you do it?

Bo said, Sam, it's not about taking sides. If you told Pop you were in love with the daughter of the man who shot dead your father, he would sit you down like a tracker with spoor and say, *You've got to know your own mind, son. Then it doesn't matter what you do.*

Sam threw the rubber ball at Bo and hit him in the chest. I wasn't even two. And Ruth was just a baby.

Bo threw the ball back. Like I said. It's Mom. She would want to know why, of all the girls in Dardan, you had to choose a Younger, and then you would have to live with her believing that you couldn't show your father's memory the respect of leaving that family alone.

Sam shook his head. Family, he said. She lives down in the Flats on Holly Street with her dad in a place no bigger than a shed. I'll bet there wasn't any talk of the old man leaving that family alone when he was scooping up their land.

Those were different times, Bo said.

Yep. Real different. Pop still lets him hunt, you know. Paul Younger.

Bo had not known, but he pretended that it was no matter. You've got to understand, he said. It's not like she believes Younger went unpunished. It's more like she doesn't want to be reminded of who our father was when he came home.

Who was he? Sam asked, though not like he wanted to know.

Not the man in that photograph she keeps on the mantel, Bo said. That's for sure. I remember him looking thin and weak. And he walked slow, like he was hollowed out of everything. There was a horse he spent most of his time with, an old gelding he called Pushkin. Mom said he used to take care of a lot of horses in town before they were married. Men brought them to him from all over the place. Something about the Lowari. The kind of gypsies he had come from. He and I just walked in the woods a lot. I was afraid to ask him too many questions. Thought he might start to cry or blow over if I did.

Sam sat and listened and considered Bo's memory of their father. That's a fair bit of him you've got in there, brother, he said.

There's more, Bo said. Scenes in my head that stand out for the season or time of day. Things he did. Or didn't do. He wouldn't eat an egg. I remember that.

Was he what they say he was? Sam asked.

I don't know. Pop says he fought same as

any man. More, even, if he was broken like that. He did what he could to save his life and come home.

Sam stared out into the hall. Sounds like someone I wish I'd known, he said.

When he got back to the house, Bo pulled his truck all the way up the drive and went in by the back door. The woodstove in the kitchen was warm. He lifted the lid and put some kindling on the coals and a small log on top of that.

Hannah, he said into the quiet.

Krasna pushed past and padded in the direction of the living room. Bo followed the dog and found his mother asleep in a chair by the fireplace, that fire not having burned for long before going out. A worn hardback of Rebecca West's *Black Lamb and Grey Falcon* was splayed spine-up on the floor. Bo pulled a blanket around her shoulders and walked back into the kitchen. The stove was burning again, and he put two more logs in the firebox and went outside to the barn.

There was enough daylight in the wood shop to work, but he flipped the light switch, stoked a fire in the potbelly, then moved to the center of the room and chucked up a cherry block in the lathe and tightened the tool rest a finger's distance from the wood.

He had the idea for a hutch when he saw the stack of letters his mother was collecting from the marines and the Department of the Navy. By February she had two small piles tied together and sitting on the table in the dining room, a table they set only for the *velija* feast at Christmas Eve and on Easter Sunday. He began to make a sketch of something with drawers in it, a shelf, and a top for writing. It was during a snowstorm in late February that he sat down in the kitchen and looked at the sketch and added four short legs to the hutch to see what it would look like set off from the floor, then measured a corner of the foyer and altered the dimensions he had drawn so it would fit there. He had some cherry set aside in the drying shed at the mill, and he told himself he would get to work on the hutch in April. Then his grandfather died.

He put on glasses and took up the new gouge. His hands were shaking and he knew why. He breathed and imagined for a moment the short-styled leg's finished shape, the shallow recess above the midpoint, then the single long-curved hourglass tapering into the foot. All he wanted to do now, though, was rough them out. He snapped on the machine, his left hand palm-down to guide the gouge, and eased the cutting edge into the spinning block. He worked in increments of a few inches across the wood out toward the tailstock, feeling the edges give way until they spun smooth and the entire piece was round. He did the same to the other three, then shut off the lathe, removed his glasses, and stepped back.

He thought he heard a car outside and looked out the window and down the drive, but there was no one. It was like that when they came to tell Hannah about Sam. Bo was stoking the potbelly when he saw the blue Nova sedan, and he ran from the barn into the house just as his mother answered the door. Now all he felt were the wood shavings under his sleeves and the cold off the glass. He walked over to the stove and fed it another shovelful of coal, the sulfur smell mingling with the sweetness of the cherry in the air. Only in the summer, when he came in after work to touch up a piece, or prep it for a long stretch on the weekend, did he open the windows and let in the smell of the mowed grass and ripening apples or the coming rain. His grandfather never had any heat in there. Bo wondered what Jozef would say when he put the stove in, but he seemed not to notice or care.

Then, on that same afternoon in November when the marines came to the door, he told his grandson he was glad to have the heat and the stove. Wished he had thought of it forty years ago.

Well, Pop, Bo said into the empty silence of the wood shop, if I can keep it warm in here for another forty, I'll be doing all right.

He walked back to the house in the spring twilight. Hannah had soup, a bowl of noodles, and a bottle of wine on the table, the last of a case of Tokaji that Jozef had bought in 1949, a '45 Tokayer Essenz. Bo washed and sat and told her he could remember the two times in his life he had tasted the wine. The Christmas Eve when he came home from college in the winter of '59, and dinner on the day he took ownership of the mill.

I had it for the first time with your father, she said. When he came home from the war. I remember him raising his glass and looking through it, then bringing it to his nose. *It's the smell of my boyhood, minus a horse or two,* he said, and I thought, *My God, he's home.*

That doesn't add up to a case, Bo said. Where'd the rest go?

Oh, you know, Hannah said, and seemed to brush the air with her hand, and laughed.

Well, to fathers and sons, then, Bo said, and they touched glasses and drank, the wine tasting to him at once sweet and earthy, like molasses and black tea. He sipped again, as though he had missed something the first time, and asked, Are you sure it's the last bottle?

Hannah nodded. Enjoy it, she said. You won't ever see that year in this house again. Don't drink it all now, though. It's for after dinner.

They bowed their heads and said grace, then ladled their dinner into bowls and ate in the new silence that had descended over them at the table. When they had finished, Hannah asked, What are you building out there?

Just roughing out some spindles, Bo said.

Hannah dabbed at the corners of her mouth with a napkin. I got a letter from Captain Foote today. He's been reassigned to San Diego. He told me that a Captain Kraynack was going to be my new contact for any information that might come up about Sam. I don't know, Bo. It feels like the world is moving on.

He had seen the mail. The folded sheet of white paper by the radio was not official-looking stationery, but it was typed, single-spaced, one paragraph with a sweep of a signature beneath the second fold.

He said, I don't think that's necessarily a bad thing.

I don't mean the war, Hannah said. I mean the ones who are supposed to be looking for him.

They've been looking for six months now, Mom.

He's your brother.

Yes. And that matters to me only?

She shook her head. Your grandfather once said something I've remembered ever since. It was just after Sam enlisted. We were sitting at this same table and I wondered out loud why it had to come to that. Why couldn't we have seen? And he said, *Finding yourself is hard, Hannah. Finding yourself in a war is very hard. You have to let him walk the path he chose.*

Bo got up from the table and hooked a dish towel around the stove handle. He turned and leaned against the sink. Leave these for later, he said, and gave a nod to the dishes. Let's drink our wine outside. It's a beautiful night.

They put on jackets and went through the house and out the front door. A gusty wind had risen since he had come in from the wood shop, and the branches of the pear swayed and ticked against the gutters along

54

the porch roof. He sat down on the top step and she in the rocking chair her father had placed there. They looked in the direction of the town, where a faint glow of lights was visible from the creek valley. A crescent moon hung like a tiny scimitar in the west.

It is a beautiful night, Hannah said, and she began to rock back and forth in the chair, the runners sounding like low thunder rising from the floorboards of the porch, and she pulled at the collar of her jacket in the wind.

Bo sipped his wine and said, I saw Ruth Younger at the hardware store today. She asked about you.

Hannah turned to look at him. What did you tell her?

I told her the truth. That I didn't know how you were.

Hannah lowered her head into her folded arms, and when she lifted it again, she said, Must be pretty far along by now.

June, Bo said. She misses Sam.

We all do.

I know, but you don't have a baby on the way.

He is my baby, Hannah said.

The distant wail of a siren rose from the town, the sound traveling far in the cold. Bo watched his mother take a breath and, against a thin spread of lamplight that shone from inside the house, push that breath into the night air like a plume.

You two boys were so different, she said, looking back out into the dark as she started rocking again. You were always complaining about food, or wanting time to read, if you weren't in your grandfather's wood shop working on something. Sam was on the move, like a restless cat. I'd be hanging up the wash, and he'd drop out of a tree like he'd been up there all night, and it'd scare the daylights out of me. Then he'd say something like *I was just studying the bark. It's got bugs in it that the woodpeckers eat.* I remember the time once when you and your grandfather went fishing. It had to be late June. Sam was five, and he knew he was too young to be invited, but he wouldn't listen to a word of explanation and went off to his room until you and Papa had gone. When he came down, I suggested we go out to the lake to fish ourselves, and he said, *I don't want to fish. Let them.* We got our bathing suits anyway and drove out to Asa Pound's dock, and we talked about school for him next year and what a big boy he was becoming. I parked the car under the pine, and we walked down to the water, and he sat in one of those Adirondack chairs that had been there since the beginning. Well, the chair must have had a nest of yellow jackets under it, because I saw him jump and scream and start twitching like no dance I'd ever seen, and it dawned on me what was happening. I dropped everything I had and ran to him, lifted him up with one hand, and pulled him in so close that I could feel those hornets stinging me. Then I jumped right off the dock into the lake, bees floating past like bubbles around our faces. And when I glanced at him there underwater, he was looking at me like he wasn't sure if he should be confused or relieved, and I could feel him hugging me so tight that I kicked to the surface and swam back because I thought something might really be wrong with him. You know? Like he was allergic and I didn't know it. But then he let go of me and pulled himself up onto the dock and got the bucket he had brought to play with, filled it with water, walked to the chair, and flipped it over, then doused the nest. Slow, too. Like he knew a good stream of water would do the most damage. And then he kicked that nest off and into the lake, flipped the chair back over, and said, *We're okay now, Mom.* Just like that. *We're okay.*

Her rocking slowed to a stop. Listen to me. Talking about him in the past tense.

Your grandfather never would.

Bo said, The night he came up from Camp Lejeune after his first tour, we were drinking beers and he asked me if getting married to Ruth Younger would cause holy hell in the family.

What did you say?

I said, Vietcong shooting at you and you're worried about who's going to come to your wedding? I'll come. Find someone else and it'll be legal.

Your grandfather, you know, thought that girl was the best thing that ever happened to him. After the marines.

What do you think? Bo asked.

She did not answer but started to rock, and for a while there was nothing but the sound of that rhythm and the wind.

I'll write to this new captain, she said. We'll see what we get back.

The moon had set, and she turned and looked down into the shadows of orchard and road on which every visitor to the farm arrived and left, bent forward and reached for her glass, then sat up and looked over at her son.

When things settle down, Bernie Lloyd's coming over to read the will.

No surprises in there, I'd imagine.

No. She paused. I've seen it. It's not that.

I'm just wondering what it's going to be like to hear my father's voice again. Even coming out of the mouth of a lawyer and from beyond the grave.

I hear that voice around every corner of this place, Bo said, and drank off the wine in his glass. It's gotten so that I've started talking to him myself.

She smiled and Bo thought she would stand and go, but she sat there for a moment and seemed to study his face in the paring of light from inside the house.

You look so much like him, she said. Your father, I mean. So much like him still.

CHAPTER THREE

He was born in 1941 and christened Bohumír Ondrej Konar because, his father said, *He will be God's peace to us.* That was the year Bexhet Konar took the exam and raised his right hand to become an American citizen and enlisted in the United States Army. The year he wrote to his wife once a week from basic training in Alabama and saw her and his infant son one more time that spring, before he boarded the troop ship bound for Southampton, England. The letters slowed then, sometimes three a month, sometimes one every other month, letters in which he would refer to a passage from a letter that she had never received. But it did not seem to her that letter-writer wrote less. Rather, the interval of time between them had stretched. In September 1944 a postcard came from Paris on which he had written, *My love and a kiss to you and Bohumír.* There was no word from him at Christmas. She listened to the news. The tide was turning in Europe after the great landing. Then, in early 1945, she received the note that said her husband was missing in action in France and presumed dead.

Bo was five when he asked his grandfather if he could come into the wood shop to watch him work. Six when Jozef started teaching him how to use the tools. Bo rode on the tractor, was put in charge of some hens in the chicken coop, and never flinched the day he watched his grandfather and Mr. Pound from the mill butcher a hog. And when he was not with Jozef in the shop, the orchard, or the barn, Bo was in his grandfather's library, reading the spines of the books that lined the floor-to-ceiling shelves. Washington Irving, Nathaniel Hawthorne, Stephen Crane (the only writer Jozef Vinich said he wished he could have met), Rudyard Kipling, Thomas Hardy, H. W. Longfellow, and H. G. Wells. There were collections his grandfather had acquired at auctions. Tomes of philosophy and theology. Local histories he had received as discards from the Osterhout Free Library in Wilkes-Barre. Encyclopedias and almanacs dating back to the turn of the century that he had found in boxes put out for junk at the edge of yards from Dardan to the New York state line. All of it belonging now to a man who had grown up in what Aunt Sue called *the ol' kawntree,* a man who had read each one of those books and placed them like stones in a wall that he built against the life he would have been destined to live had he remained in that old country.

When Bo was seven, his grandfather pulled up to the house in the truck with another man sitting in the front seat next to him. It was a wet spring then, too, one of torrential rains, and the two men waited in the pickup, as though they were talking, before they got out and walked slowly (in spite of the rain) up to the front porch, where Bo and his mother stood waiting. Hannah and the man embraced and remained in that embrace for a long time before he said, Where is my son? Hannah stepped back. The man knelt down, held out his arms (so thin they looked to Bo as if they were lost in the sleeves of the green coat the man wore), and said, I've missed you, my Bohumír.

For the next two years Bo came to know something of his father. Bo walked with him in the woods, walks on which there were long stretches of silence that Bo wanted to fill with questions but dared not. Walks on which they had to stop and rest often, on a lush patch of crow's-foot, or the bald dome of Summit Rocks, where they could see most of the two-thousand-acre stretch of the Vinich land. It was there on the rocks one day that Bo asked his father the question that gnawed at him the most, Did you kill any Germans in the war? Becks looked at his son and back out at the land and said, Yes, son. And then I ran away from the war and hid so that I wouldn't have to kill any more. Then he stood and walked off the path and into the woods and pulled up a tree of sassafras, snapped the root in two, and inhaled the wood and cinnamon smell mixed with dried leaf and dirt. So that I could come home to this, my Bohumír, he said, louder for the distance he stood from his son. All of this.

On the farm, Bo listened to him sing strange and mournful songs as he carved horses and birds out of blocks of wood. And Bo remembered the day his mother went into labor. The doctor came to the house and Bo and his father waited in the kitchen together, trying not to listen to the sounds. When they were told that another Konar boy had been born and that Hannah was doing well, the man knelt down and hugged Bo like he had on the day he arrived home in Jozef's pickup, and said, A good man is good to his brother, Bohumír. Promise me you'll be good to him when I'm gone.

And on a night in March in 1950, Bo went to sleep with his father's kiss on his lips and woke in a house that would never hear his steps again.

He understood what they told him. That his father was walking in the woods in the morning, in the high meadow above the creek bend, when a man named Paul Younger, whom Jozef Vinich let hunt on his land, shot Becks Konar. It was an accident, they said. Younger was hunting deer out of season, but Jozef Vinich had given him permission. The herds were thick and needed culling, and Paul Younger needed the food. The man was no more guilty of directing the path of a ricocheted bullet than he was of wanting to feed his wife and baby daughter. Most asked why Becks Konar was in the woods at all that morning. Bo knew the answer. Because he missed them. Paul Younger waited for Hannah at the cemetery, took off his hat, and told her he was sorry for her loss. After that, Bo drifted back to the side of his grandfather, back to him for advice, instruction, and comfort, back to the man he had never stopped calling Pop.

■ ■ ■ ■

Everything Jozef Vinich taught his grandsons in the years after their father died came across in a language of discipline and correction. The ax swing when they split wood. (Center! Helve straight.) How to sharpen the Morseth on an Arkansas bench stone. (Don't turn that blade over until you can feel the burr.) And, at the age Jozef alone believed each of his grandsons was ready, where to hunt and how to shoot. A discipline one learns more by observation than by talk, he told each one in turn. He never reminded Bo of the morning they went into the woods to shoot the deer-killer dog. He waited for the fall and took Bo out again, for squirrel and rabbit. Each time the lesson was the same. They sat on the steps of the back porch before they left and Jozef intoned softly into the morning air, You're my shadow. And if you can't be my shadow and only my shadow, then you can stay home. Then he would turn and make his way through the orchard for the woods, Bo right behind.

Jozef Vinich was lean and fair-haired and stood five feet five in his boots. To Bo and Sam he seemed Herculean, a man incapable of weakness. Unassisted, he could lift whole barrels of apples or bundles of wood in a leather sling as though they were no more than cotton wool or straw, in spite of the missing fingers on his right hand. (From another war, their mother said, so that Bo wondered when he was young how many wars there could possibly be.) They knew Jozef had once walked from the mill in West Dardan to the house and arrived at dinner and sat down as though he had come in from the barn. And they were certain there was no part of the perimeter of the Vinich land he could not reach on foot and with his rifle within hours of setting out, recounting to them later details of his patrol. The eight-foot black snake. An albino doe. The feces from a bobcat he had never seen but knew came over from the state lands to hunt for grouse. He spoke in a voice so low-pitched and sonorous that it seemed to resonate from his entire frame.

This was who had shaped Bo's world for eighteen years, except for the long days he had to suffer through the boredom of high school, a young man of some privilege in a town where land meant wealth. A young man who was at times shown affection in that town, at times ignored, though he sought out neither. It was something else he was looking for, something of which he caught a glimpse in the books he had pulled down from his grandfather's shelves. Something of a world that existed beyond Dardan and the banks of the Salamander, a world through which he would travel as a rite of passage, those books (and others he might find) his maps along the way.

In the early spring of 1959, he went to his grandfather and said he had been thinking about it for a long time and he would like to go to college.

College? Jozef said. He stroked his chin with his pistol-shaped hand. I hadn't expected that. In time, you know, you'll take over the mill and half of that land out there will be yours.

I know.

Then what is it? Jozef asked.

This town, Bo said.

Jozef laughed and looked in the direction of that town as though he could see it from where they were in the barn, inspecting the fuel lines on the Farmall. How could he have known the worlds that rested between the covers of every book he had acquired and read would someday make his grandson curious enough to want to see what those worlds might have to offer.

There's a lot more out there than this

town has to offer. That's for sure, Jozef said. Let me think about it. In the meantime, find a place that's not going to let the privilege of having some big letter sewn onto a sweatshirt go to your head.

Bo went to an old school on the Chesapeake Bay in Annapolis, Maryland, that read the books of the ancients because they believed the ancients still had something to say. He could not believe his luck in those first autumn months at having found such a place among the brick walkways and buildings whose foundations were older than the nation entire. Inside the Great Hall, rooms of wooden tables and stone fireplaces reminded him of reading at home so much that he would arrive early to class in the morning and sit alone and speak to his grandfather as though he were sitting in the next chair. Euclid reminds me of you, old man, he'd say. Difficult and right.

There were several women in his entering class of sixty undergraduates that year, but only two were in his first-year seminar where they read the Greeks, and one left after a week. The other was named Ann Dvorak. She was tall with wide, sloe-colored eyes that she kept hidden behind black-framed glasses. She tied her long brown hair in a kind of knot on her head, up off her shoulders and away from her face, and kept it twisted around what looked to Bo like a stick stripped of its bark, sanded smooth, and varnished.

For the first month she seemed not shy but aloof. Toward the end of that month, she took off her glasses in class and stared across the table at him, and he could not help thinking that she looked as though she had just walked out of the workshop of a Renaissance sculptor. She caught him staring, winked, and put her glasses back on.

Most of the other men at the college were older than eighteen. Several were veterans of Korea. Of those, more than a few thought Miss Dvorak (as she was called) was more arrogant than intelligent, and they wondered how she had gotten there and when she would leave. But Bo was drawn to her, wondering if there was at work in her the same desire to see beyond a horizon without fear of leaving something else behind, something known and comforting and seemingly incapable of change.

He had not cut his hair at all the year before he went off to school. His mother said to him one day, You have your father's hair, and so he let it grow because he liked the idea that he could evoke the man. When he got to the school and Hannah sent him some money for a barber and lunch, he used it to buy a Loeb copy of Aeschylus and a book for his grandfather on sundials. He kept what had become long and loose black curls pushed back behind his ears, or in a ponytail if he was playing basketball, and for this reason people began to believe he was from someplace other than a small town in northeastern Pennsylvania, although no one knew where.

They were reading Thucydides in the fall, and Miss Dvorak asked a question on the virtue of self-mastery and the perception, in the speech of the Corinthians from Book One, of the Spartans as warriors too cautious and slow.

Is it rather, she asked, a deeper understanding with the intimacy of men and war, as King Archidamus suggests, in the heart of the individual as well as a nation? Then she quoted, *When a great confederacy, in order to satisfy private grudges, undertakes a war of which no man can foresee the issue, it is not easy to terminate it with honour.*

No one spoke for a few moments, until someone offered dismissively from across the table, You know, Miss Dvorak, that real Spartans wouldn't have treated women very well.

It's comforting to know that I'm not in

the presence of real Spartans, she said. Except there, on Mr. Konar. That's a Spartan's hair. That's what an Athenian would see when he closed in to do battle with the Lacedaemonian. A man free to stand or die. An honorable man. That's what I mean by self-mastery.

Bo knew by her glance that she was asking him to take her side. He looked down at the table, down at the old and blackened stain and shellac holding up against the penknives of undergraduates wanting to etch their initials onto its surface, then up at the crystal wall sconces that gave off a light more steady than the books themselves. Then he turned back to the faces of the fourteen men, one woman, and two tutors (who held their beat-up Jowett translations in front of them like explorers not two leagues off from their discovery) and said, It's fear of the Athenians and their increasing power that leads the Spartans to war, Thucydides says in the end. Not the speeches of their allies. But that doesn't mean they can't act honorably, even in fear. If we are speaking of self-mastery, that seems to be the difference. How we act. What we do. I think the cautious Spartans knew that best. The difference between the honorable man and the belligerent fool.

Later that evening he saw her with some other students in the campus bar. She walked over to him and pushed her eyeglasses up on her head. Let me buy you a beer for coming to my rescue, she said.

Did I? he asked.

I thought so.

He pointed to her glasses. Don't you need those to see?

They're just for show, she said, and tucked them into a pocket on her sweater. But don't tell anyone.

I will stand or die, he said.

They talked in that bar until last call, and then they walked the cobblestones back to campus and continued on past the dormitories to the edge of the playing fields, where a small creek flowed out to the river that flowed out to the bay. There they sat on the bank and talked about their families. She was from Parma, Ohio, a town from which she, too, longed to leave and yet wondered if she ever could. She'd gone to an all-girls Catholic school, graduated at the top of her class, and, after working behind the counter of a bakery for six months, begged her father to send her to college. Her mother would not hear of it, but her father told her if she could scrape up half, he would give her the rest. And so she worked at the bakery until she had what she needed.

She had listened to her parents speak Slovak all her life, but she had never learned it with any fluency because, they said, You don't need to. As the sky brightened, the sun rose, and Bo listened to her slur her speech as she practiced saying his name the way his father used to say it, as if rolling an ice cube around on her tongue. And he felt as though he were in the presence of some goddess who had come to deliver a message of courage to those whose fates had yet to be measured.

On Friday afternoons they went to dance lessons in the Great Hall, and on Saturdays they attended the school's waltz parties and swing balls. He would dress in one of the two suits his grandfather bought him at a clothier in Wilkes-Barre, and she would wear a gown that her grandmother had owned from the twenties. All of the young women there were townies, or girls from Baltimore visiting one boy or another. She danced with him alone, the two of them gliding across the floor with a grace she had brought out of him, taught him how to feel, then said, Now you lead. And she moved before his every step as if she were his mirror, their eyes locked, their bodies close, the hint of tea rose rising to him from her shoulders, a reminder that he drifted in the wake of this dancer for a short time. *But I have her,* he thought. *We leave this wake together.*

They stayed on campus over the Thanksgiving break, ate turkey sandwiches at the only open shop on Main Street, and took a six-pack of National Premium back to her dorm room, which had a fireplace. They sat near the hearth and drank beer, and Bo read out loud to her from a letter he had gotten from his grandfather the day before. Jozef wrote with news of the farm and the mill, greetings of people who had asked about him, and finished with a recounting of his younger brother's first hunt. Sam had been given a break-action .20-gauge for his ninth birthday, and he and Jozef went turkey hunting the first week of November. *The little guy snuck up to the biggest bastard in the rafter,* Jozef wrote, *twenty-five yards maybe, waved me back, and took the bird down with the only shot that H&R would give. Then he said, I sure wish Bo was here to see it.*

Ann laughed and said, I sure wish I could meet them.

You will, Bo said.

They turned up the record player and

listened to *Come Fly With Me* and *Songs Our Daddy Taught Us,* then turned it down for *Everybody Digs Bill Evans* and fell asleep next to each other while the needle softly hissed and bumped against the end of the album on the turntable, like the heart beating in his chest.

When winter recess came, they took the same bus together to Harrisburg, where she would change for the westbound Greyhound to Pittsburgh and go on to Cleveland, and Bo would head north to Wilkes-Barre. He let that bus go without him, and they drank coffee and ate apple Danish from a vending machine and talked about the spring and traveling west to work in the state parks for the summer. He held her a long time when they announced her bus was boarding. They kissed and she said he tasted like sugar and apple jam.

I'll miss you, he said, though he wanted to say *I love you,* because it was true.

I know, she said.

As his bus pulled into the Wilkes-Barre station, he saw his grandfather and kid brother sitting in the front seat of the pickup. He gave them each a hug on the depot platform and they walked together to the parking lot. He threw his duffel onto a crust of snow in the open truck bed and

Sam said, We've got a new dog, Bo! Her name is Krasna because Mom says that means *beautiful* in Slovak. Bo opened the passenger door and there was a black Lab puppy asleep on the seat. Sam scooped her up in his arms and slid in between Bo and his grandfather for the drive back to the farm.

Ann wrote to him as soon as she got home, the letter arriving with the mail on December 24. It was not a long letter. She told him that Parma felt like a world flat and without depth, and she could not wait to get back on the bus in the New Year. She wrote in the same cursive hand with which he had watched her fill entire notebooks with commentaries on translations and directions for mathematical proofs, and it smelled faintly of her tea rose. He waited until the twenty-sixth to write back, telling her of Christmas with his mother, grandfather, and younger brother, the living room where the tree from their own woods stood, and the longing that he had for her. Then he walked down to the post office in Dardan to mail the letter, the thought coming to him as he crossed over Salamander Creek that he was prepared in that moment to walk across Pennsylvania and into Ohio just to be with her.

He did not know until the New Year, when every student received a letter from the dean saying that Miss Ann Dvorak had been struck by a car and killed on Christmas Eve as she walked home from church, that he would not be going back to college. The day after he received the letter he walked down the hill again into Dardan in the snow, and he went to the barber and told the man to give him a regular. The following week (the year was 1960), he went to work at the roughing mill and never looked beyond the tree-studded horizon of Dardan, Pennsylvania, again.

CHAPTER FOUR

The house settled into a new rhythm after Jozef Vinich died. Hannah collected the daily evidence of her father's presence (flannel shirt on a hook, boots in a closet, a copy of Steinbeck's *Travels with Charley* on the nightstand in the room where he slept) and put them with the other things of his that she had taken from his dresser drawers and boxed and stored in the attic. She swept and dusted and aired out his room on the first day the temperature rose above fifty degrees. But there was not much more to do in his absence. One morning she walked into that room as if to wake him, wondering why he had not risen, until she pushed open the door and realized (once again, for it happened often) he was gone. She sat on the bed she had made the day before, looked out through the glass on the doors that opened onto the balcony above the front porch, and breathed in the air of the room.

She used to love the smell of her father's room. It was like cedar and dried leaves in October, with just a hint (she swore) of root beer. She ran her hand along the quilt that covered the bed and felt the desire to lie down on it and sleep, so tired had she become of maintaining the weeks-long pace and process of mourning. But the sun was already filtering in and the day promised to be a beautiful one. She stood and patted flat the depression she had made on the bed and went downstairs. Bo would have fed the cow, but the chickens needed to be let out, their waterer filled and the feed trough checked. Then she would get started on the flower beds. And then, well, she would know the next thing when she saw it.

Bernie Lloyd drove up to the house on a Monday morning in May at nine o'clock. Hannah met him at the door and showed him into her father's study, then told Bo they were ready. When all three were in the room, she opened the safe and took out the folder on which was written will in black ink and handed it to the lawyer, who put his briefcase on the desk and produced a similar folder, which he put down next to the original.

Jozef Vinich had designed and built his

home around two main chimneys, one for the fireplaces that sat opposite each other in the dining room and the kitchen, the other for the large fireplace in the living room. On the other side of that wall was the study, where he kept a smaller collection of books and an old six-drawer captain's desk by the window facing west. Two days after he had gotten the letter from Dean Smith informing him of Ann Dvorak's death, Bo had come into this room to tell his grandfather he was not going back to the college. He knocked on the door of the study, heard the command *Come!,* and went in. Jozef was closing a thick leather-bound ledger on his desk. He stood, placed it on the bookshelf behind him, next to the book on sundials Bo had just given him for Christmas, and sat back down at the desk that had nothing on it but an ink blotter and an old steel dagger once cleaned of rust yet blackened and aged and resting where a paperweight might have been if there had been any papers. He motioned for Bo to take the chair opposite him and opened the conversation by asking what he was looking forward to reading in the spring semester.

I won't be there this spring, Bo said. I came in here to tell you that.

It's the girl, Jozef said, as though it was a

matter of fact.

Bo nodded.

Jozef reached down to open a side drawer on the desk and pulled out a letter that he unfolded on top of the blotter and began to read out loud: October eighth, nineteen fifty-nine. This place, Pop. I have found people who are so oddly like me, and yet not, and for this reason I want to be around them, as though I once was for a long time and have returned.

Bo remembered the words and where he wrote them, the corner desk and wooden chair where he sat, the anticipation of being with Ann after he dropped the letter in the mailbox. His grandfather rose and walked to the fireplace and put a log on the fire. Bo told him he could not imagine being at the college without seeing her there. He thought of their night alone in the dorm room, remembered the sound of the record when the music stopped, as it thumped and turned and thumped and turned, and he told his grandfather he had felt as though the stones of the buildings themselves were alive at that school.

And now they're just stones, he said.

Jozef stood at the mantel and stared down into the fire. That's the nature of loss, he said, and lifted his head and looked at his grandson. You are both lessened and left behind. There's nothing to be done but the work that's been given, so the part of you that's lessened doesn't become lost as well.

Then that's what I'll do, Bo said. I'll work. Here.

Jozef walked back to his desk and sat down. Your work is there. The work you asked to do. You don't want to know what it is you might have become? he said, as though curious.

Bo told himself he would not give in. He stared straight ahead and said, I've thought about it, Pop, and there's nowhere else I would have gone afterward but back here, to work on this land. Would it be worth the discipline to study the books and the languages and the mathematics regardless?

Jozef put his arms on the desk and held out his hands. He remained there for a moment, looking at the boy who had become, in such a short time, a young man. Remained there as if he wanted to memorize Bo and call him to mind one day, when he would need to be reminded never to put an obstacle in the young man's way.

It's discipline just the same, Bo, he said. That's what shapes us, no matter what the trade or how we ply it.

You're disappointed, Bo said.

No. I just thought you had found a place of your own. That's all I've ever wanted for you. Jozef picked up the letter, folded it, and placed it back in the drawer. There's work at the mill for now, he said. Until you find something else. You can help Andy in the tally shed. He's about the best teacher you'll find anywhere.

The chair where Bo had sat that day was gone, and the desktop where Mr. Lloyd laid out the papers of his trade was empty of all but the old blotter. Where the dagger had gone, Bo did not know.

It was a short last will and testament. Hannah was given the house and all of the land until she saw fit to pass her inheritance on to her sons (not *fit to pass her inheritance on,* as though there might, in the fullness of time, be someone else who would be the beneficiary of her love and good fortune, but *on to her sons*). The savings account in Jozef Vinich's name held at United Penn Bank was to be withdrawn, used to pay any and all creditors and taxes owed, the remainder divided three ways, distributed, and the account closed.

Bo had already purchased his grandfather's share of the Endless Roughing Mill two years prior, so there was no part of the business to be passed on. But there was one final paragraph in the will. Mr. Lloyd looked across the desk at Bo, then put his head down and read.

To my grandson Bohumír Ondrej Konar, eldest son of Bexhet and Hannah Konar: Separate from the two thousand acres of land that my daughter, Hannah Elizabeth Vinich Konar, is now in possession of, effective immediately and in perpetuity, I leave twenty acres of land and the house that stands at the top of that land, from the border with Rock Mountain Road to where the state game lands and the trees of the Vinich/Konar land begin (there being two iron rods in the ground at the highest and lowest points of that property).

Mr. Lloyd closed the folder. Well, Hannah, he said, they match sure enough. I can file this one with the probate court for you if you'd like. Save a trip.

She thanked him and offered him coffee, which he declined, saying he had a full day ahead of him and had to get back to the office. She walked him to the door.

Bo was in the study, sitting and staring at the cold fireplace in front of him, when his mother came back in.

Did you know he was going to give all that

to me? he asked.

Your grandfather and I went over everything.

What about Sam?

Sam's not here. No one else could man-
age that land as well as you. He saw that
when you took over the mill.

Suppose I do. Make it a place to live. What
about you? You're going to run this farm by
yourself?

I'll get by. It's not like he left you a house
in California. Besides, this place is no longer
the farm it was. You said so yourself.

Bo drummed his fingers on the blotter
and glanced down at the drawer from which
his grandfather once produced the letter Bo
had written to him from college. He opened
it and found it empty of all but some dust
motes and the faint smell of dried ink.

Hannah said, Are you going to sit around
here and wonder why things are the way
they are? Because I've got to get to the bank
and the store and mail some letters.

No, he said. You go. I need to head over
to the mill and check on some orders coming in.

Good, she said. Lock up on your way out.
I'll take Krasna with me. Almost as an
afterthought, she went over to the bookshelf
and picked up the ledger he had seen but

never opened, the leather cover a deep rosewood with a light brown rectangle in the center, on which were embossed the letters JV.

This is part of it, she said. The first part. So you'll see how it came into his hands. What you're being asked to keep. She put the ledger on the desk and walked to the door.

Hannah? he said.

She turned.

Was it welcome? he asked.

Was what welcome?

The sound of his voice.

Yes, Bo, she said. Yes, it was.

He sat in the chair behind the desk, the silence of the house falling around him, and he wondered how it was a man who had worked and acquired and tended his whole life could leave behind all he had acquired with less than a page of words. He did not write, *To my grandson Bo, I leave the wood shop and all of its contents.* Or, *To my grandson Sam, I leave my gun and rifle collection,* on and on like that, some precise and well-considered checklist of matching talents. Jozef just handed it all down to the next, as though it could be held in both hands, whole and without fear of it in any way splintering or breaking off. In life he lived every day with the separation of the wood shop and the barn and the tractor and animals (what was left of them), the gun collection and the loaders and the cabinet and the walls of the house and the land on which it stood, farm or forest. But not in death. *You are both lessened and left behind.*

Bo pulled the ledger toward him and opened it to the first page, the entry marked:

9 April 1921 — $100 in Miners Bank and this book to record what I will build.

The next entry came right after, cramped and without white space on the page, although several weeks had passed.

31 April — Hired at Cording mill Leaving Brookside for flat above store in Dardan Will ask Štefan Posol once more in one month for his daughter's hand.

Two months and still no space more than the black ink that separated each written line like a guide.

4 June 1921 — Married Helen Posol today She sleeps while I write this by candle flame Cording has given me a week off

paid and left a ham and a bottle of wine
by the stairs

Beginning with that entry, a gap of one to
two lines appeared between the last word
and the subsequent date. They were not
long, the entries he recorded, not even when
his daughter, Hannah, was born on the
twenty-second of February in 1922. Each
was, as he had promised from the outset, a
record of acquisition, the growing spaces
consisting of the months and the years (such
as 1923, the only entry written in that year,
on August 27, when Jozef was made a shop
foreman at the mill and given a five-cent
raise in pay) that would remind anyone
reading that the man lived most of his life
in ordinary time.

Bo saw it then, in an entry dated *8 October
1924,* mention of Walter Younger, who appeared as a man to whom Jozef Vinich
looked up. In an uncharacteristically long
passage, Cording, Erskine Pound, and Jozef
had skirted the Younger land with a surveyor
from the state from whom they wanted to
acquire timber, and the house at the hill
came into view. *What has that man done?
He has built what I would build, too,* Jozef
wrote at the end of the paragraph that began
with numbers of acreage and a rough tally

of pine and hardwoods. And then it was the Christmas of 1924.

With Helen and Hannah at Posol's for *velija* feast Talk in Brookside of WY and troubles four years into prohibition Flat's cold and the girl's sick I will not spend another winter here

So it began, what the man seemed destined to acquire, what Bo's mother told him he was being asked now to keep.

1 June 1925 — purchased 100 acres on Rock Mt from WY $50 Says you can't farm it

Two months later.

1 August — WY offered another 200 acres for same price/acre as previous Can't afford but he's hungry Countered with half and he walked

Two weeks.

15 August — 200 acres attached to previous 100 $85 Now have what I want to start building Foundation and framed by winter (Though I had promised myself and my

wife) we'll wait until spring to move into the house

The next several entries recorded board feet of two-by-tens, two-by-fours, bags of mortar, and pounds of nails, along with costs and delivery schedules. Names of men Bo had heard about or known as a boy, men whom his grandfather knew and trusted his entire life, and men who would show up and then disappear like minor actors in a play, weak adversaries, or opportunistic friends. Bo turned several pages that consisted solely of figures, amounts in the tens and hundreds, added, subtracted, divided, and added again, until the number with which Jozef Vinich ended the columns on the page equaled the number with which he began: *2,000 acres.* Written and circled in the top right corner as though a reminder of some goal. Then the longest entry Bo had seen:

24 December 1925 — (With Helen and Hannah for *velija* feast) Mild winter House framed and tight WY showed up this week to see progress Miss Emma Cording showed EP and me work orders and profits '26 looks good Her father is a lonely man WY has gone to her and offered to

sell his land but she knows what it's worth
That it's not just a house I'm wanting to
build Days still when I wish my brother
could walk this land with me like we
walked in Pastvina before the war, my
father and the horse out ahead of us, the
man the same age that I am now

The clock struck noon and Bo looked up
from the book, watched the door swing
open, and waited for his grandfather to walk
into the room. Krasna pushed it with her
nose and came up to him for a sniff and a
pat on the head.

Bo exhaled and shook his head. I thought
you went with Hannah, he said. All right.
Sit down if you want. I'm just reading.

The dog walked over to the fireplace and
lay down in front of it as though folding
herself up on top of her paws. Bo turned
back to the ledger.

The initial recordings of land purchased
gave way to a spare accounting (into the
summer of 1926) of the building of the
house where Bo and his brother had grown
up, and then the gradual acquisition of farm
machinery long rusted and animals Bo had
never seen, until October of that year, where
he found a note in all capital letters, as
though a signpost.

KEEP YOUR ACCOUNTS ON YOUR
THUMBNAIL This my father always said
to me and I did not believe it possible or
even desirable I am now more than what
he wanted to be Have more than he ever
held Which will mean more to let go of

The years thinned out on the page through
'27 and '28, with the writer's attention
drawn only to his wife and daughter and
house, the sparseness of details so striking
(recorded without day or date but rather
just the passing remark of season, *Winter '27
Hannah's fifth birthday First of May — Planted
blossoming pears*) that Bo wondered what
else must have occupied his grandfather's
mind. Something for which he was waiting.
Something he welcomed. Something he
feared. He turned the page and found two
entries. One on the verso.

29 October — Cording brought the mill to
a halt

The other on the recto.

Miss Emma drove to the farm this morning
to say that her father had taken his life
God rest his soul

The whole of 1929 summed up in these

handful of words, the year itself not even written down, both pages otherwise un- marked but for a note at the bottom of the recto.

New Year's Miss Emma has renamed us Endless Roughing Mill

Us, Bo thought, and when he turned the page he saw what he had wanted to see, though sooner in the ledger than he had expected.

22 February 1930 — Last 1,020 acres of water forest and field up to game lands from WY for a good price (because it'll save him) and proviso he and family not be evicted from house or 20 acres of field (where he has a right to farm) until his death Offered to let him keep the 20 but he said no and I feared for him for a mo- ment because he seemed desperate

Bo wondered what the price was and sup- posed he could have looked it up at the town hall (those twenty acres hanging on to the final thousand like bracket fungus on a log that was his now), but he knew he never would. He turned to one more entry that spoke of the land. It was dated March 1 of that year:

Miss Emma Cording sounded pleased that WY has sold all he owns scolding me even for letting him stay on as a tenant and I said nothing in reply She is a harder woman than I know

Bo turned the page and found a sea of ink-lined white space, then saw writing on the next page, as though it were a new book altogether, for his grandfather had begun to punctuate and compose a clearer line.

April 1933. Easter. The boy they once called Bexhet has found me. He has been given the Branch for a name and (though it will be difficult for him) intends to stay. Hannah is mesmerized in his presence. I will have to tell her now from where he has come.

Bo closed the ledger and put it back on the shelf.

Come on, girl, he said to Krasna, and she lifted her head from the floor. Let's get in the truck. We've got work to do.

Outside in the driveway he opened the tailgate of the pickup and lifted her rump and pushed her paws first into the bed. You won't be doing this much longer, he said.

He got in the driver's side and glanced

over at the passenger seat and noticed, for the first time since his grandfather had ridden with him last at Christmas, a pair of the man's old leather work gloves still pushed into the fold of the bench seat. Bo leaned over and pulled them out and laid them next to him. He thought again of the days when he and his grandfather drove to work together and spoke in the front seat of the pickup about matters of business, or the days when they never said a word to each other (out of exhaustion or contentment, it never seemed to matter) and Dardan flicked by in scenes framed by the window of the truck. Then as now, it was a place of peace where he had found himself, found his labor and his rest. Bo turned the engine over and backed down the drive.

CHAPTER FIVE

He had heard some of the men around his grandfather's time call it a planing mill, but it was known in Dardan as the Endless Roughing Mill, a place where lumber came in on logging trucks from the Allegheny Mountains and was air-dried, then cut to shape and kiln-dried and sent out to the local lumberyards or sold to contractors, freight yards, and the mines. When Jozef Vinich arrived in America in 1919, he worked on whatever construction crews would hire him during those years of boom in northeastern Pennsylvania. And when he went to Helen Posol's father in 1920 and asked the man for his daughter's hand in marriage, Posol laughed and said, You need to settle down. Jozef asked what he meant, and Posol said that a man needs a business. Jozef never told the father of the woman he loved that he was worth a hundred dollars in the eyes of the Miners Bank. But he understood. In the early spring of '21 he hopped the train out of Wilkes-Barre to Dardan and walked the remaining four miles west to the edge of town, where the Cording Mill (as it was known) was hiring a tallier.

In those days, the mill consisted of a warehouse, tally shed, straight-line ripsaw, two roughing planes, and a kiln. Jonathan Cording was a reclusive man, one of the last of the lumber barons in town. He had lost his only son in the battle of Belleau Wood and carried his grief like an empty watch chain that he pulled from his pocket hourly and seemed surprised to find the watch no longer there. He hired Jozef as the second of two handlers on the tally crew. But Cording's inexhaustible well of sorrow, and the crash of '29, nearly drove the business into the ground. On Christmas Eve of that year he leaned over the barrel of a twelve-gauge shotgun pressed between his knees and pulled the trigger.

Cording's daughter, Emma, saved the place by asking the workers to put what money they could back into the mill and become shareholders in the company. Four of them — laborers, mostly, who stacked boards, swept floors, and shoveled sawdust and wood shavings — left and migrated to the coal mines in Wilkes-Barre and Nanti-coke. Four others put in as little as twenty dollars of their savings and hoped that Miss Cording knew what she was doing. Jozef, the yard foreman, the mill manager, and the supervisor put in two hundred dollars each, which she matched with the ten thousand dollars she had gotten from her father's insurance settlement, and Cording Mill became the Endless Roughing Mill.

There were days at a stretch when the saws were silent and the owner-operators still came in because they could not tell their families they had no more savings and they would soon have nowhere to work. But in 1930 there was a run on gold found in the Swatara Gap, and the Endless Rough-ing Mill sold nine thousand board feet of pine a week to a local contractor for the shanty towns going up. By the time the rush was over in 1931 (there was some gold but not enough for an industry to grow) and the National Guard bought the land for a state park, the lumber was sold and the money banked, and Endless Roughing made profits into '36 supplying WPA proj-ects. By 1940, Jozef Vinich and Erskine Pound, the supervisor, were the sole owner-operators of the mill, everyone else having sold their shares to these men when it looked like the profits were about as good as they were ever going to get. Then they began gearing up for another war in Europe.

Twenty years later, when Bo came home from college and took the job working in the tally shed with Andy Jones, he told himself it would be temporary. But he was still at the yard in '62 and had no plans to leave. He loved the acrid smell of the green woods and the syrup scent of pine as loads of these logs came down the grading chain and dropped to the floor, their presence recorded in the echoes that rose to the rafters of the corrugated ceiling before anyone ever made a scratch in the book. He apprenticed in the milling sheds (where he spent another two years breathing the incenselike heaviness of the air that carried on it the rips and whines of the planes and saws) and learned the business side of lumber in the back office with his grandfather. By the time Bo became the owner of Endless Roughing in 1970, he had worked every job in the mill and still shoveled shavings into the kiln furnace in the months when they were shorthanded because no high school kid wanted the job.

Bo pulled into the yard at noon and walked to his office with Krasna at his heels. Jeff

Lamoreaux, the mill supervisor, was sitting behind Bo's desk and fanning a pile of work orders. Jeff had worked in sawmills in Georgia since he was fourteen. When he was twenty, he moved with his family north to Wilkes-Barre and then to the mountains west of the city, where he showed up one day at Endless Roughing with a letter and a short résumé. Jozef hired him not long after Bo started working.

Jeff dropped the stack of orders on the desk and stood. Where've you been, boss?

The lawyer read the old man's will today, Bo said. Looks like I've got my own house. That place atop the field on the other side of Rock Mountain.

That was your grandfather's? Jeff asked, shaking his head. Damn. The things I don't know.

Bo took off his jacket and hung it on the back of the door. What's come in?

Jeff pointed to the desk. Heatin' up all over the place. And not just local. Wilkes-Barre. Hazelton. That means they're buying lumber.

It's just a seasonal bump, Bo said. We'll bust our asses for a few months and then have to sit on them all summer.

This one might last. We should be ready for it.

Bo nodded. You got the help you need?

I could use someone with a little skill around a saw. I'm tired of teaching them and losing them.

All right, Bo said, and sat down. I'll pay three-fifty an hour to anyone who knows what he's doing.

How about two more to sweep and shovel?

Buck-seventy-five. That's more than they'll make at the Dairy Queen. Maybe someone will take to it and stick around for a change.

Will do, Jeff said. He pulled a cigarette from where it was resting on the top of his ear and put it in his mouth.

I thought you quit? Bo asked.

Tryin'. One after lunch. One after supper. I just don't think this one's going to last until supper. He reached down to scratch Krasna's ear and turned to Bo. You here for the rest of the day? Because I got to head over to the kiln to keep an eye on those boys from Mansfield. Good Christ, there's a tree stump down in Georgia that knows more about the inside of that thing than they do.

Bo laughed. I'm here. You go take care of that. You found them, remember?

Don't remind me, Jeff said, and walked out the door chewing on the filter of his Marlboro.

Bo picked up the work orders. A stack of

eight. Maybe this time it would last. Maybe they could buy a moulder, a multihead, and set up a finish shed and get into the business of more custom profiles. Bo signed them all and called the dog and went outside to walk the grounds.

He ran into the foreman, Dave Cummings, coming out of the break room. Dave told Bo he had seen Asa Pound in town and that Bo ought to check in on the guy. He's torn up about your grandfather.

Bo had seen Asa at the wake and the funeral and he had seemed fine, kept it in, but Bo knew he was not fine. The Pounds were their best friends in Dardan. Jozef and Asa had run the mill by themselves once old Erskine let his son have his share of the place. The two men were undivided and of one mind when it came to matters of business, aloof and silent when it came to matters of the town. Asa and Maryann's son, Will, was right between Sam and Bo in age, the three of them placed five years apart, as inseparable as their guardians. Then one morning in the summer of '65, Sam and Bo came in from fishing and Jozef and Hannah were at the kitchen table, Hannah crying and Jozef looking like he had seen a ghost. Sit down, boys, he said, and told them that Will had been driving back from a ball game in Philadelphia that night when a trucker who had fallen asleep at the wheel crushed Will in his car between the truck and the mountainside. Will had asked Bo and Sam to come with him, but Sam had schoolwork to do, and Bo hated the idea of being anywhere near Philadelphia. So Will had driven down alone.

I'll swing by the house tonight or tomorrow, Bo said to Dave. I was just thinking about him and the times my brother and I used to have with his son out at the lake.

Don't let it keep, Dave said, and Bo thanked him.

He walked past the planing shed, heard the saws going and the ductwork humming, and he kept on walking. He skirted the kiln and the pond that was surrounded by rhododendrons and blueberry bushes that Jozef had planted a long time ago, and he ducked into the tally shed.

The air felt ten degrees cooler in there and smelled of dirt and tree bark and a hint of grease as Bo walked past the grading chain. Old Andy Jones was not around, but that was all right. Bo was in no mood to talk. He went over to the makeshift tally desk of eight cinder blocks and an old door and looked into the book Andy kept meticulously and could see they had received two loads of ten thousand board feet the Friday before. Bo told himself to remind Andy to check the schedule for any double loads. Krasna seemed curious about a mouse that had found a corner of the shed in which to hide, until Bo called her away, and they walked out and over to the parking lot and got back into the truck.

He drove into town and took a left at the lights and headed up Old Lake Road, then veered off onto Rock Mountain Road. Signs for the state game lands were posted ahead of him, and he took a right turn onto a dirt road that looked as though it disappeared into the forest but looped in an S through the trees for half a mile and came out into a clearing. And there it stood at the edge of a field, the house, exposed and weathered like an unintended cenotaph no one returned to or even remembered anymore. He parked and left Krasna on the passenger seat and walked up the front yard of grass and weeds left uncut and brown and pushed flat along the ground from the winter's snow and spring rain. He stopped at what was once a brick pathway that led to the front porch, but was barely visible now where it had cracked and moved and been covered by the overgrowth along its edge. He heard the warble of birds and looked up and saw doves sitting in the recess of a decorative tympanum above the front door.

He knew now that Walter Younger had built the house — a three-story clapboard — sometime before Jozef Vinich built his on the other side of the mountain. It had a large porch that ran the entire length of the front, tall windows on the first and second floors that made the facade seem delicate and light, and two small gablet dormers built into the roof of the third floor on the east and west sides. Two chimneys rose through that roof. And in the direction of the field, there was a timber-frame barn that had weathered to a silver so bright the afternoon sun glinted off it like a shard of glass broken and left in the dirt.

Bo surveyed the front from the bottom step of the porch and reckoned the house had been painted last in the mid-sixties, but the siding had held it well, and only on the south- and south-west-facing sides was there any peeling. As he got closer, he saw a rotten fascia board on the north side where one of the wooden gutters had pulled away. He could see, too, that the window frames were shedding some paint, the glazing raised here and there, but not much, and it oc-curred to him that Walter Younger had known what he was doing when he built this house. Jozef Vinich had known it, too.

Bo kicked through the grass and got up close to the foundation, took out his folding knife with an awl on it, and poked at the mortar between the bricks. It was sound. He went around to the back and stood at the full basement door that led down steps cut into the hill on the eastern slope and tried to imagine where his grandfather might have hidden a key, since neither Hannah nor the lawyer had handed him one. It would be close but not too close. Part of the house, a place where he could pick it up upon arriving and hide it when he left. Bo walked back to the front and noticed one side of the latticework under the porch swung on a hinge and was closed with a latch. He opened it and saw a space the width of a deck of playing cards between two bricks in the foundation just below the sill plate. He put his thumb and index finger inside the gap and pulled out a key.

The basement was cool and smelled of the earth floor and coal dust from the bin that had been emptied and swept clean. Bo opened the ashpan on the furnace and that, too, was empty. The water had been shut off at the main where it came in from the well, and the water heater was gone. He probed the frames of all six windows with the tip of his knife and then retraced his steps in a U-shape, looking up at the floor joists for any cracks or sags. He pulled a wooden crate away from a corner and hoped he would find some mouse droppings or a snakeskin or some crack in the foundation below grade and a line of damp, but there was nothing.

The basement stairs came up into the kitchen, where there was a soapstone sink, an old wringer washer in a corner, and a Glenwood cookstove. He went over to the sink to have a look at the plumbing and noticed there was a gap between the back of it and the wall. He pulled on the sink to see how well it was anchored and heard something metal fall and clink on the floor. He bent down and picked up a small silver teaspoon, so plain and spare in its design that it looked deliberate. On the back of the handle was the silver mark bk. Bo put it in his pocket.

He walked out into the main living room and went back and forth across the bare wood floors, feeling for any lifts or loose boards. He stopped at the fireplace and knelt down on the stone hearth, opened the damper, and peered up that chimney. Nothing except sky, but he would have to put a cap on it. The room was bright, and it had warmed considerably in the sun all day, so he opened the windows to see what the cross-breeze was like and to check the sash weights. Then he went upstairs.

On the second floor he found some water damage in the bathroom. He took his knife and stabbed the watermark, and plaster crumbled into a claw-foot tub.

Now we've got some work to do, he said out loud, and walked through the rest of the bedrooms, checking the walls and ceilings. But the house had weathered its abandonment well. He went up to the third floor to see if there was any evidence of squirrels or more leaks, then climbed down and went out through the front door. He walked over to his truck and hopped up inside the bed so he could see the full surface of the roof, then jumped down. It would be good for at least another five years.

He let Krasna out of the truck and they walked over to the barn, a post-and-beam design built into the rise of the hill. There was a green cockerel weathervane at the top of a cupola, and it turned gently with the breeze. Two twelve-foot doors on sliders opened at the level of the driveway, and Bo tried these and went inside. He figured there was a little over a hundred square feet of space but nothing on the floor other than a rack of garden tools and two moldy bales of hay. He kicked one bale, and a garter snake nosed out and slid away toward the open door and disappeared into the grass outside. A set of stairs along the wall rose to an upper section of the barn, and he walked up, testing each step for loose boards. At the top was an area large enough for a tractor, and there were two doors that hung on hinges and opened out. He threw the bolt at their center and pushed on them and looked across his twenty acres of field. He knew that a man who rented the place in '64 had grown potatoes. It had been a cornfield for a short time before that. Who brought in the hay bales or left them, he did not know. Spring shoots of orchard grass and clover were coming up. *The old man would have planted those,* he thought. The soil looked healthy. He would need the summer just to do repairs on the house, but he could try growing some winter wheat in September. And he knew a man who had a tractor with a plow and a harrow who might be interested in a lease. Krasna came up and around from the side of the barn and lay down in the shade beside the door. Bo looked over at the far edge of the field, a landscape familiar, though from a different angle, the angle he and his grandfather once approached this land from the farm, and stared at the house, and he wondered why it sat alone and unoccupied on that hill as though waiting, though for what his grandfather never said.

The rifle crack made him jump, and Krasna stood up. It was a large-caliber round, and it came from the creek.

Stay, Bo said to the dog.

He walked at a pace across the field, the lay of the land moving him toward the edge of the woods. The breeze had picked up, and he felt the air cool as he approached the trees. *There's no wall,* he thought, and kicked at the grass as if to make one appear. But the ground had been plowed right to the closest maples, and he knew whatever fieldstone had been collected went not into building a border but into the foundation of Walter Younger's house, like his grandfather's. Bo walked another two hundred yards downslope and came to the black and white sign for the game lands, the iron rod driven into the ground, woods on one side of it, weeds and grass on the other. Then he crossed over.

He could smell the moss and wet rocks. The leaves on the trees had begun to emerge only the week before, their cover like a thin and silvery wash against the sky. Bo scanned the stretch of creek where hepatica and trout lily were beginning to bloom in white and yellow patches, and ferns unfolded in the shade and wet cover of the bend. He looked farther downstream, where the brush thickened, and he saw a man squatting over something on the ground. Bo moved closer and the man stood up and said in a flat voice, You'd get yourself shot in-season stomping around here like that, Konar.

It was Paul Younger, Ruth Younger's father. He had on army-surplus fatigues and pants, and he wore a thick black headband without a hat. Not a mark of hunter's orange anywhere on him. He took a cigarette out of a pack in his vest pocket, lit it, dropped the match, and pushed it into the soft ground with his boot. He took a long drag and Bo could see the scar that curved down his cheek like an age line, too graceful and clean to have been received in any way other than slow. It was said around Dardan that there was not a stretch of woods in Pennsylvania where Paul Younger had ever gotten lost. Or would. Bo had seen him in town only from a distance. He had to be in his sixties, although Bo was not sure, wondering if he just had one of those images of the man in his mind that defined perception regardless of age, an image shaped by the memory of the day he had come up to Hannah at her husband's funeral with a black hat in hand (the face not scarred then) and tried to speak to her. But she put her arm around Bo, turned her back, and walked away.

Bo stood five yards from him now and could see it was a doe Younger had brought down.

You always hunt out of season? Bo asked.

Season, Younger said, and spat. I'm doing these woods a favor. He wiped his mouth with his sleeve. Your brother showed me this spot. Deer love those cattails over there. To bed. I can come over the escarpment upwind of them and have my pick. Any day. Any season.

Close up, the man looked gaunt and filthy, his gray-flecked hair greasy and strewn with bits of dried leaves, the skin in his neck lined with dirt. He had likely spent the night in those woods. Maybe two. And something about the way he described his method of hunting these lowlands beneath the curve of the creek reminded Bo of Sam recounting how he, too, had lain and waited for the buck he bagged and brought home all by himself each year.

My brother? Bo asked.

Used to hunt with him here all the time.

That boy had a gift.

Bo regarded the man before him, a man like his grandfather in many ways, save the one way that counted most. He could lay claim to no ground for his own — ground, that is, on which he could hunt with impunity, and for this he seemed a man lost. Bo remembered what Sam had said about him, and he remembered the arguments Sam and Jozef got into over whose land this rightfully was, land Sam believed should belong not to the Youngers or the Viniches but to anyone who would walk through it, take what he needed, and leave the rest in peace. You're living forty-nine states too far to the east there, son, Jozef said to him. You and Mr. Younger might believe it to be a wilderness, but you'd be the only two in this town. God didn't give it to me, the bank did, and that'll do for now. Bo wished he could conjure his grandfather's ledger and sit down with this man among the cattails where the deer he sought to kill loved to rest, and say, *Look here, Mr. Younger. Each man has had a part in this. But something peaceful could be born out still.*

He said, Hunting's over, Mr. Younger. And my brother's not here. You want permission, you ask. Now, do what you need to do with that thing and stay off my mother's land.

Your mother's now, is it?

Younger stood and sheathed the knife he had taken from his belt and turned to face Bo. I guess when she's gone, it'll be yours. Or maybe some of it's yours already. And tell me, Bo Konar, when the Good Lord takes you, whose land will it be then?

Bo said, I don't imagine it'll matter to you anyway, will it?

Younger smiled. Now you're catching on. They told me you were the smart one.

What about the game commissioner? Bo asked. You're pretty close to land where the state has some say about who hunts and when.

Younger scoffed. Game commissioner couldn't find his ass with both hands. Do you know what the fine is for poaching out of season?

It's not much.

Do you know what this doe will bring besides food?

No, but I bet you do.

Younger nodded. I hunt deer when there's room in my freezer. I've been doing it since I was a boy and my daddy owned this land, and I intend to keep doing it until I don't need to eat anymore.

Younger paused and looked like he was about to turn back to the task before him,

114

but he pushed his boot again into the ground where he had thrown the match, and said, About your father. Your grandfather knew I meant him no harm. Your brother, too. You know how many times I've relived the moment I pulled that trigger? How many times I see him in that second before I pull it? He said this to the ground. Then he lifted his eyes and said to Bo, Your mom —

My mother won't forgive you, Bo said so fast he wished he had not.

Younger scratched his head and looked at his fingers as though he had caught something in them. Yeah, well, that'd make two of us, he said.

They stood looking at each other, and Bo could see Ruth in him. Something around the mouth, though, was different, something that could not be inherited, and Bo felt all of a sudden like a man coming home after a long time away and finding another family in his kitchen and wondering if he has walked into the wrong house.

What do you want? Bo asked.

Younger pointed to the doe, and Bo stared at it as if measuring not the dead animal but what his response ought to be. The same, or different from those others who had come before him?

All right, he said, but this is between you and me. No one else. You hunt alone, and you keep your mouth shut about it.

Younger drew the back of his hand across his forehead. Just until your brother comes home, he said. Then we go together, him and me.

Bo took a deep breath and let it out, and Paul Younger turned back to his kill. Bo watched the man as he rolled up both of his sleeves and slid his arm through the shoulder strap of his rifle and pushed it behind him. He took his belt knife back out, knelt down, and began to work the blade along the underside of the doe, fast but steady, stopping only to wipe hair off of the choil. He leaned closer to the ground as he sliced past the belly and slowed around the bladder. When he had cut the animal open to the anus, he stood and looked at Bo one more time, then walked over to the creek side, bent down, and washed the blood from his knife and hands.

CHAPTER SIX

Late that spring the rains returned as though it were April, and it seemed there would be no end to them, except for single days or hours when the clouds parted and the sun came out and the ground dried enough for anyone to believe that something besides mushrooms and more ferns might grow. On a day like that (long enough after the day she had written last, so the postmark was as much a surprise as a reminder), a Friday, Hannah received a letter from the new casualty assistance officer. She handed it to Bo when he came home from work. He opened a beer, went outside, and sat down on the front porch steps. It was the longest letter they had received regarding Sam. It read:

Dear Mrs. Konar,

This is in reply to your letter of April 17, 1972. Regrettably, there is no new information concerning your son Corporal Samuel B. Konar. The search is continuing. As you know, the officers' board that was convened to investigate his status had, after sixty days, found no evidence to recommend a change to deceased. That remains the case these more than seven months later.

The letter went on to say the welfare of the American servicemen captured or missing in Vietnam was a matter of the utmost urgency, and the president desired all to know that his administration would not set the matter aside until every American was repatriated and the fullest possible accounting of the missing was given.

Then there was another paragraph, and Bo was surprised by the change in tone. He read closely, as if he might be the recipient of some code meant to tell him more about his brother than protocol would allow. *On a personal note, there is one further detail I can add, which may at least give you the chance to talk to someone who knew your son in Vietnam. Captain Burne Grayson has retired and is living in the town of Abas, West Virginia. He was on the ground the day Corporal Konar went missing, and his testimony has been instrumental in keeping your son carried in that status.*

The letter was signed, *Sincerely, J. A. KRAYNACK, Captain, U.S. Marine Corps Head, Casualty Section, Personal Affairs Branch,* and at the bottom of the letter was a handwritten postscript: *#1 Morning Ridge. It would not be out of line to go visit. Good luck. Jack.*

After Bo came home from college in the winter of '59, the farthest he had ever traveled from Dardan was a trip to Johnstown, Pennsylvania, to look at a saw he did not buy. It was a Mattison and had been poorly maintained and then stored for years in a barn near the river, so its parts were either seized or decayed beyond repair. Jozef had told him to go. You never know what you might find, he said, and four hours later Bo found out he had wasted his time.

So he sat there on the porch, the air smelling sweetly of peonies and wet grass, and he wondered if he should go to this place in West Virginia and listen to a man he had never met tell him about the last days of his brother's life. And he decided he would not.

The screen door slammed, and Hannah came out and sat down in the rocking chair.

It's the most we've ever gotten, she said.

And we've still got nothing.

That's just what it feels like. We don't

know for sure. Maybe we should go see this Captain Grayson. Maybe he could tell us something, if he's so inclined.

Why wouldn't he come see us, if he was so inclined? And why wouldn't he already have told it to the marines in charge of this stuff?

She didn't answer. Bo put the letter down on the porch and banged some mud off of his boots into the beds below.

Maybe I can get a number and call him first, he said. We could drive down together.

Hannah rocked. What about Ruth? she asked.

I'll take the letter to her, Bo said. He was working a stick into the lug sole of his Chippewas, and he pretended to be distracted. When he finished, he banged that boot, too, and said, She's the one who ought to make the visit, you know.

She won't drive down there pregnant like that to visit some man she's never met.

I didn't mean down there. I mean up here. Invite her into this house, Hannah. It's not like when that baby comes you can just ignore her, Sam or no Sam.

Bo, Hannah said, I lay up most nights thinking about the same thing. And the closer I get to becoming a grandmother, the more sleep I lose over it.

Well?

Yes, she said. I wish that it were.

She got out of the rocker and walked down the steps of the porch and picked up the garden trowel and hand rake she had left on the grass and put them in the wheelbarrow.

You know, she said, turning to look up at Bo on the porch, if Sam had ever felt the loss, ever felt what it was like to have your father around and then to know he was never coming back, he'd have stayed away from her, no matter how beautiful she is. Not out of anger. Out of sadness. That's all I want, Bo. I just want them to stay away. Is that too much to ask?

In the morning, after Bo had gone to the mill, Hannah drove over to St. Michael the Archangel church and parked behind Father Rovnávaha's Scout in the rectory lot. She got out and knocked on the front door, and the housekeeper said that the priest was in the church hearing confessions, so Hannah walked along the sidewalk and went in by the back door and sat down.

The church was built in the 1920s by Father Bozak of Swoyersville, a revered World War I chaplain who was wounded badly with a company of men at the second

121

battle of the Marne. He vowed, the story went, that if he lived he would build a church of stone just like the ruined one in France where he lay waiting for someone to find him, while all around the men of his company cried out in their final hours for a medic, their mothers, and God.

Stone turned out to be more practical than symbolic in that part of Pennsylvania when the priest came home and announced his plans to build a church west of the city for the people of faith who lived along the Salamander. Catholics kept mostly to their neighborhoods in Wilkes-Barre. Jozef once said that in 1921 he remembered seeing, against the night sky on the hill where the church now stood (the whole valley clear-cut and stripped of trees for the mines), three crosses almost two stories high, burning to remind Dardan what could happen if they let the immigrant papist have his way. But that only steeled Bozak, who was said to have threatened the burning of his church with the fires of hell, unleashed by a man who knew what those fires looked and felt like. And so St. Michael's was built. The stone quarried in Pennsylvania. The timber cut in the Endless Mountains. The hands that raised it from the town itself, men of all faiths and no faith, hired and paid, their names etched on a plaque in the nave.

Inside, it was quiet and still and Hannah felt like she was nine again, when she came there with her mother on Saturday afternoons to confess to Father Blok in the dark of the confessional about hiding some hardtack under her pillow, or not wanting to help her mother or father around the house. Once she blurted out that she hated the farm and wished she could live like other boys and girls who did not have to milk cows and gather eggs or weed patches of tomatoes and cucumbers. In those days, the old priest looked to her through the screen like he might be asleep. But she could hear him breathing, waiting for her to finish, and he said, Your sins are not grave, Hannah. She was shocked to hear a priest tell her she had done nothing wrong. He went on, Imagine, there is a part of the world where right now a girl like you is praying that she might not lose her mother, because her father was lost when the soldiers came into town. And after that, she wants for one thing only. Food. What did you have for breakfast this morning? She told him, Fresh eggs. He said, Ahh, fresh eggs, as though they had appeared on a plate before him in that tiny booth. Did you thank God for them? Hannah said no. Then for your penance, thank God for the food before you when your mother places it on the table. And then take a moment to thank God for her, too. Will you?

The air smelled of the same candle smoke and slight perfume of frankincense and gardenia that she remembered, and it still sounded even in its silence like every voice uttered was a whisper and that whisper would echo forever if she just sat and listened long enough.

When there were no more lines outside the confessional, Hannah slipped inside and heard the screen slide. Father Rovnávaha greeted her with a blessing.

Good morning, Father, she said. I wanted to ask if you'd like to come for lunch tomorrow. I need your advice and your counsel and, well, I need it sooner rather than later. I thought this might be as good a place as any to find you.

Hannah, Rovnávaha said. He sounded exhausted, though it was only morning. For lunch with you, I would tell the pope himself to wait. What time?

Come at noon if you can. We'll have chicken soup.

Noon it is.

There was a short silence between them, then Rovnávaha said, Is there anything else you need to talk about?

No, Father, she said. We'll save that for another conversation.

She sat reading in the living room with the front door open so she could listen for the priest, the telltale downshifting every vehicle did to make the hill. He was right on time at twelve, and she went out on the porch and watched his small truck come up and over the rise through the trees and pull into the drive.

In the church, and when he made sick calls at the hospitals in Kingston and Wilkes-Barre, Rovnávaha wore his full black clerical suit with a high white collar. But in town, when he ran errands or traveled to the homes of parishioners, he dressed in khaki trousers and a tab-collar clerical shirt that he rolled up at the sleeves, with a faded jean jacket over it if there was a chill in the air. He got out and stared up at the sky that had clouded over again, walked up the front steps of the house, and gave Hannah a bottle of wine.

Will it ever stop trying to rain? he said, and she smiled and told him she had given up on the spring and was pinning all of her hopes on summer.

They had the chicken soup with fresh

bread and they told stories of Jozef and laughed at most of them and did not speak of anything or anyone else.

When they were finished, Hannah cleared the bowls and plates and made coffee. Rovnávaha sat, swirled the last of the wine in his glass, and waited for her to tell him why she had asked him to lunch. She put out cups, saucers, a sugar bowl, and a creamer and sat down, one hand resting on the table, the other in her lap.

She said to the priest, You know, Father, when Becks went missing during the war, there were days I used to leave Bo with Papa and walk up to the bend, where he and I hiked when we were young. I could speak to him there. I knew he was alive. So I wasn't surprised when Father Blok called me one day to tell me he had heard from a Hungarian priest who was a friend of his that a man named Konar was being held by the military police and was suspected of desertion. All I could help thinking was, *He is alive.* I trusted while the others doubted.

When I went to Brooklyn to visit him in prison, he told me what he had done, the weeks on end of fighting in French villages, the rain of mortars in the forests, the man next to him with no arms or legs, the dead. He had no desire to be anywhere. Less desire to fight. So when he got the chance, he fled and found a *kumpania* of Rom who took him in like one of their own, which he was in a way. Until the war was over.

But when he came home finally, he was a changed man. I would wake up in the morning, his side of the bed cold, and I would go outside and find him walking out of the woods as though he had spent the entire night there. *Where were you?* I'd ask, and he would say, *I couldn't sleep, so I went up to the bend to listen to the stream.* And I knew I had lost him. Lost the part of him that had years earlier, when he was a boy yet, run from Europe to come live with us on this farm, because his own grandfather said to him, *Go find the man they called Vinich.*

She stopped, put her head down, and dabbed at her eyes with a napkin.

Go on, Rovnávaha said.

So even though two years had gone by, two years in which we had Sam, and Papa was talking about Becks taking over the mill, and he seemed to be coming back to us, I wasn't surprised when they told me he'd been shot by Paul Younger on the ridge that spring. It was like I had been expecting it all along. Like he had willed it somehow. I know it was an accident, and I can't imagine what Paul Younger must carry around with him still. Like some kind of millstone. But I carry one, too. And I can't forgive him, Father. I don't want to forgive him. To me he's just another man with a rifle who took my Becks. And now Bo wants me to invite him and his daughter into my home. Feed them. Welcome them as family because of what Sam and Ruth have done. But it's not what I want to do. I don't want to call them family. If I had my way, I would make them leave this town altogether. Only that would bring me peace.

Rovnávaha leaned back into his chair. He had heard the story of Bexhet Konar from Father Blok when he first came to St. Michael's as a young priest, one week after they buried the man. Information during the war was often passed through the Vatican, and there was talk of an American soldier with Romani blood who had been found by the Resistance, separated from his unit and wandering the Ardenne Forest. They killed many, many Germans, Tomáš, Blok told him in a tone more of wonder than of disapproval, as though Becks Konar might have been a part of that resistance. But he was, in the end, just a lost and tired soldier who waited too long to return to the war.

The story Rovnávaha knew firsthand and

heard from the lips of Paul Younger was how Becks Konar had died. Paul Younger had chosen Rovnávaha for confession over Blok (Rovnávaha understood) because the new priest would not have known anyone yet in the town of Dardan, and Paul Younger would be judged for his own sins. What Rovnávaha would never tell Hannah was how hard the man wept that day when he confessed to having been unfaithful to his wife with a prostitute (which was why she had left him when their daughter was three months old) and the belief that this sin was what had guided the bullet into the heart of Becks Konar. I couldn't stop the blood, Father. I couldn't stop it, he said as he wept like a boy, the two of them in that dimly lit room for so long that the parishioners outside gave up and went home. Rovnávaha did his best to convince Paul Younger that God does not hold a man's sins as a weapon against him but loves all men regardless of those conditions they place on themselves. To which Younger replied, Then God is more of a fool than I guessed. And he rose from that confessional, never to set foot in St. Michael the Archangel church again.

What Rovnávaha said to her was, It's time, Hannah. It's time you thought of the gift that Sam and Ruth have given to you and

Paul. The chance to forget what misfortune has shaped the past, and to forgive one another. And yourselves. Once and for all.

Except my husband and my son are both gone now, she said.

Rovnávaha leaned forward and took her hand. After what you just told me about Becks? he said. You believe that? In your heart, you believe Sam won't come back?

She shook her head and told him she thought every day about Sam and knew he was still alive, just as she had with Becks, no matter how much time had gone by. There were days when she would try to imagine what her son might be doing or thinking at that moment. What kind of pain he might be in. And she would be overcome with her own pain and the desire to escape into sleep, where she would see her son in her dreams.

And I don't welcome them, Father. Those dreams. I never have. Because the people of them are not people but ghosts. And my son is no ghost.

Then welcome the Youngers, the priest said, and you welcome Sam. Into this house. And your grandchild with them. All you have to do is say the word, open the door, and put food on the table as you have for me, as you have for your sons, and this will all be healed. I promise you. It will all be healed.

She let his words settle into the quiet and then said, I can do that for the girl. But him, too?

He needs it the most, the priest said.

She pulled her hand back to her side and bowed her head. Outside, gusts of wind pushed against the loose screen on the open window above the sink, and she glanced up at it but did not rise to close it. There had been a phoebe calling near that same window in the morning, and she watched young squirrels jump from the apple trees and thought this day might turn out to be fine. But all she could see now were the undersides of leaves on those trees pulled back by the wind and black clouds gathering in the sky, and then the rain as it poured down once again over all of Dardan.

■ ■ ■ ■ ■

PART 2
WHILE THE
EARTH REMAINS

■ ■ ■ ■

CHAPTER SEVEN

Solstice approached, but the light from day to day lengthened as though from behind a veil, so flat, thickset, and general were the cloud cover and its rain, from sunup to sundown. What had been a world of lush green in May had turned cinereal in hue as it leaned toward saturation and growing rot in June. Those who moved through this, intent on their desire to work and live regardless, walked hunched and ashen as well. Some believed in omens and portents yet would not say so. Others hoped — out loud in the stores and bars and diners, and quietly in their homes to themselves — that if this branch of storms had to bend down upon them for whatever reason God might allow, it would not break over them in those mountains.

In the late spring of 1972, low pressure was stationary over most of the Northeast, and Pennsylvania, from the border with

New York's southern tier to the Mason-Dixon Line, saw more rain in three weeks than it had since the flood before the war, all the old folks said, and they meant the flood of '36. The rain was a follow-on to the deep melting snowpack that had been accumulating in the higher elevations since December, so that long before the first day of summer, the ground was sodden and gave like a sponge wherever it was not covered with pavement or concrete, until those surfaces, too, began to crack and buckle.

On a Monday, June 19, after the television anchorman announced a U.S. declaration of victory against NVA forces in the months-long battle of An Lộc, and a short-lived airline pilots' strike, the local weatherman reported that over the weekend a tropical storm from the Yucatán had drifted across the Gulf of Mexico and become the first hurricane of the season. It came ashore again near the Florida panhandle, tracked across Georgia, and went out to sea around North Carolina on the twenty-first before coming back ashore, grown now, near New York and pushing inland. On the twenty-second, that same Pennsylvania weatherman forecasted light rain for the Wyoming Valley from the weakened but dogged low as it moved north, but he intoned cautiously that a nontropical front was coming in directly from the west, and he did not know what might happen when the two met. On the twenty-third, the rains came hard and never let up, and the creeks and rivers of northeastern Pennsylvania's towns and cities (the waters already held at bay with stacked sandbags and whispered prayers) rose to a height that the work of those hands could no longer hold.

Bo pulled up to the mill on Thursday night and unloaded his pickup of food, two transistor radios, batteries, and three full five-gallon fuel cans. He took a Mossberg twelve-gauge and a box of shells from the metal cabinet where he kept it locked and sat in his office watching the news and footage of a river that seemed to hover above the city of Wilkes-Barre in its false banks like the slime trail of some outsize gastropod. He had sent the men home and made himself watchman, not knowing who or what would come down that highway in the night. The pond behind the tally shed was rising, but the men had sandbagged it well, and there was enough surrounding forest that Bo believed it would not be a threat to the heart of the mill. Now all he had to do was wait and see just how bad the hurricane that had drifted north would be for the folks who lived along the Salamander and the Susquehanna.

Ruth Younger went into labor that night. Her aunt Mary, who had midwifed a handful of animals and two other babies whose mothers could not get to the hospital, walked one street over on the Flats in the dark and rain and put water on to boil and asked her brother to cut up some old bedsheets for rags, turn off the overhead light in his daughter's room, and bring in a lamp.

The Flats in Dardan were a plateaulike stretch of stone fields on the creek's plane just before it dropped into the cut of Troy Pass. Between the wars, anyone could get cheap land there and build a cheap house on it. Paul Younger moved into one of the last saltboxes to be erected in the 1930s. Before the first flood. When his father, Walter, passed away and Paul found out the twenty acres of Younger land that he had planned to farm belonged to Jozef Vinich.

He finished cutting up the bedsheet with his wife's old sewing shears and wondered where she was, if she would even care that her daughter was having a baby. *She left me, not the girl,* he thought. When he was done,

138

he took the towel-size remnants into the room at the back of the house. What had been panting and cries in the early evening were screams now, and he watched his daughter writhe until his sister said, She's going to be fine.

He went outside and stood on the porch and smoked and drank coffee and stared at the swollen creek. He had never seen it this high, and he began to go over in his mind a plan to get Ruth and the baby and him up to higher ground, as soon as that baby decided to be born. And what ground after that? They could stay in Dardan, even though it looked more and more like Sam Konar was not coming home. Or they could go. West, it would have to be. Let the baby get a little older, pack up the car, and head out to California. Oregon, maybe. He liked the sound of Oregon. They called those mountains the Cascades.

He had gone inside to make another pot of coffee when Mary pushed into the kitchen from the bedroom and stopped by the wall. She looked tired and pale and her voice trembled when she spoke. She needs to get to a hospital.

Now? Younger put his coffee down. How long have I —

Mary glanced in the direction of a windup

cuckoo on the wall as it struck five. I'm going to call an ambulance, she said.

No. I'll get the car started.

Paul, the baby's back to front. She needs a doctor.

And she'll get one sooner if we get her in that car and drive, he said, and went outside. Mary could hear the Country Squire struggling to turn over, and she went to the phone and dialed and got an operator who took her address, and then the line went dead.

It took another five minutes for the two of them to get Ruth into the back of the station wagon, where they had put the seats down, and lay her sideways on a bed of blankets and pillows, her head behind the driver and her feet touching the back of the bench seat on the passenger side.

Mary yelled to Ruth as though she were hard of hearing, You're going to be fine, honey! The baby just needs a little help to come on out, that's all.

There was a contraction, and Ruth howled and pitched forward and vomited. Paul jumped into the driver's seat and Mary grabbed him by the shoulder. They'll be here any minute.

We don't have a minute from what I can see. Now get in the car.

Mary shook her head and got in on the passenger side, and Paul Younger gunned the old Ford out onto the road.

Bo woke from a dream too shifting and dim to survive out of sleep. He had been sitting in the chair against the wall, and he grabbed the shotgun and stood and went to the door and looked out at the rain and the dark. He passed a finger through the corner of both eyes and turned to check the clock and heard the police scanner on his desk request an ambulance at 26 Holly Street. It took a moment for the address to come to him. Sam had told him years ago, *She lives down in the Flats on Holly Street with her dad.* It had to be. She had said the baby was due in June. He wished now that he had checked in on her at the store every week, not just to take her a letter. But there was work. And there was the house. *A good man is good to his brother, Bohumír.* Jeff was due in around seven-thirty. He could call the hospital then. He walked over to the desk and picked up the phone, and the line was dead. He dropped it and grabbed his oilskin duster from a hook on the back of the door and put it on to keep the shotgun dry, then he ran outside and across the yard to his truck.

He listened to channel nine on the CB as

he drove in the direction of town, but he heard no further mention of Paul Younger's address in the Flats. He switched over to nineteen and asked for a break and got a trucker going the opposite direction out of Dardan on 118.

As he came down the long hill into the town center the clutch slipped on the Dodge and he whispered, Not now, braked the truck to a slow crawl on the blacktop, and thought, *They could only have gone one way.*

He still had Dardan to get through, and as he approached, all he could see in the drab dawn were the lights of police cars and what looked like hooded monks of yellow and black along the creek, passing burlap sacks from where one monk half-filled a bag with sand, twisted the top, and passed it to another monk, who passed it along to another, who stacked the bag on top of a crude bunker near the bridge. The traffic light was flashing red, and Bo was making his way toward it when a policeman in a rain poncho walked out in front of him. Bo slammed on the brakes and the truck skidded to a stop. He rolled down his window and the policeman came over and said, Nothing but National Guard trucks getting through, Mr. Konar.

Bo recognized him as the brother of one of the boys who used to work for him at the mill, a kid Bo fired for coming in hungover and smoking outside of the break room. His name was Kozick.

You haven't seen an ambulance head down to the Flats, have you, Jimmy?

The cop looked past Bo to the passenger side and shook his head. Sorry, Mr. Konar. Everyone down there's coming out. You're going to have to go around the long way if you want to get up to your place now.

The wipers seemed to beat in time to the gusts of rain against the windshield, and Bo took in the scene of sandbaggers, cops, and evacuees coming up from the neighborhoods along the creek in the light.

All right, he said. I'll try my luck on the back roads. He pointed to the line of sandbaggers. Looks like they need you over there.

The cop turned around fast, and Bo punched the gas and shifted hard through all three gears, right through two sets of lights and out onto the long stretch of highway that wound down along Salamander Creek into the pass.

He switched the CB back to channel nine to listen for any traffic that might be coming after him, but all he heard with any clarity was a 10-52 for a heart attack. In his rearview mirror he saw a state police car moving fast in his direction, then crossing the highway at a gap in the median and heading back toward town with its lights on. He came up fast on the sign for Elm Street that led into the Flats, and he downshifted and pumped the brakes to make the turn, the back wheels skittering before coming to a stop at the old stringer bridge. Bo got out and stood on the highway side and watched the water coursing and splashing as it surged past, the entire structure throbbing in place, and he wondered if it would even be there when he needed it. He could hear more sirens heading in the direction of town, and he knew that if he drove over the bridge, he was not going to find Ruth at the house anyway. He got into his truck and backed out onto the highway.

He kept his speed at fifty. A line of army-surplus trucks lumbered toward him from out of the valley in the westbound lane like a diminished caravan of returning soldiers. It occurred to him that he did not know what he was looking for or what he would find if he got all the way through the pass into the town of Luzerne and was stopped by rising water. Another state police cruiser came around the bend behind the convoy, slowed down, and hit the lights. Bo accelerated and felt the rear end of the pickup lift with a gust of wind so that he was looking at the berm, where fresh skid marks led into a wire guardrail that was pushed over like an old fence. He kept his eye on the spot, hit the brakes, and counter-steered. The truck swerved and planed and slid to a stop on the narrow shoulder.

He jumped out and ran over to the gap in the guardrail and could see the wreck below nestled among the trees. He got back in his truck and reversed it to the edge of the ravine, then got out again and reached into the bed for the rope and crawled underneath and tied it fast to the truck's frame. He looked up to see the lights of the statie approaching, then he heaved the other end of the rope down the bank and disappeared along its length.

The station wagon had pushed a good-size maple out by the roots and come to rest on top of it. Bo dropped headlong, his boots cumbrous in the terrain of wet rocks and leaves, the duster too heavy, and his hands losing their grip on the sopping rope. He could see the back wheels of the car spinning in a groove of dirt, and he swung around to the driver's side, where Paul Younger was slumped over the steering wheel, blood seeping from his ears. Bo felt for a neck pulse and pushed the dead man's foot off the accelerator. The wheels stopped and the engine idled and Bo reached over and shut the car off. He went around to the passenger side, where Mary Younger lay in the dirt and leaves next to the open door. He peered in the back at the flattened platform of blankets and pillows smeared with vomit. That door was open, too, but he could not see Ruth. He heard footsteps and snapping branches and looked up to see the trooper bounding down the hill along the rope.

Bo left the car and strode farther along the bank in the direction of the creek, and that was where he saw her, leaning against a tree on the slope as if she had crawled on her hands and knees and then stopped to rest. She had on a T-shirt and was white and naked from the belly down, her eyes open, her face without mark or bruise or trace of blood, and she held the baby in her arms.

Ruth! he shouted above the roar of creek water. He approached and slowed. He could see the scarlet pool in which she sat, the rain having washed her clean as she bled into the ground. She seemed to gaze right through him. He knelt down and put his ear to her lips and felt her breath, then took off his coat and draped it around her shoulders. He reached to take the baby, inert and gray and also washed of mess by the rain, and she held tighter, squeezing the tiny mass to her breasts, and Bo could see the cord and the afterbirth that clung to her. He knelt close and whispered, It's Bo, Ruth. I'm right here.

Ruth looked at him then as though she had come out of a daydream and let him take the lifeless form from her. It was a girl, and he pulled out his knife and cut the umbilicus and held the baby to his shirt, cupped his hand to catch the rain, and poured the water over her head three times.

There, he said, now you can go be with your father.

He placed her back in Ruth's arms and whispered, She's beautiful, and Ruth pulled her baby in close, huddled under the cover of the duster, and began to wail.

Mary Younger's heart had stopped beating by the time the firemen had gotten her to the side of the highway in a litter, and she could not be revived. One of the paramedics came over to Bo and said they had to get out of there fast if Ruth was going to live. Bo knew him from high school and said, I'll follow you, Chip.

He made a move for the door, and Chip put his arm out in front of him. Listen, Bo. We can't get a coroner for those two. You're going to have to bring them with you in the back of your truck.

The other paramedic stepped out of the ambulance with a small bundle of white sheets, and Chip took them from his partner along with two rolls of one-inch adhesive tape. We'll wrap them, he said. Then we go.

They worked fast, and when they were finished, the two paramedics lifted the white statuettes into the truck bed and Bo slammed the tailgate shut. What about the baby? he asked.

She's with her mother, Chip said. Keep that radio on channel nine. We're headed to Dardan College. They've set up an emergency care unit there.

There was no traffic on the highway in either direction. The state police cruiser drove escort with its lights on, and the ambulance followed, the sound of its siren muffled and hollow in the rain. Bo hooked a dry rag over the gun on the rack in the cab so that he could not see into the bed through the mirror, and he gave the ambulance fifty feet. As they passed over the bridge at the first set of traffic lights on the outskirts of town, Bo thought he could feel the road move. Pools of rain grew on the asphalt and exploded when the ambulance drove through them. At the top of the next rise, he could see Dardan Center, the ground appearing to move like a sheen of mercury, and he realized that it was not ground but water. A growing sea without visible crest or wave, Dardan appearing to shrink as they sped into that sea. Sidewalks. Curbs. Everything at the edges disappearing beneath a brown and swirling cover as it erased all discernible terrain.

The police cruiser was the first in, stalled, and was swept aside. The ambulance slowed and drifted right and scraped along a telephone pole until the mirror caught and held. Bo steered to avoid it but felt his truck being pushed in the same direction and then lifted, so that he was surging backward into a speed-limit sign that hooked his front bumper. He watched Chip open the driver-side door of the ambulance, step out into water up to his thighs, lose his footing, then hug his way along the vehicle to the back. Bo climbed out of the pickup and stood on the edge of the floorboard, hoisted himself onto the roof, and dropped down into the bed. He could see an outboard-powered johnboat with two men in it zigzagging down Main Street as the current sped its progress toward them. Bo felt the pickup shift and list against the sign as the water ran faster, and the rear end began to sway back and forth like a trout's tail in a stream. Still he would not look down. He watched as the boat pulled even with the ambulance and the paramedics slid Ruth out on a stretcher and onto the thwarts, and the man at the tiller shouted, There's another one right behind me!

And there was. With two men in it. It raced past Bo and swung around and pushed up against the truck, and the man in the bow grabbed the bumper and dropped the tailgate just as the ambulance that was caught on the telephone pole in front of them slipped and crashed hard into the front grille of the pickup. The truck shook, and the man at the bow of the john-boat could not hold on. Bo dropped to his knees and watched as the bodies he had been carrying slipped into the water. He stood, ran the length of the bed, and jumped in after them.

His feet hit bottom, but the current was fast and he could not stand against it. He struggled to keep his head above-water, and he could just see the bodies as they canted on the surface and began to sink. Then he closed his eyes and dived, grabbing at whatever lay in front of him as he swam, until he felt a patch of something tear in his hands. He reached with his other hand and pulled the body in close by the head until he hugged the entire length of the corpse he knew was Paul Younger by the feel of the unshaved jaw. He kicked to the surface and spat.

Don't let go! he heard a voice from the boat holler. It came toward him and swung around so that water sloshed over its sides. The man in the bow threw a life ring, and Bo had to take two hard strokes with a free hand to grab it. They hauled him over the gunwale first, then tried to lift the body but left it knocking against the side of the boat.

There's one more, Bo said.

The man at the tiller shook his head. There's no time. They'll find it. Help me with this one.

The boat turned hard, and Bo and the man reached into the water together and rolled the body onto the deck. The helmsman waited until the bowman yelled, Go!, and the boat throttled up and rode through that brown sea toward the only stretch of dry hillside visible in the town.

CHAPTER EIGHT

Bo slept for a few fitful hours on a couch in the basement of Alumnae Hall at the college and woke to the sound of a Chinook thumping overhead. He sat up and turned on an AM transistor radio he had found and listened to the news, until the sound got lower and lower and then there was no sound at all. He pulled off the back and took out the nine-volt battery, held it to his tongue, and felt the weak pulse of voltage. He put it down on the armrest of the couch and walked out into the hall.

A clock said four-thirty. He passed a line of empty gurneys and went up a flight of stairs to the ground level. He saw a woman with a clipboard walking ahead of him, and he followed her until she turned and stared him down. She had on green scrubs and blue jeans. A small silver Saint Francis medal on a chain sat in the open V of her shirt. Bo stammered and asked if he could see Ruth Younger, who had come in after a traffic accident.

Family? she asked.

No. I found the car and helped bring her in.

The woman did not check any papers or pick up a telephone or even nod. The Younger woman was airlifted to the VA hospital, she said. They're taking critical cases up there.

He turned to go, then turned back. There was a baby who came in. It had died. Do you know where they might have put her?

The woman shook her head. There's no morgue here, she said. Not yet.

Bo walked outside. Rain was still falling, the wind gusting hard. He set off across a lawn, and by the time he reached the middle of it his face and clothes were soaked, but he put his head down and walked on, moving in the direction of a row of tall pines toward a thin white cross that he knew was the college chapel. He remembered coming here as a boy with his mother to see a sister of mercy whom Hannah helped by translating the letters of a priest hiding in Czechoslovakia. Bo would sit in the sisters' dining room and drink hot cocoa while Hannah took that week's correspondence and they spoke of the weather, Europe after the war, and the fruit trees back at the farm. That was all he knew of the campus that should have been quiet in June but was buzzing with trucks and ambulances, then the loud and lumbering sound of another helicopter dropping out of the sky onto the big lawn.

As he angled toward the yellow-brick and glass-fronted building, he saw Father Rovnávaha's Scout drive through the archway of the college entrance and take a right turn onto the road along which Bo was walking. It occurred to him that the priest came to say Mass for the sisters on Friday afternoons at five-fifteen. *So it's Friday still,* he thought, and Rovnávaha braked to a stop and jumped out of the truck, ran over to Bo on the sidewalk, and embraced him, whispering, Jesus, Bo. Jesus, I'm so happy to see you.

Bo put his arms around the priest below the shoulders as if hugging a giant. He felt the dry back of the man's jacket with his hands and said, She's gone, Father. My brother's girl is gone.

The priest thought he meant Ruth and held Bo at arm's length and pushed the wet hair out of his eyes and said, She's gone to a hospital. They'll do all they can.

Bo shook his head and dropped to the ground and did not say another word.

Rovnávaha sat down on the ground with him, leaned back against the rear tire of the truck, and hugged him as close as he could, as close as he would if it were his own son in his arms whom he had found and rescued from the rising waters of a flood.

After Mass and dinner in the refectory of the convent, the mother superior insisted Bo use her phone to call his mother, and he sat in the nun's office, walls adorned with nothing but a crucifix, and he studied the titles of books on her shelf before he dialed the number at the house and told his mother where he was and that he was all right. She asked about Ruth. He was silent for one moment too long, and she said, Bo?

There was an accident. She's not good, Mom. I can't tell you about it now.

He hung up and went back out into the refectory. The sister gave him a hot tea, and he sipped at it and listened to her and the priest talk until Rovnávaha said it was time he got Bo home, and they went outside and climbed into the Scout.

They drove west, away from town, past the cemetery, and into the mountains on two-lane roads that came back around to the road that skirted the Vinich land, the only way they could get to the farm until the waters receded.

After a while Rovnávaha said to him, Everyone seems to have seen you, Bo, but no one knew where you were. You even had a few cops after you, from what I heard.

The priest kept looking between his passenger and the road, but Bo just nodded and turned to look out the window, his eyes opening and closing on the countryside. Some improbable farmer was in his field on a tractor under the leaden sky. Bo thought again of the days when his grandfather used to drive him around like this, when Bo was younger, and he remembered a story Jozef told him about purchasing his first truck, going out for a little spin at nine o'clock in the morning and coming back at nine o'clock at night, he loved it so much.

The evening air was warm and thick, the rain still steady, but Bo rolled down the window and hooked his elbow on the door and let his arm dangle and rise in the slipstream. He stared at the mountains, the creeks, and the pastures, and sniffed on the breeze the smell of wet and manure. Like his grandfather, he had come to know every field, stand of forest, body of water, and mountain knoll that made up this landscape through which they passed, and he heard Jozef say, When I left Pastvina, I came to where I was reminded of it the most, the time before the war, a time when I had a father and a brother and I knew peace, and death was, for a time, at least, a thing distant, and I believed that all things were possible and unbound and worth fighting for, even when I knew it wouldn't last forever. Bo thought of Sam. He wondered if there would come a time when they, too, old men around a table in the house, would tell stories to each other, to their sons or grandsons, stories of what they had fought for as younger men, what secrets they had held, until the scared eyes of Ruth clutching her baby rose to him, and he shook the vision from his sight so hard that he flinched.

Rovnávaha said, Bo.

He turned from the window and looked at the priest.

I called the chaplain at the VA as soon as I heard. He saw her come in. She's not giving up.

She won't, Bo said.

They took Paul and the baby to a funeral home out on 309. Not much else they could do.

Bo shook the rain from his hand, rolled up the window, and rested his head against the glass. He stared out at the steep hill they were skirting, the house and barn on that hill in the distance telling him where they were and what he had yet to do. Rovnávaha stopped where the pavement stopped, got out and turned the hubs, then jumped back inside and shifted the Scout into four high and turned onto the logging road. They passed through the game lands and climbed the escarpment and came back out onto Vinich land, and they followed the back road right to the bottom of the hill that led up to the farm, where Hannah was waiting for them on the porch.

Bo remained in his room until Sunday morning. When he came down to breakfast, Hannah was cooking bacon and eggs. She asked him how he felt and he said, Like I was drowned twice and the second time wasn't good enough, so they had to drown me again just to make sure.

Well, you missed a whole day. Lots of news about the flood. Nixon declared Wilkes-Barre a disaster area. Rain's supposed to clear out today.

He asked if she had heard anything else about Ruth, but she said she had not. Father Rovnávaha told me everything, Bo. I'm sorry. Folks are talking about you. Someone from the *Dardan Post* called.

He sat down without speaking and she put

158

a cup of coffee in front of him.

I still keep seeing her, he said.

Ruth?

The baby. I never felt so weak in my life, knowing there was nothing I could do.

Hannah sat down and touched his arm and said, You did more than anyone could have. Or would.

On Monday he moved a cot and food out to the mill in his mother's car and stayed there, since it took so long for him to drive the back way through the mountains from the farm, and on Tuesday morning a tow truck pulled his pickup into the yard. The driver unhooked it and told Bo he had orders from the Dardan police to deliver it there. Inside on the driver's seat was a note that said, *We all heard what you did for the Younger girl. I told them to tow this to the mill. We've got your shotgun at the station. Jimmy Kozick.*

Bo called Rovnávaha every day that week to ask if the priest had heard anything from his chaplain friend, and on Thursday afternoon at five o'clock the phone in the trailer office rang. Bo picked it up and it was the priest. He had heard from Father Romanelli that Ruth had woken up, and although she was weak, she was out of danger. He asked Bo if he wanted to see her.

159

In what? Bo asked. That helicopter you got parked behind the rectory?

How long does it take you to drive to the college from the mill? the priest said.

In Hannah's Dart? No more than fifteen. If I wake up before the National Guard.

Let me see what I can do. I'm going to have to pull strings thick as rope, but I've got an idea of who to call. You just be ready tomorrow.

Bo woke at five the next morning, pink sky visible through the open blinds. He rubbed his eyes and rose from the couch, turned on a desk lamp, and took a sip of water from a canteen. The rest he poured into the coffee percolator, then scooped grounds into the basket and plugged it in and sat down and began to go over the work orders that had arrived before the flood.

At six-forty-five the phone rang. It was Rovnávaha.

It's now, Bo, he said. I'm at the college. Head to the back lot. They'll give you fifteen minutes, like you said, then they're lifting off with or without you.

Bo was there in ten. He parked the car and ran toward a Huey that had a red cross painted on the side and nose below the cockpit, and UNITED STATES ARMY on the tail boom. He could hear the high-pitched

160

whine of the engine powering up, the two rotor blades spinning at a medium lop, Rovnávaha and the crew chief waiting at the open door. Bo approached and put his head down, and the crew chief put his hand on Bo's shoulder and directed him onto a bench seat and yelled, Buckle up! Rovnávaha sat down next to him. The chief spoke into a headset on his flight helmet and closed the door, and Bo could hear the engine revs climb, the rotors sounding like a tribe of angry swordsmen trying to come at them two at a time from the top. Then the fast *whup-whup* of the blades and the whine of the engine became one continuous, punctuating drone, and the helicopter shook with that beat as it slipped sideways and tilted forward and lifted off from the field in the direction of Dardan Center. Bo felt like his body might split in two and remain buckled in the canvas seat, but he looked down at the highway to his left and tried to pick out landmarks he might recognize in the morning play of shadows and light. Sam had tried to describe this once, his first trip on a marine helo in the jungles near the DMZ, the noise and shaking, the canopy of forest rushing by no closer (it seemed) than arm's length, until they gained some altitude and it resembled a sea

161

of green leaves from horizon to horizon, and the sheer impenetrable distance of it made him wonder if they would fly above its surface until they were swallowed up in that sea, never to be found.

When the helicopter banked right to follow the course of the highway through the pass, the sun rolled into Bo's eyes with a glare like a knife so that he had to look away and down at the floor. He glanced at Rovnávaha, who had his thumbs hooked into the chest straps of the seat belt and his eyes closed, and Bo wondered how the priest had made this happen. How he could summon the military in the midst of a catastrophe to do what he called simply the will of the Lord.

There was another medic inside the helicopter and two people strapped into stretchers placed symmetrically on the floor behind where Bo and Rovnávaha sat. The crew chief knelt before one of the stretchers and flicked the IV tube with his finger, then swung around and sat down across from Bo. TUCKER was stenciled on a nameplate over his left breast, and he shouted to Bo above the engine roar.

Padre tells me your brother's a marine!

Bo nodded.

Still in-country?

Bo nodded again.

Late for marines to be in 'Nam. Where is he?

Missing! Bo yelled.

The man looked at Rovnávaha, who still sat with his eyes closed, asleep, for all anyone knew, and he shook his head and looked out the right side of the helicopter and pointed, and Bo could see the city of Wilkes-Barre as though frozen in a mold.

There were four people in white coats waiting for them as the helicopter landed. Tucker and the other medic got the stretchers off and handed them over to the hospital personnel, then helped Bo and Rovnávaha jump out. Tucker tapped his watch and said, Thirty minutes, Padre.

We'll be here, Rovnávaha said, and he and Bo walked across the tarmac to an open door and down some stairs to where a 6 was painted on the wall, and they went through that door and came out into a hall and walked toward another group of doors with a hand-painted INTENSIVE CARE on them.

Bo held the image of her in his mind from the day of the flood, the eyes vacant, the body mostly naked and white, bloodless but for the smear the child made when Ruth pressed it to her breasts. And so the thin, waiflike girl who lay in the bed amid the IVs and machines that seemed to do all but breathe for her startled him, and he stopped. He felt Rovnávaha take him by the hand and lead him to the side of the bed, where there was a chair, and Bo sat down.

The priest moved over to the foot of the bed and said, Ruth.

She opened her eyes.

Bo's here.

She turned slowly to her left and tried to lift her hand but placed it back on the bed. Bo watched her looking at him, the eyes empty at first, then brightening, and the lips turning up slightly, and she said, Bo. You have another letter for me?

He tried to smile, but he felt like the muscles were gone around his mouth, and he said, No, Ruth. I just came by to see you.

Thank you, she said, and reached for the bedrail again. He took her hand and held it, and she closed her eyes.

Rovnávaha motioned for him to stay and then left the room.

Bo put her hand back down on the bedside and studied her face. Lips cracked and ringed in a chalky white. Stitches at the cheekbone. Her black hair matted and cut short. Raccoon bruises around both eyes.

Ruth, he said. Do you remember anything?

She opened her eyes again and turned to look at him and nodded. The baby, she said. She cried when I held her, Bo. I want to hold her again. She glanced down at the foot of the bed where the priest had stood, then back to Bo.

Let's wait until you're stronger, he said.

They're all gone, aren't they?

He waited and said, I'm sorry, Ruth.

She closed her eyes and he thought she had gone to sleep, but she lifted her hand and took his and squeezed it and, without turning, said, Won't they want to know what I called her?

What do you want to call her? Tell me and I'll make sure they know.

Clare.

Clare what?

Clare Frances.

All right. I'll tell Father Rovnávaha. He'll say the Mass. My mother and I both will be there.

For my father, too? He'll do the funeral, the priest?

Yes, Bo said.

She tried to lift her hand to her face but could not for the IV. Bo took a handkerchief from his pocket and pressed it gently to her cheek.

They sat for a while, hand in hand without speaking, until her grip slackened and he leaned back in the chair and watched her breathe and wondered where it was she would go when the time came. Whom did she have now? Bo lifted her hand to his lips and kissed it, then placed it back at her side and went to find Rovnávaha.

The priest was standing in the hallway by a large window that looked out onto the valley. Bo came up beside him and said, The man who serves the Lord and commands all others. Thank you, Father.

Rovnávaha nodded, his eyes unmoving from the view outside. She's lucky to be alive, he said. The way they had her in that car saved her. But they had to take out her spleen. She needed lots of blood. Romanelli told me he gave her extreme unction right away, she was so bad.

She just wasn't ready, I guess, Bo said.

No, Rovnávaha said.

They watched as a bank of clouds skipping west blocked out the sun for a moment, then reemerged, brighter somehow, and they could tell all of a sudden what was water and what was mud by the way the light was or was not reflected on its surface.

Rovnávaha looked at his watch. Our ride's leaving.

Bo said, She told me she wanted the baby's name to be Clare Frances. She wants her buried with her father. And you to do the funeral.

The baby will be taken care of, the priest said. There are rubrics for the unbaptized. Let's go.

She was, Bo said. I did it. In the rain.

Rovnávaha had begun to walk down the hall, and he stopped and turned and looked at Bo. Was she alive when you got there? he asked.

She bawled like she was mad as hell at that storm, Bo said.

The priest moved his head from side to side as though looking for a way out of a room. And did you say the words? I mean, you knew what to do?

Bo straightened in front of the man, the two of them standing eye to eye in the empty hospital corridor, and he could not help feeling he had gained a victory when, until today, every struggle was becoming a losing one. And it was Rovnávaha who, for the second time, had handed it to him.

Bo ran his fingers through his beard from the ends of his mouth. I said the only words there were to say, Padre. If that girl's not counted among the believers now, then I don't want any part of them.

Rovnávaha put his arm around Bo's shoulders, and the two of them walked back up the stairs that led to the roof.

CHAPTER NINE

Two boys who had grown up on the Flats and now had no house to go home to found a Daisy Red Ryder in fair condition among the boxes and bins of junk that began to appear along the roads in Dardan. There were a handful of BBs left in the magazine, and they hiked down along the rushing creek until they came to a place where a fallen tree had lodged up against a huge stone, and they saw more rats than they had ever seen in their lives, scurrying in and out of the cover of that tree. They came within ten yards of the pack and the older boy who had found the gun commenced firing, plinking some of the smaller rats off the stone into the water but doing little more than making the bigger ones jump from the sting and turn back to whatever it was that had gathered them.

The wind shifted then, and on it came a stench that halted the boys as if they had

169

walked into a wall. The older one lowered the gun, and his friend reached down and picked up a rock to throw, because it seemed all of a sudden that the rats were swarming toward them like some bristling black carpet that moved of its own accord. They turned and tried to run with their hands covering their noses, but the younger boy tripped and fell, eye level with the mass of squealing rodents. He dropped the rock where he lay and began to scream. The older one ran back and grabbed him by the arm and pulled him up, and they took off along the creek as fast as they could until they came to a group of firemen flushing out a hydrant.

The paramedics knew it was Mary Younger from the strips of sheet and tape that clung to the tree branches, and by the broken leg bones cleaned of flesh and exposed. They matched her dental records and sent the body to the funeral home where Paul Younger and baby Clare remained, and all three awaited their burial as a family.

And so it was, two weeks after the flood had come, the ground stable enough for a backhoe to dig three graves, that Father Rovnávaha said the funeral Mass for the only lives from the town that had been lost, and who would be placed side by side next to Walter and Augustin Younger, patriarchs of a family who had lived in Dardan for over a hundred years and had been winnowed down to one.

Bo called on every workman at the mill to come and help bear a coffin. Hannah did the readings and the Psalm, and she wondered in her heart at how she had come in this life to be a woman asked to put to rest in peace the man whom she had hated for killing her husband, even when she knew that hate was not the reason why Becks had died. Maybe if they had had their dinner, broken bread at the table in her house, she would have felt something for them now. When she read out loud the words of Saint Paul, *We shall all be changed,* she thought of Sam, who had given her a grandchild, the child who might have changed them all forever. And now that child lay wrapped in a shroud. When the priest rose to read the Gospel, she listened to the Beatitudes, listened to him pause on *Blessed are the peacemakers,* and still she felt nothing.

After Mass she rode with Bo out to the cemetery and listened again to the priest, his voice tired and breaking as he shouldered the weight of laying to rest two generations of one family. And yet he spoke of the promise of inheritance, an inheritance not of riches, land, or a home but of a kingdom, one so unlikely and yet so certain a place that it had been prepared and was waiting for them from the foundation of the world. *A kingdom,* she thought. Her faith was once that strong, but she doubted it now, doubted not that there was a promise but that the promise claimed was a gift to hold, a joy that could assuage all sadness. No, she had come to believe that the only thing one could be certain of was loss. The loss of others as one lived on. Loss as the last thing one left behind.

Rovnávaha lifted his eyes from the book at that moment and said to those gathered for the committal, Just as the covenant of God with those few who remained on the earth remained amid destruction and devastation, only the sun and what they carried had not been lost. And so He promised *seedtime and harvest, cold and heat, summer and winter, day and night. Not one of these shall cease.*

Then the priest put his head down and prayed the prayer that promised every tear would be wiped away, closed the book, and said to those at the graveside, Go in peace.

No floodwaters ever touched Endless Roughing, and Bo and Jeff Lamoreaux

172

gathered in Bo's office every morning at seven-thirty and honed their plans for letting the town use the yard as an early staging ground for cleanup and recovery efforts, then shifting back to full running of the mill once rebuilding in the town began. But on the day after they buried Paul and Mary and Clare Frances Younger, Jeff found Bo standing by his old Dodge pickup, parked beneath a pine near the tally shed. The rest of the yard was filled with pallets of government-issued cheese, powdered milk, boxes of iodine, and plastic bottles of bleach.

Bo had his hand on the top of the tailgate, and Jeff said from behind him, You coming to work?

Bo turned and nodded and slapped the inside of the truck. I was just thinking that if my brother was here, he'd have this thing running in a heartbeat.

Jeff shook his head. Have I not taught you anything, Bo Konar, since the auspicious day that I came to this mill? You know I raced your brother once. And won.

Bo laughed. Are you telling me you can get this thing running?

Jeff said, You just got to say the word.

Over the course of the week, they pulled the wheels and scraped the mud and rust off the brakes, then cleaned and repacked the wheel bearings. They dropped the oil pan and hosed it out, changed the oil, transmission fluid, and final-drive lube, then siphoned the fuel out of the gas tank and replaced the filter. The cylinder heads of the engine were dry, and Jeff said that they could only hope there wasn't any water in the carburetor float bowls. Then they pulled the front bench seat and took a wet-vac to whatever cavity still held water, and wiped down the dashboard and the doors inside with diluted bleach, of which there was plenty in that yard. A friend of Jeff's in Noxen had a junk '63 Dodge pickup, and they took its radiator and the bench seat for twenty dollars and a case of beer. They bolted the seat in last.

It was a Friday night when they were done, and Bo stood leaning against the wall of the shed with his arms crossed. Jeff poured a little gas into the carb to prime it, then climbed into the driver's seat and put the key in the ignition. The engine labored to turn over, caught once, and stalled. He pumped the gas to fill the lines, tried again, and got the same. He looked over at Bo, who shook his head, but Jeff held up one finger, pumped the gas pedal three more times, then held off when he could smell it, and let the whole thing rest. He looked like he had fallen asleep with his hands on the wheel when he lifted his nose, sniffed, and turned the key again. The engine sputtered and pushed blue smoke out of the tailpipe. Jeff stayed hunched over the wheel and listening, revved the engine slightly, then a little more, until it was idling fast but steady and the exhaust had cleared. He jumped out and bonged the hood with his fist. There you go! he shouted at Bo.

The truck rattled and coughed out the back every few seconds like a steam train lying on its side, but it kept running and did not sound like it would stop.

Bo smiled and kept shaking his head. I should have had you replace the clutch, too, he said. Then I'd have a new truck.

You should have got your ass to dry ground when you saw the waters come, is what you should have done, Jeff said, then stepped back and worked a cigarette from a pack. He cupped the match in his hand and leaned his head toward it. The bad news is, he said as he inhaled, dropped the match on the ground, and toed it with his boot, you won't be driving this thing two months from now.

Summer settled in toward the end of June,

and the town began to dry on the high pressure and string of hot days that stretched into July, so that whenever talk turned to the weather, people shook their heads. Hannah went back to tending a small garden she had begun in May, but the sudden heat scorched the late and puny shoots that had managed to come up, shoots of everything from tomatoes and peppers to pumpkin and squash, which already had white leaf mold on them that jumped from plant to plant. Only the rhubarb she grew on the border of her garden seemed to thrive. That and the lettuce she planted from seed wherever she ripped out the rangy and ruined squash. Each day she stopped and made toast and tea at ten-thirty and waited for Bo's morning phone call from the mill, during which he would ask how her plants were doing, and she would say, It's just one lousy summer all around.

When the Salamander rose, it rose fast, but it fell fast, too (not like what the Susquehanna did to the Wyoming Valley), and toward the end of July, Dardan ran something like the town it was before the flood, even if it no longer looked like it. The front-end loaders that had scraped the roads of mud were gone, and the steady stream of trucks hauling refuse was replaced by another stream delivering lumber. Every now and then the lopping thud of a helicopter echoed in the mountains as it flew up through the pass but did not land, the sound fading into the distance.

Logging trucks pulled in to the mill three and four times a day. The saws and planes hummed from seven in the morning to seven at night. Bo put coffee on his tab at Ruby's for all the men, and he hired a lunch truck to come to the yard every day at noon. He left Jeff in charge of the office and went out into the sheds and talked with the men on break and thanked them for pulling together, told them where they stood on orders, how much he anticipated to complete before the summer was over. Most of these men his grandfather had hired, the skilled ones, anyway. A few Bo had brought to the mill. They were older than he was and had families and mortgages, and some spoke of sending a kid to college. Jozef had told him the hardest thing he would have to do was sit behind the desk in his office and listen to their requests for a raise, knowing what expenses and burdens were behind that need for more money. You know, the truth is, son, Jozef said to Bo the day he handed over the mill, our money really does grow on trees. Just not in every season.

And Jozef was right. Bo decided he would tell the men who worked for him what he could about profits and loss and quarterly revenue. Though he knew that most of them feared for what they might do or where they might go if Endless Roughing ever closed down, it was Bo who feared it more. Feared he would lose their respect and then their skill, and this alone would be the death knell of the mill that was his now. And so he never said no whenever one of those men knocked on his door, even after he had shown them the books and the margins thin as plywood, even after they nodded, as if to understand that the grandson of the man who had brought them into this trade was hiding nothing and wanted only to make the business run for everyone. Even after he told them that another fifteen cents an hour was all he could give them when they had come in hoping for twenty-five.

Friday of the first week of August, Bo asked Jeff to close up the place, and he got in his truck at four o'clock and drove up to the hill house.

He had not been there since before the flood. The grass, thick and stocky, was overgrown from the steps at the top of the drive all the way to the field's edge, so it looked like there was no difference between what was lawn and what was not, but for the tips of what grasses grew in each place. He stood at the bottom of those steps for a minute and reminded himself there was only one more full month of summer left, then fall, and then what did he have this house for, if just a place to come and watch the weeds grow? He walked toward the barn, slid open the bottom door, and went inside. He scanned the garden tools left on hooks near a corner, took down a sickle, went back outside, and walked over to the front of the house.

Hannah's going to want to know where the hell I've gotten to, he thought, and high-stepped through the tall rye grass and Queen Anne's lace until he stood on the nearly covered stone walkway, took his shirt off and tied it around his waist, then held the sickle in his right hand and began to mow in rows, one long sweep after another, moving outward and up the hill toward the porch and around the side of the house, his swing as even as the pendulum of a clock, until a low even matte of fallen grass lay over the sloping front yard.

He leaned the sickle against his hip, untied his shirt and wiped his face, then put it back on and buttoned it up to his neck and buttoned the sleeves. He walked into the barn, replaced the sickle and picked up a bamboo rake, went back outside, and began to gather into piles all that he could carry under one arm. Then he picked them up two at a time and walked them to the edge of the field where bunches of switchgrass swayed in the evening breeze, and he dropped the cuttings into the dirt furrow that acted like a border along the entire length of the back lawn. When he was done, he wiped his forehead with his shirtsleeve and surveyed the lawn in the late afternoon. There was plenty yet to mow, but he had cleared all of it from around the house so that the place did not look so derelict. He said out loud, as though the old man were right next to him, All right, Pop. Tomorrow I'll get a lawn mower up here and finish the rest, and then I'll call some builders and the bank and we can get on with it.

The house cast a long shadow down to the east, and Bo turned and looked up the hill where the sun was an orange ball hovering above the top of the field. He walked back to his truck and got in, turned it around, and drove down the road through town and up to the farm.

He found half a chicken with roasted carrots and parsnips in the warming tray of the oven, washed his hands and got a beer from the refrigerator, and sat down at the table to eat. He was finished reading the newspaper and drinking a second beer, when Hannah came into the kitchen and sat down across from him. She did not ask why he was late, and he did not offer.

She said, Father Rovnávaha called me this afternoon. Ruth Younger's going to be discharged as soon as she knows where she's going to live.

Bo looked up from the paper. There's nothing there now, he said. That house in the Flats? It's gone.

They know, Hannah said. They tracked down her mother. She's living in a trailer in Florida somewhere. Ruth said she'll be all right if that's where she has to go. They're waiting to hear back from her.

Mom, Bo said, and folded the paper and pushed it away from him. He stood up and walked to the counter and stared out the kitchen window with his back to her, then turned. I held your grandchild. You can't live in that past. Not anymore.

Hannah's eyes were fixed on the table and she said nothing. Years ago, when she cornered her son Sam and asked him if it was Ruth Younger he had been driving around town, and he stood defiant and said

181

yes, that it was, she came at him with an anger that had been building up for two decades. She grabbed him by the arm and dragged him up the stairs (and he let her, knowing that to fight against her would be far worse) to her own bedroom and pinned that arm behind his back so he was forced to the ground in front of the nightstand, where a photograph of Becks and Hannah Konar sat from the summer of their wedding, the two of them browned and windblown, standing in front of the paddock where they kept the horses. She spoke into her son's ear as he tried to wriggle out of the painful position but dared not rise and disobey his mother: I want you to see what you lost to a Younger. Then she pushed him hard so that his face slammed into the brass handles on the drawers, and he looked up at her and said, I'm sorry, Mom. But she's not the reason he's gone.

She drew a deep breath and looked up from the table at Bo. I told Father Tom she's welcome here. Until she can get on her feet and go back to work and rent a place, or —

Bo waited for her to finish, but her voice hung there.

Or what? he said.

Or until Sam comes home and they sort things out and find a place of their own.

Bo shook his head. I'll go get her Monday morning in the Dart.

Can you go in to work late? she asked.

I own the place, he said.

She stood. We'll need to clear out a room. She can stay in Papa's.

She won't make the stairs.

Yes, she will, Hannah said. I'll take care of her.

She picked up Bo's plate and utensils and brought them to the sink and rinsed them. They stood side by side, Hannah facing the window, Bo looking down at the table.

Hannah said, I was thinking the other day about how hard it's becoming to keep this place. There's so much to do. Grass mowed. Trees pruned. Chickens fed. One day Miss Wayne's going to give up the ghost, and then what?

Then you won't have to feed her, Bo said. Besides, weren't you just talking a little while ago about getting an actual milking cow?

It was just talk.

Well, I'll do what I can. I'd do more if it weren't for the mill. It's humming. This flood year's going to turn out to be our best year yet.

Good, she said. That's good. Old Father Blok used to say, *The Lord works, too. It's hard to let Him, though.*

Well, I don't know about the Lord, but my men are working their asses off, and it's my job to make sure it's not for nothing.

On Saturday morning Bo put the Briggs & Stratton from the barn into his truck and drove to the hill house and cut the rest of the lawn. By the time he had finished, eleven o'clock, a thermometer on the north side of the barn said it was eighty-five degrees. Cicadas whirred and he raked up the mowed grass and pulled it to the edge of the field and left it with the grass he had cut the day before. There was no rain forecast, so he went inside the house and on each floor opened the windows a crack at the top, then went outside, loaded the mower on the truck, and drove back to the farm.

Hannah was in the kitchen baking bread in spite of the heat, and she asked Bo if there was anything he wanted her to pick up at the store, since she was going out later to shop for the week. Bo thanked her and said he had what he needed, then sat down at the desk in the foyer and picked up the phone.

He called Matt Devlin, a plumber friend of his in Dardan, and asked how he was making out with all of the repair work going on after the flood.

It's a dream and a nightmare rolled into one, Bo, Matt said. I got plenty of business, but it's business I don't want. You been in any of those houses? I'm doing a few in Kingston and Forty Fort, and I can't get the smell out of my nose. It's toxic shit, man, like dead animal left under a wet rug and forgotten. And you can't tell anyone they ought to do it the right way when the wrong way costs a lot less.

Bo asked if there was any chance he could do some work on a house in Dardan. New water heater, Bo said, sweat some pipes, hook up propane, and put in a gas stove. New kitchen sink. Then redo a bathroom. I'll give you what they're paying you in the city.

There was quiet on the other end of the line, and Bo added, I'll need an electrician, too, and a good carpenter. Someone who does drywall and can fix a porch right. There's steady work into September. By then they'll be wanting you back in the city to fix all the hack work the fly-by-nights did in the first place.

Matt said, All right, Bo. You got a deal. I know just the boys. You give me the address and I'll swing by on Tuesday at five. We can have a look and I'll get some numbers back to you by Friday. How's that sound?

That sounds good, Bo said, and hung up the phone.

Chapter Ten

The air was thick and unmoving when Bo left the farm at sunrise on Monday morning and stopped at St. Michael's to pick up Father Rovnávaha. They drove out of town through the pass and across the river into Wilkes-Barre on the Market Street Bridge, then followed detours through the warrens of streets and avenues, past buildings that bore watermarks like the bows of square and overladen boats that had plied their way through a foul sea before coming back to anchor. They had rolled down the windows in the car for the heat, until the noise of the machinery hauling refuse and mud and the smell of that same mix made them roll the windows back up and sweat for the few miles it took to rise out of the valley on the east side.

In the parking lot of the VA, the priest took a moment to slide a white tab collar into his black shirt, then opened his door

187

and got out. Bo sat in the driver's side. Rovnávaha came around the back of the car and said through the window, You coming?

You go, Bo said. I'll wait here.

It was twenty minutes before he saw the man's towering figure reemerge and pushing Ruth Younger in a wheelchair. Her black hair was brushed and came down to just below her ears in an uneven bob. She wore a New York Jets football jersey with the number 12 on it, and it was tucked into a pair of Levi's cinched with an army-surplus web belt at the waist. Bo got out of the Dart and put his hand on the fender so he had something to lean against. Ruth stopped halfway to him, lifted herself out of the chair, and walked the last ten yards to the car. She had a slight limp and pointed to the outsize Keds sneakers she wore, as though these alone were the reason why she had spent so much time in the hospital behind her. He reached for her and hugged her, his arms wrapping around her entire body, so slight had she become, and he let her head rest against his chest. He looked up at the priest, who was watching them and nodding, then said quietly to the top of Ruth's head, We'll get you some clothes that fit. I'm just glad you're here with us.

She sat in the backseat of the car with her

shoulder against the window glass. As they drove back down into Wilkes-Barre, the priest talked about what had been torn down and what was being rebuilt in Dardan, as though the destruction and decay in the streets of the city were not what they would find in the mountains, and that this might be a comfort to her (though she had lost her father and her baby, and the house on Holly Street along the Flats had been swept with the others off its foundation and down into the pass). Bo glanced into the rearview mirror and saw her turn from the window and face the front to ask the priest if he knew whether the Phillies had won their game against the Cardinals.

Talk about what needs tearing down, Rovnávaha said. They lost six to nothing. Twitchell was on the mound.

No sound rose then from the back, and when Bo peered in the mirror again, Ruth was not in view. Rovnávaha looked over his shoulder and saw her lying down with hands under her head and feet and knees curled up on the seat.

She's asleep, he said, and looked back out at the houses and streets of the city along the flood plain, the morning like any other but for those whose work it was to decide in the single block of home or business that made up their world what could be saved and what could not. Rovnávaha seemed to study the landscape and then spoke as if he and Bo had been having a long conversation on the ways of God and men, waving his hand at the scene outside and asking, Who is worse off? These folks pulling trash and soaking rugs and furniture from their store? Or that girl in the backseat who lost in one day what most would mourn in a lifetime?

Bo shook his head. You tell me, Father.

It's not for me to tell. Each would have to stand and speak, plead his or her case, and even then, who could judge? Do we know what was inside that store? he said as his head followed a sign on a building they had just passed. Clocks. No doubt generations of clocks and the knowledge to repair them. Were they lost? he asked, and Bo said nothing. The clocks, yes, the priest went on. The knowledge, though? I would say no, if they are horologists worth going to with your timepiece. But she is as alone in this world now as her great-grandfather Augustin was when he stepped off that ship in New York Harbor from Galway. Or your grandfather, he said, and turned to Bo. Aliens, Scripture called them. No land. No country. Only God, though for some, not even that.

Augustin? Bo asked.

The priest looked over his shoulder again to make sure Ruth was asleep, and then turned to the front. Augustin Younger, he said. I never knew the man. He's the thing of stories now, I suppose. Blok knew him. He and Father Bozak used to dine often at Augustin and Klára Younger's house. It was Augustin Younger who told Bozak when he came home from the war, *There's need of a church back here, Father,* though Augustin never had need for one himself, I was told. Fell away but couldn't stand seeing anyone hate the Church just because it was the Church.

Like another man we once knew, Bo said.

Two trees, same forest, said Rovnávaha. Your grandfather would have liked Augustin Younger, from what Blok said.

It was Paul's father, Walter, he took the land from, Bo said.

Not took. Your grandfather bought it fair and square. Lots of men from that time forgot how it came to them in the first place, the priest said.

How did it? Bo asked. Come to the Youngers, I mean.

Well, Augustin wasn't a Younger then. He was Patrick Kelleher, son of an Irish silver-smith named Bartley Kelleher.

191

BK, Bo said.

You know? Rovnávaha asked.

Something I found.

Rovnávaha looked at him and said, Well, Patrick arrived in New York Harbor from Galway on a Sunday in February 1863, hoping to get to Mass at the cathedral on Mott Street, the story goes, after which he was told he'd find help getting lodging and a job. But recruiters caught him at the docks and said there was plenty of work and food if he joined the Union Army. So the boy took up the uniform and musket and blanket roll and marched south and became a soldier between Newark and the fields of Gettysburg. In July of that year he was one of the few soldiers of the Irish Brigade left standing. Still he marched and lined up and fought wherever they told him to line up and fight, and lay down to sleep whenever they told him the fight was done, until the priest whom the brigade had paid to march with them announced one morning in April of '65 that Lee had surrendered to Grant in a courthouse in Virginia. Patrick was eighteen.

Rovnávaha reached into his clerical shirt and pulled out a plain cheroot, rolled down the window halfway, and lit the cigar with a black crackle Zippo he took out of the front pocket of his trousers.

You don't mind, do you? he asked, and Bo shook his head.

The priest drew on the cigar and blew the smoke toward the window and said, Now, somewhere along the way, Kelleher had been folded into the 116th Pennsylvania and become friends with a kid named Michael Zlodej from a town called Dardan.

I know that name, Bo said.

Of course you do.

No, I mean Zlodej.

I know. If you listened to your grandfather at all, you would have heard it when he talked about his own father. Kelleher and Zlodej fought side by side from Maryland into Virginia, and the Irishman thought his luck was catchy, until the Pennsylvanian took a musket ball straight in the belly and died slow and angry, cursing the Confederates and begging Patrick to tell his family in Dardan he had died with the Lord's name on his lips. So Patrick swore he would, and when the war was over and they discharged him in Baltimore, he set out north to Havre de Grace, and followed the Susquehanna across the Mason-Dixon Line, until, after weeks of walking, he came to Wilkes-Barre and crossed at Market Street and walked west to the town of Luzerne. There was a creek there that poured out of a rocky pass, and Patrick was told all he needed to do was stick to the slopes and rising hills that the water skirted and he'd come to Dardan. The Pennsylvanian, he said, used to speak of his town as a cross between Mount Ararat and the Garden of Eden. Patrick thought he was exaggerating, mixing biblical metaphors, but as he climbed into the mountains and got closer and closer to town, he no longer thought the Pennsylvanian's evocation of paradise and the land on which an ark might settle was wrong.

Rovnávaha smoked and looked out the window of the car as though considering the truthfulness of these words as well, then went on. The Zlodej family lived west of the town center, and after a month of journeying on foot to the last place in America he ever expected to journey, that Irish boy who had turned from stranger to soldier back to stranger sat down in the kitchen of a log cabin and ate a bowl of venison stew with a glass of water so cold in the heat of summer that he choked on it as though it were the first time he'd ever tasted water. And when they asked him what his name was, he remembered whose feast day fell on the twenty-eighth of August, and he said in as flat a voice as he could so as to press the

Galway from it, *Augustin.* And then he remembered the sign he saw along the Susquehanna as he passed through the town of Sunbury, the Young Family Funeral Home, and he said to them, *Augustin Younger's my name.*

And he told the father, mother, and twin sister of the one they called Mike, that the Pennsylvanian had died bravely in battle, and that his last words were a whisper of love and farewell to his family, which Augustin Younger had come all that way to deliver, for he had made an earlier vow on the fields of Gettysburg never to utter the name of the Lord again.

Since he had nowhere to go, the family took him in. The father got him a job rounding up rattlesnakes with the crews felling timber for the railroad companies. He met the truck in Noxen before the sun was up and drove out to Williamsport and hiked into the eastern Alleghenies with leather boots to the knee, a knife, a hooked stick, and a burlap sack. The men were paid by the snake, but after the first day, when the others were bringing in twenty and thirty snakes a day, Augustin had none. Nor did he fare any better the second and third day, so that by the time it was Thursday of the first week, they called him Saint Patrick,

and the foreman who ran the hunt gave him
five dollars for his time and sent him back
to Dardan.

He'd have been just another mick in the
coal mines if he hadn't gone into the feed
mill to buy a ticket on the light-gauge train
that ran to Luzerne and seen the help-
wanted sign for a laborer to unload the feed
that came to the mill on the same train. He
took the sign down and gave it to a man
behind the register and said he could start
right there if the man was expecting what
was on the twelve o'clock. The man glanced
up from his till and asked the boy where he
was from, and Augustin said, Not from
anywhere since Gettysburg, but I assure
you, sir, I've lifted my fair share of dead-
weight.

The man, George Dockens, told him the
pay was a dollar a day. Six dollars a week if
there was nothing left to stack, sweep, or
unload when it was time to knock off on
Friday. Augustin worked through that Friday and the next, and by the time it was
Thanksgiving, George Dockens had put
him in charge of the books and rented him
a room and asked him to close up on
Saturday evenings.

Rovnávaha finished his cigar and flicked it
out of the car as they drove past an old

lumberyard at the light. He spat a piece of tobacco from his mouth and said, Now comes the part about the girl. When Klára Zlodej, twin sister of the Pennsylvanian, rode into Dardan, she made a point of coming to the feed mill, first for nothing more than chicken feed and then for nothing at all except to see Augustin, how he was faring, and — the way she told it to Blok — to see if there was any light behind those dark green eyes of his that betrayed a fondness for her. But she saw nothing, or at least nothing she could tell, until the week before Thanksgiving, when she came to hand-deliver an invitation to him from her mother to share Thanksgiving at their table.

Augustin read the note and looked up at the girl, saw the same sharp features and full mouth that seemed so alive and combative on her brother, and he knew that this town to which the Pennsylvanian had sent him as an emissary of his last words was the town where he would live, the young woman in front of him the woman he would love, and the dirt and dust he swept off the wooden floorboards of Dockens Feed Mill every afternoon dirt and dust of the same into which he'd be buried. So he folded the note, slid it into the front pocket of his leather apron, and said to Klára, Tell Mrs.

Zlodej that her invitation is what I'll be thankful for on that day. And they were married the following summer. Walter was their only child, born in the spring of 1880.

Bo glanced into the mirror to see if Ruth was still asleep, rolled down his window, and accelerated onto the highway.

So how'd they get all that land? he asked Rovnávaha.

Slowly, the priest said. Every couple of years Zlodej would buy a parcel here or there until he owned pretty much all of the outerlying forest, before most of it was clear-cut. The timber alone in those days made him a rich man, though you never would have known it. When he died, it all went to Klára, and the Younger family became the largest landowners in Dardan.

And what happened to Walter? Bo asked.

Walter was brought up in the business, and when he learned all he wanted to learn about provender, he secured a loan from his father to become Dardan's sole beer distributor. That was 1910, the year Paul was born. Walter made a fortune throughout the years of World War I and into the early twenties, until Prohibition shut him down. There was nothing he could do but go back to running the store that was still known as Dockens Feed Mill and begin selling off, piece by piece, all the land that his mother and father had passed on to him and that he had believed he would pass on to his son, Paul, were it not for the bills and the debts he ran up to float his business, his appetite for gambling and whiskey, and the occasional whore in the Wilkes-Barre brothels.

Bo started and looked into the backseat and said, She might hear you.

Oh, I have no doubt she's heard all this before, Rovnávaha said. Every word of it. From her father. And none of it good.

Ruth did wake, just as they turned off the highway into Dardan and went over the bridge and Bo downshifted and drove the long road that wound up to the farm.

She had never been to the Vinich home, had never even set foot on the land. When they got to the house, she sat up and looked out at the porch columns and tall windows. The gardens and fruit trees in the front yard. The balcony on the second floor, with its wrought-iron railing and glass-paneled French doors through which white curtains swept out and around the glass like waves rising and receding on a shore. She slid to the other side of the seat and scanned the orchard. Rows of apple trees hung with green fruit, and chickens pecked and scratched around a stand of them in the back.

Bo, I won't stay long, she said nervously, the sleep still in her voice. You'll tell your mother that, won't you?

Bo turned around in his seat. And where are you going to go? She's been waiting for you. We've got a room all set upstairs. He pointed to the balcony. That's the one. And a nurse is going to come this week to check on you.

I won't need a nurse.

I don't think it's for you. I think it's to make sure we're taking care of you all right.

I'll be all right, she said. Two weeks and I'll be out of your hair and you can get back to your lives.

Rovnávaha turned around, too, and said, Ruth. It's what we talked about. This is going to be home for a while. Bo and Mrs. Konar both want you to stay here.

Hannah had walked out onto the porch and down to the car but stood at a distance as Rovnávaha helped Ruth climb out of the Dart. Krasna moved from Hannah's side and went to Ruth and licked her fingers. Ruth bent down to pet the old dog, and when she looked up, Hannah was standing in front of her.

She likes you, Hannah said, and stepped

forward and took the girl's hand. Come on inside, Ruth. I'll bet you're hungry. I have lunch all ready for us.

The men followed the women as they walked slowly, arm in arm, up the front steps and through the door, Ruth's eyes taking in every detail as she entered the house, and Bo wondered what his brother had told her and what he had not about the world that had shaped the young man whom she loved. The young man who could move from his world to hers so seamlessly, without drawing attention, that he hunted with her father on his grandfather's own land. The young man who had promised her that, after he came back from Vietnam, he would never leave her again. And she had believed him.

Where is he now? Bo wondered. *Now that she is here?*

Hannah had made a mushroom soup and barley salad with fresh tomatoes for their meal. They let Rovnávaha speak once again of what they had seen in the valley, and Hannah mentioned that, though the week was meant to be hot, there was a nice breeze coming through the doors and windows upstairs. Ruth was quiet except to say that she had never tasted a soup as good as this one, and Hannah thanked her and told her she expected her to do nothing around here for a while but eat and sleep.

After they had coffee, Rovnávaha asked Bo for a ride back to the church. Bo said he had to get over to the mill as well, and they left together in Bo's truck.

Hannah saw them out, and when she came back to the kitchen, she found Ruth trying to carry a stack of dishes to the sink before she stopped halfway and left them on the counter and leaned against it holding her side. Hannah ran to her and Ruth said, I'm all right.

You need some rest, Hannah said. Let's get you to your room.

They went down the hall and turned in the foyer for the stairs. Hannah asked if they were too much, but Ruth shook her head and said, It's about time I started moving some more.

At the top of the steps, they walked to the end of the hall and Hannah opened the door of the room that was her father's. The curtains on the balcony doors lifted and swayed, and Hannah walked across the floor and tied the curtains back and turned to face Ruth. This is where you'll stay, she said. It's the biggest room in the house. And the brightest. You can use the balcony to read or sleep, and you can put your clothes in that chest of drawers there.

For the first time Ruth smiled and held out her hands.

Hannah laughed and said, When you get some clothes.

Ruth looked across the room at a dresser with three photographs on top of it, and she walked over and held one up: Sam as a baby, with Hannah, Becks, and Bo huddled around. She put it down and moved to the next one of him, in hunter's orange, holding the head of an eight-point buck. Then she picked up the last one, a color photograph of the young man in his marine dress blues, his jaw looking as though it had been carved out of a block of wood.

I put those there for you, Hannah said. I had them in my own room and thought they might help you feel a little more at home.

That's kind of you, Ruth said. She looked back at the one of Sam as a baby. This was his father? Your husband? she asked.

Yes. That's Becks.

Ruth stood and stared at the photograph, then said, I remember once when we were in high school and Sam came over for dinner and my dad cooked us up some venison stew. Sam really liked it, and my dad really liked him. They talked about hunting and cars and all kinds of things, and afterward, when he was saying goodbye to us, my dad said, Don't make yourself a stranger around here, Sam Konar. Sam told him he had no plans to and they shook hands. That night my dad was sitting up watching the TV and I came out of my room to ask if anything was wrong. He said, There's not a morning I rise when I don't wish I hadn't shot that boy's father. Today I wished it twice.

Hannah sat down on the bed and looked at her hands and then out the window at the top of the cherry tree in the yard.

He carried that with him every day of his life, Ruth said. My dad. He never stopped being sorry for it.

It was an accident, Ruth, Hannah said, and turned to look at the girl. We all knew that. I hope your father did, too.

He did. But you know, he took pride in his skill as a hunter. And although I know now she was just looking for any old reason, it gave my mom a reason to scoot. That hurt him.

She still held the photograph of the family and she traced her finger along its border. He was handsome, she said. Those eyes are something. Like Bo's.

Hannah stood from where she sat and patted the bedspread. Why don't you get some rest, Ruth, she said.

Ruth put down the photograph. I'm not

tired. What I'd really like to do, Mrs. Konar, is take a bath. I haven't had a good one in I can't remember.

You call me Hannah, Ruth. And I'll draw you a bath.

On the side of the room opposite the windows was a white door, and Hannah went through it and Ruth could hear the plug chain drop and water running. Hannah came back through the door with a bath sheet.

Ruth turned to face the wall and said, Now, don't look. She let the baggy Levi's drop to the floor and tried to pull the football jersey over her head but could not. Hannah helped her the rest of the way and wrapped the large towel around her so she was covered from her breasts to her thighs. Then she kicked the jeans and shirt to the side of the room.

I've got some sundresses you can wear, Hannah said. We're about the same size.

A dress would be nice, Ruth said.

Hannah led her to the door of the bathroom and stopped outside. Let that water get as deep and hot as you like, she said. There's soap and shampoo and everything right on the shelf.

Ruth stood with her hand on the crystal knob. I can't, Hannah, she said. I mean, do this by myself.

Hannah nodded. I wasn't sure, but that's okay.

She walked Ruth to the edge of the tub and tested the water temperature with her hand, turned the cold tap up a little higher, then helped Ruth unwrap the towel. Ruth put her left arm around Hannah's shoulder and blushed when their eyes met. Hannah could have lifted her into the tub all by herself, she was so light. Ruth touched her scar with her right hand and said, Still tender. Then she sank slowly into the bath.

Hannah took a washcloth from a rack on the wall, knelt down on the floor, and lathered the cloth with a bar of Pears soap. She washed Ruth's back and neck, and soaped along her arms and under her arms, being careful of her abdomen. Then she rinsed the cloth and began to rinse the lather from Ruth's body with water that she wrung from the cloth and let pour over her arms and neck.

Did they tell you what happened? Hannah asked.

I remember some, Ruth said. Father Romanelli, the chaplain, told me the rest. Over a couple of days. There sure was time to stretch it out. They were good to me there, though.

Hannah helped her raise her legs and lathered the cloth some more and washed Ruth's thighs and knees and feet, water splashing back into the bath the only sound that echoed off those tile walls, until Hannah heard the sobs and looked to see Ruth's eyes pressed closed and her lips trembling. Hannah rinsed the soap and dropped the cloth into the water and leaned forward and hugged her. It's all right, Ruth, she said. It's all right.

Ruth broke into a long aching cry as Hannah pulled her in closer and rocked with her in the bath, holding her as she shook and gave no words to the grief that had overcome her, until her breaths evened out and she wiped her eyes with the back of her hand and pushed a sigh from her as though she had come to the end of an unwanted task.

They told me the bleeding was so bad I might have died if they hadn't — She stopped and lowered her head and breathed again. I can't have any more babies, she said.

Hannah held her tighter and did not say a thing.

Ruth heaved to catch her breath and said, It's like I've lost not only what family I had but what family I dreamed of having.

No, Ruth, Hannah said. That's not true.

I've dreamed of having you in my family. You and Sam. And here you are. And I know that Sam's coming back here, too. You wait and see.

Ruth nodded, and Hannah rose from the floor and took a bottle of shampoo from a cabinet and wetted Ruth's hair with the telephone-handle faucet and worked the shampoo with her fingers, then rinsed it slowly.

I'm taking you down to Marie's on Friday to get this bob cleaned up, she said. Then she took the towel off the rack and Ruth stood, stepped out of the tub, and faced Hannah, who dried the girl's hair, wrapped the towel back around her, and kissed her. She led her out into the room and sat her down in a chair at the desk by the window, closed the doors that led to the balcony outside, and said, Stay here while I go get you some clothes.

When she returned, Ruth was asleep on one side of the bed, still wrapped in the towel. Hannah undid it gently, pulled back the sheet and covered her, and walked downstairs to the kitchen.

It was four o'clock in the afternoon when she heard Ruth coming down the steps. Krasna stood up from the floor and wagged her tail and strode along the hall, and the two of them showed in the kitchen a minute later.

I slept, Ruth said.

You needed it. Bo will be home in another hour or so. We're going to have chicken on the firepit tonight. I asked Father Rovná-vaha if he wanted to join us, but he can't. So it'll just be the three of us.

I saw chickens when I came in, Ruth said. Are we eating one of them?

No, Hannah said. You saw Celeste, Venus, and Renée. Celeste is too old and dear to me to eat. She doesn't even lay. Tonight's chicken is just a roaster I got at the Acme.

I wouldn't know the difference, Ruth said.

Oh, I bet you would.

My dad said he kept chickens as a boy. Best eggs in the county.

I'll make you some tomorrow morning, Hannah said, and you can decide.

Bo pulled into the drive at five-thirty and came in the back door and said, I'm a mess from this heat. You're going to have to wait until I take a shower.

Go on, then, Hannah said.

When he came down the stairs and into the kitchen, he wore jeans and a T-shirt and was in his bare feet.

You feel better? Hannah asked.

I feel human.

They put the bird on a spit over the fire Hannah had made in the afternoon, and wrapped russet potatoes in foil and laid them in among the coals. They set the picnic table outside under a winter banana-apple tree and put out the tomato and cucumber salad Ruth had helped chop, and while their dinner cooked and they drank iced tea and cold beer, Hannah told them about the summer Jozef and Becks had built the firepit with fieldstones from the woods over by the paddock.

They spoke Slovak the whole time, Hannah said. Not a word of English. Well, Papa spoke and Becks did what he was told. They spent all of one Friday gathering the stones, then got up early on Saturday morning and started laying them out one by one. They rested Sunday morning, while my mother and I went to church, and they picked up again when we got home. By supper it was finished. Chimney and all. My mother thought it was a thing of beauty and wanted to cook on it right there, but Papa said, *No, no. That mortar needs a few days to cure.*

Where was Becks from? Ruth asked.

Only my father knew that, Hannah said. He told me he had been at Becks's birth and that he had saved the boy's life. This was just after World War I. My father was walking home after spending six months in an Italian prisoner-of-war camp. He came upon a Romani woman. A gypsy. Which was strange, because gypsies never traveled without family. But she was pregnant and pretty far along. It turned out the father was a Hungarian army officer and the girl had run away. When her time came, she told my father that if she died, he was to take the child to their camp on the banks of the Sajó River. And she did die, so my father picked up the boy and started moving fast. The war wasn't over along that border, and he risked imprisonment if he got caught by the Hungarians. But he did what he had promised the girl. And then he came to America, never giving a second thought to that gypsy whose life he saved.

Who would believe that? Ruth said.

Well, that's not the end of it, Hannah said. When I was a girl of eleven, this boy showed up one afternoon at the front door of the house. His hair was flattened from his hat, and his eyes were a blue like dusk set in almond shells, just like Bo's over there. And he asked in this heavy accent if Mr. Vinich was at home. I just stood there, speechless. My mother came to the door and told him Mr. Vinich was across town at the mill, but she expected him within the hour. He stared back at her, and my mother took him by the hand and led him into the kitchen, leaving the rucksack that he carried out on the porch.

We were drinking tea like a party of polite mutes when Papa came in by the back door and the boy looked up at him and rose to his feet and began to speak in Slovak, animated and expressive as he tried over and over to explain why he was there. When he finished, Papa didn't move, and that boy ran from the kitchen and returned with his rucksack and took an old rusted knife and a sling of coarse cotton from it. Then he said his name was Bexhet, which seemed to hang in the air as the final word. My father sat down in his place at the table, smoothed his hand along the weave of the cloth, and said to me, *I wondered when he would come.*

Ruth shook her head and said again, Who would believe that?

No one, Bo said. That's who.

Hannah said nothing, and there was quiet for a long time.

When the chicken and potatoes were done, the three who had gathered ate and spoke of the food and how pretty the sunset was, although they could see an ominous bank of clouds rolling in from the east. And when they were finished, they sat at the garden table in the twilight and watched the coals of the fire pulse red and an ashen silver without flame, sat like sated guests at their own feast, silent once again and not wondering what came next, for all that they had strived for in the course of the day lay in the past, and what anxiety each carried lay, at least for the moment, in that past as well. There arose around them the hungry *peent* of nighthawks as these birds swept and dodged near the barn for moths and mosquitos in the warm night air. The brash, uncanny cry of a northern mockingbird joined them for a few minutes, and then the calls ceased. The night grew darker, and with the dark came the low hooting of a great horned owl from somewhere in the trees, and still the three did not move or speak. Not until they could see the flash of lightning and the thick curtain of clouds that had assembled and stalled in the heat, followed by a low rumble of thunder.

Hannah stood from the table and said with some regret in her voice, We should go inside. The wind picked up then and shook the trees in gusts, and they cleared the table of everything and had to run the last few feet into the house as the skies opened and their world knew rain again.

CHAPTER ELEVEN

Ruth did little more the next day than sleep and eat and sit in the room that had been given to her and stare at the photographs on the dresser. After the nurse left, Hannah knocked to see if she needed anything, and Ruth said no and waited in the room for the next meal and then for the dark. That night Hannah left a pair of sandals, a dress, and some fresh underwear by the door.

In the morning Ruth came down the stairs after Bo had left for work and thanked Hannah for the clothes that she was wearing.

Well, sit down and have some coffee, Hannah said, and I'll be back with those eggs I was bragging about for your breakfast.

Where are you going? Ruth asked.

Out to the barn.

Can I go?

Sure, Hannah said, and pointed to a bench by the door. You can slip on my gardening boots there and grab that basket.

The morning air was warm, though it was not quite six-thirty. They walked through the orchard, where the smell of rotting ground apples that had fallen early mixed with the smell of weed pollen. Ruth seemed to want to walk fast but was laboring to do so, and Hannah asked how she was feeling.

Better, Ruth said. Just stiff from sleeping. And hungry now, too.

We'll take care of both of those, Hannah said.

Inside the barn she turned on the light and showed Ruth where they kept the feed for the cow. Take a handful, she said, and drop it in that pail of hers. She'll eat.

Do you milk her?

Not anymore. You're standing in the cow equivalent of a retirement home. The next stop for her's that great big pasture in the sky.

That's sad, Ruth said.

Why? She's had a good life.

How old is she?

My father bought her a year after Becks died, so she's getting close to twenty. We had a couple of cows then, and a bull. We got all our milk right here. But you've got to keep them calving, otherwise they stop. Hannah patted Miss Wayne. This old girl is the last one left.

215

They went into the chicken coop and Hannah opened the cages and let them out into the yard. Two flew at each other and broke off. The rest set to scratching in the grass.

You just leave them? Ruth asked. Like the ones I saw the other day?

Same ones. I'll put them back into the coop before we leave later.

Why don't they fly away?

I suppose they would if they could. But they know where the food is. And where the hawks and raccoons are not. Krasna helps, too. I remember when that dog was a puppy and she came racing past me on her way to the henhouse and caught up a new pullet right in her mouth. Mr. Vinich walloped her so hard she never went after a chicken with an open mouth again.

Hannah reached into a nest box and pulled out an egg. Bring that basket, she said. Ruth walked over and held out the basket and Hannah placed the egg inside. You can check all of those boxes and see what you find, she said to Ruth. There should be an egg or two in each one.

There were five nest boxes and Ruth got four eggs. A black-and-white-speckled hen came back in from the yard and clucked around her feet.

That's Celeste, Hannah said. She's my favorite. She and Miss Wayne are on the same plan. Hannah reached down and picked up the hen and stroked her along the back and the hen let her. Ruth put the basket on the ground and held out her arms and Hannah put Celeste into them, Ruth gathering up the hen and petting her in the same way.

Looks like you made another friend, Hannah said.

After breakfast they went upstairs to Hannah's room and took from her wardrobe two more dresses, three blouses, and a pair of Lee jeans Hannah said she had bought back when a woman would not be caught dead in jeans. Then she rummaged around in the corner of the closet until she came up with a pair of brown Frye harness boots. Size nine, right?

Ruth nodded and took the boots. Where did you get these? she asked.

I bought them right here in Dardan a few years ago. I used to wear them, too. They're nice and broken in. Hannah reached into a drawer and pulled out a pair of socks and tossed them to Ruth. Put them on, she said.

Ruth put on the socks and boots and stood with her hands on her hips and her head turned to one side. How do I look?

Like you missed your call.

Ruth laughed. No, she said, and gathered up the clothes. I didn't.

The two of them walked down the hall to Ruth's room and hung up the dresses in the empty closet. Ruth sat on the bed and bent down to take the boots off, and Hannah said, Keep those on. There's someplace I want to take you.

They had another coffee in the kitchen while Hannah packed a picnic basket with some sandwiches, banana bread, and a thermos of tea. Then they went outside and locked the chickens back in the coop and got in the Dart and drove west, out past the lake and farther into the mountains, where Hannah turned onto a back road that crossed over a large freestone stream and wound up and into hills with which Ruth was unfamiliar, until they came to a farm that looked as though it had been dropped down onto those hills from above. Corn grew in green and yellow rows across the rolling field, and there was a modest two-story farmhouse at the end of the drive where Hannah stopped the car. Beyond that there were two barns, one of wood and painted red, and another that looked like a stone cabin from another century to which was attached a long light-framed shed.

A man with silver hair and wearing brown overalls came out of the red barn and walked over to the car. Hannah got out and the man said, Hannah Konar, I have not seen you in a blue moon.

She held out her hand and the man pulled her in close and hugged her, then held her by the shoulders and said, I missed seeing your father around here in the spring. Have you been faring all right?

As well as can be, Virgil.

Well, you have made my day. And who is this pretty little thing? he said, turning to Ruth.

Hannah said, This is Ruth Younger, Virgil. She's staying with us for a while.

Hannah waited to see if the Younger name registered any sign of recognition on the man's face. If it did, he was polite enough not to show it. He stepped over to Ruth and took her hand and said, I am pleased to meet you, Ruth Younger.

And Hannah said, Ruth, this is Virgil Kravits. The man with the chickens.

I've been called worse, Virgil said. What brings you two girls around?

We came to see you about some started pullets. We'd like to get the flock back up to twelve.

Got some nice healthy ones. Barred

Rocks, I think you have. Don't you?

Yes, Hannah said.

Any cockerels?

No. Just hens.

All right. And how many will get you back up to twelve, as you say?

Seven.

He nodded. You still got Celeste, don't you? You were always partial to her, I could tell.

Hannah smiled and said, Partial to the underdog.

Underdog, he said, and laughed. He turned to Ruth. Been like that ever since she was a girl and her daddy brought her out here to buy some chicks. She left with some babies, all right, but she had convinced her father to take two hens who had their feathers bit and their eyes about scratched out. Rosemarie had them slated for the pot that night, and I had to tell her Hannah Konar came by and rescued them. So we had vegetable soup for dinner.

They had walked away from the barn and toward the stone house, where they entered and were descended upon by the din of hundreds of chickens and roosters squawking and clucking, so that Ruth backed up and put her hands to her ears. Hannah waved for her to follow, and they went through a door into the wooden shed and over to a sink, where there was a bar of lye soap in a metal dish bolted to the wall, and they all three washed their hands and shook them dry.

The noise was lessened in there, though higher-pitched, and there were fenced-off areas of smaller, thinner-feathered chickens running around feeding troughs and watering pans.

These here are the pullet cages, Virgil said just below a shout. I got some Barred Rocks right over there, Hannah. Let's go and pick out your seven.

They walked to the front of a six-foot-by-six-foot pen, where several small chickens strutted around and pecked through scratch and wood shavings on the floor. Hannah watched them and the man waited, and then she started to point to the ones she wanted, and he nodded and said, Done. I'll have George bring them over to you tomorrow in the truck. We've got to do a few errands in Dardan.

He took the women out through a door at the far end of the shed and they stood in a dirt yard that backed up onto one of the cornfields.

I'll put some feed and grit in with that order, too, Virgil said. And don't forget to keep the new ones separated from the older girls until they all get used to each other. Otherwise you're going to be breaking up fights. Or worse.

Will do, Virgil, Hannah said. Tell George he can come around whenever it's convenient for him.

Virgil held out his hand and he and Hannah shook. Then Virgil turned to Ruth and said, It was nice to meet you, young lady. You enjoy those chickens, hear?

Ruth thanked him, and she and Hannah walked back down the drive to the car.

You do that every year? Ruth asked.

Used to. In the spring. But I've been wanting to get some new hens. And started pullets are easier than chicks.

How do you know he'll bring you exactly the ones you pointed to?

Hannah shrugged. He just will. That man was raising chicks three days before water flowed. Besides, it doesn't really matter which ones I pointed to and which ones he brings. There'll be seven Barred Rocks from that pen. The selection is a kind of ritual we go through. We have ever since I was a girl and my father brought me here. He had me convinced that every chick I pointed to was one that wanted nothing more than to be with me on our farm.

It was close to twelve as they drove down the mountain and around the bend that dead-ended at the lake. Hannah took the shore road going east past the parking lot of a restaurant called the Sunset, a white shack with a neon sign on the front that said PIZZA. It sat alone in a dirt parking lot dotted with boat trailers next to a launch ramp and the marina, which was no more than a few slips on a marsh with a narrow cut for access to the open water. Hannah drove over an old stone bridge and kept going along the lake road into more forested terrain, a few summer shacks built back against the hillside, and then there was just road, tall trees, and the dark green water of the lake, into which an occasional dock jutted out from the shore.

When they got to Asa Pound's place, Hannah pulled over on the opposite side of the road and parked under the shade of a broad white pine. She reached into the backseat, where she had put the picnic basket and some towels, and they got out and walked across the road and down the steps cut into the bank that led to the lakeside and the dock. They walked to the end of it and sat down in two Adirondack chairs.

You know whose place this is? Hannah asked.

Ruth nodded. Sam told me about Will once when we were driving past.

Hannah pulled one of the chairs closer to the edge of the water and said, I haven't seen Asa out here since his son died. And yet every spring these Adirondacks come out. And every fall they disappear.

She dropped the towels and the picnic basket on the boards and watched a pair of mallards swim toward the dock, dive and come back up, then move along the edge of the lake in the direction of the breeze.

Becks and I used to come out here on hot days in the summer before we were even married. That was the late thirties. We'd swim all day and collapse on this dock and wake up shivering and mosquito-bit because the sun had gone down. My father would be mad as hell when we got back to the house, but I knew he envied us. That freedom just to be young.

Hannah opened the picnic basket and took out the thermos of iced tea, sandwiches, and banana bread, and she and Ruth drank and ate and threw the crumbs in to the ducks, who had come around for a second pass.

When they were done, Hannah said, I never believed that nonsense of waiting an hour before you swim. There won't be enough sun to warm a stone around here in an hour.

She pulled her dress over her head and slipped out of her bra and underpants and jumped into the water, surfaced, and yelled to Ruth, You better hurry! It's not getting any warmer.

Ruth turned around and took off her dress and underwear, slid her hand through her hair as though she had more of it than she did, and turned back to the water and jumped in. Hannah had already begun to swim out, but she waited as Ruth stroked toward her. When they were side by side they swam away from the dock through patches of warm and cold, where currents from the deeper part of the lake rose toward the surface and then slid back into the dark of it. They settled into longer, more powerful strides as they went, Ruth letting her ears fill with water each time she turned for air, so she felt as though she were swimming deaf to all but Hannah Konar's strong and gently knifing splash across the deep lake, until they reached the middle and Hannah stopped and treaded water, then pointed to a place off in the distance. Ruth turned and could see a worn rock peak that rose out of the forest of hardwoods like an old watch cap on the head of a solitary man just before he hunched down into his shoulders and disappeared.

It was Solace Mountain, Hannah told her, a mountain tucked so deeply in among the others surrounding it that it could be seen unobstructed only from the middle of the lake.

Ruth stared at the distant hill. Her teeth chattered and she worked her arms and legs in the water and said, Sam and I were going to climb it that summer he got arrested. That night was the last time I was out here. Seems a shame now.

Hannah nodded and lifted her chin as though to point in the direction of the dock and said, Let's get back.

The sun was still high when they climbed out of the water, and they sat wrapped in towels in their chairs for a long time with their faces turned in that direction.

When they had stopped shivering, Hannah said, I'm sorry if coming out here has got you thinking about Sam all over again. I could tell when we drove past the Sunset. You were looking in there like it was the last place you wanted to visit.

Ruth peered out of the fold of her towel at Hannah and was struck not for the first time at how much Sam resembled his mother.

No more or less than any other, she said. I'm just trying to keep it all together so you don't think I'm some kind of flower girl who was too delicate for your son.

I don't think that, Hannah said.

Ruth got up and pulled her chair closer to the water and sat back down. She stared out into the lake and smiled and said, That's what I thought when I said more than two words to him. It wasn't the first time I'd seen him, and we exchanged glances, you know, the way high school kids do. But that fall I had become a cheerleader because a friend of mine, Janey Landis, was on the squad. And after a practice where the coach had been yelling at everyone to look at Konar, Konar did it right, Konar gave his all, the team came charging off the field into the locker room and I wasn't looking where I was going. Sam crashed right into me. Knocked me down. It wasn't that hard, but he was strong. I stood up before he could help me, and said, Wow, now I know how the other guys feel. He gave me that wink of his and said, *No, you don't,* and ran into the locker room. I remember thinking Sam Konar could probably do whatever he wanted to do in this world, and I wondered what that was like.

Hannah stared down at the bleached-out

cedar planks of the dock and said, I could tell whenever he'd been with you. He had a look. A calm look. Like he'd found an answer to some question that had been bothering him.

But it bothered you, Ruth said.

Hannah shifted in her chair and looked up. Sometimes. Yes, she said. The funny thing about raising boys, Ruth, is that they're so easy to get so close to for so long. It's like their heads have a gear in them that always makes them turn back to find out where their mother is. No matter what they're doing or where. Then one day that gear shifts and they look elsewhere. They know you're there, but they're moving in a different direction for a different reason. Whatever reason it is they've chosen. And Sam chose you.

But didn't Bo get you used to that?

Bo had this sweetheart at college who died while she was home on winter break. That became the reason he never left Dardan, I guess. But Sam was different. He wanted to move from day one. And I knew that gear was going to shift fast. It's just — Well, no. I didn't get used to it. You never get used to it.

The breeze had died, and the last of the sun was at their backs so they were warm sitting on the dock now.

Ruth said, That mountain got me thinking all of a sudden about the night Sam raced that boy from Williamsport, because I swear we were going to climb it the very next day. Did he ever tell you the story? About the race? It wasn't like what the cops said.

No, Hannah said, and shook her head. He never told me.

Must have been that gear had shifted, huh?

Hannah nodded. Must have been.

Ruth told her how, on that night in June 1967, when Sam had just graduated high school and turned eighteen, he and Ruth were celebrating at the Sunset with some friends. It was about nine o'clock and a guy no one had ever seen pulled into the parking lot in a brand-new Barracuda 383. He walked into the restaurant and started hitting on Ruth as though no one else were in there. Sam stood up and told the guy to leave. The place got quiet, like there was going to be a fight, and then Sam looked out at the car — red and chrome and catching the glare of the streetlights — and said, Why don't we race for her?

The guy thought he meant Ruth, but Sam said, No, the car.

The guy sat down as though thinking hard about whether Sam Konar's 426 Hemi was worth it. I win and I get your Dodge? he said, and Sam asked what was under the hood of the Plymouth. The guy told him it was a four-barrel, which Sam already knew, but he opened his eyes wide and said, Your driveway will look like a Mopar ad.

And then they were all out on the road where those races happened, a quarter-mile stretch along the creek that flowed out of the lake. The drivers started at the bottom when a spotter at the top gave the signal that there was no traffic coming, and they raced on the slight uphill that drifted gently to the right and then flattened out for the last hundred yards. Ruth was the flagger and the Barracuda jumped the start, but Sam had guessed he would and let him go and watched the car head into the bend too fast, fishtail, and slow just enough for Sam to sprint past and win by a hood length.

There was a lot of shouting and threatening in the air, and the guy who drove the Barracuda insisted on two more runs, best out of three, saying that where he was from, no one bet a car like that on one race. Sam grinned his boyish grin and said, Well then, you'd better go back to where you're from and think hard about what's yours and what's not before you open your mouth again.

They knew that at any minute there were bound to be cops, and then the guy just tossed Sam the keys, jumped into the front seat of his friend's car, and was gone.

Sam looked stunned, Ruth said. He'd expected to win, but he hadn't expected the guy to give him his car. He had no title, no registration, and he told me later it crossed his mind that he was being set up. But he pressed the keys into my hand and I drove the 'Cuda home and parked it in my father's backyard. Never once thought about what might happen to me or to Sam. Until I woke up to police flashers and my father outside talking to the cops. All he said to me when he came back inside was, *I thought you two were smarter than that.*

Hannah said, The police came to the farm that day, too. Looking for Sam. And he tried to run. I had never seen him do anything like that. Mr. Vinich came out and told the police to leave and not come back until they had a warrant for whatever it was they were looking for. While they were gone, he went into the wood shop, pulled Sam out by the neck, and threw him onto the ground by the driveway. *Nobody runs in this family,* he said. *Now sit your ass down and don't move. The police can do what they want with you when they come back.*

All was shade except the last few feet of the dock, where they had pushed the chairs as the sun dropped, and Ruth leaned back in the Adirondack and said, I had never seen him so scared in that courtroom. Like he couldn't just do whatever he wanted to do anymore. And that scared me, too.

Hannah reached over and touched her hand and said, We're close to a place I want to take you. If you've got strength enough for one more thing today.

Okay, Ruth said.

They dressed and walked to the car, and Hannah drove back around the lake and out of the basin of mountains, where there was all of a sudden more sun, as though another afternoon remained before them, and they drove in the direction of town with the windows down until Hannah slowed and took a left turn onto a road that a sign partially obscured by overgrown sumac said was Myrtle Ave. She drove down this road as though she knew it well. By distance and direction of the town Ruth could tell only that they were not far from the college. Hannah stopped the car beneath a wrought-iron arch decorated with scrollwork and a gold-painted sign at the top that read OUR LADY OF SORROWS CEMETERY, and Ruth knew where they were.

Hannah said, You haven't asked to come see these graves, but I know you think about them. If you're ready, we'll go in. If not, we can go back to the house and come back another time. You just tell me.

Ruth looked up at the gently sloping hill on which row after row of headstones seemed to grow out of the ground — some flat, others curved at the top, many looking like monuments in worn granite capped with flanking angels or a single cross — without uniformity or order but for the worn paths that visitors had trod to come and go from their loved ones. And she said, I wanted to ask you but didn't know how.

It's all right, Hannah said. It's the kind of place I know my way around.

She put the Dart in gear and drove up the main access road, then began to angle the car toward the far corner. She passed the row of graves where her husband and father and mother lay, but she said nothing and drove on. When they were nearly to the back of the property, she stopped the car at the edge of a chain-link fence long overgrown with ivy, which separated the cemetery grounds from practice fields in the distance.

They're down that path, Hannah said, and pointed through the open window.

They got out of the car and Ruth reached

for Hannah's hand and they walked through grass that had not been mowed in a few weeks, until they came to three rectangular patches of earth that were dirt and stone and slightly rounded, though it was clear that the earth had settled some. At the head were freshly laid grave markers flush with the ground, the edges sharp and newly cut, as were the names on the stone. Paul A. Younger. Clare Frances Younger. Mary E. Younger.

Hannah said, Bo had these placed here. In the spring you can decide what you want to do for a headstone. We can help. She let go of Ruth's hand and backed away a few steps, and Ruth knelt down on the ground.

The baby's grave was in the middle of the three, and she put her palm flat on the earth of that one and curled her fingers as though trying to grab a handful of the rock and dirt. But the months of summer sun had baked it hard, and she uncurled her fingers and let the dirt lay where it was. Then she sat back on her heels and put her face in her hands and shook as she cried, though she made no sound. Hannah came forward again and knelt beside her, as if they were two women mourners brought together by those whom they mourned. Sisters, someone might have thought they were, if seen from a distance.

Or a mother and daughter. Regardless, they were women who, after a time, rose and wiped their eyes, then walked across the grass to the car and drove down the road into town and back to the place where they were not strangers and there were chores to do and food to consider. In the evening around the kitchen table, they made a decision to go out to those graves every Sunday after Mass with fresh flowers, which they placed in six small vases (each woman with three), then knelt and prayed for those whom they loved and missed. And the next week did the same.

CHAPTER TWELVE

On the Friday morning before Labor Day that year, Bo woke and closed his window against the cold air that had come in with a front and pushed out the last stretch of heat and humidity of the summer. He washed and dressed for work and went downstairs, where he found Ruth sitting at the kitchen table. She was dressed in one of Sam's flannel shirts, and the jeans and boots Hannah had given her, and she was drinking coffee from a mug with USMC printed on it in blue.

Morning, he said.

Good morning, Bo. How'd you sleep?

Like fall is in the air.

She was reading the paper from the day before. She turned a page and smoothed out the fold and said without looking up, Coffee's ready.

Bo took a cup off a hook and filled it. He leaned against the counter and studied her as he drank but said nothing. When he had finished, he put the cup in the sink and called Krasna and said to Ruth, Last time, all right? You've got it down. They're chickens, not thoroughbreds.

Ruth pushed the paper aside and said, I just don't want Hannah to worry about whether I'm doing it right or not.

He shook his head and she picked up her egg basket and they went out the back door.

When he and Ruth stepped out onto the porch, the light was murky and there was a stiff breeze that shipped and swayed the limbs of the apple trees, the world of the orchard looking to Bo like it had been alive in the darkness and the players had suddenly run back to their places. The air smelled of cold and turning leaves, and Bo glanced at the thermometer on the smokehouse as they passed.

Temperature dropped twenty degrees last night, he said.

I don't mind it, she said. I always liked the fall.

When they got to the barn, Bo followed her inside and said nothing as she went through the steps of feeding Miss Wayne. Ruth said over her shoulder, as though it were a casual conversation, that the old cow was eating less these days, and Bo said, She won't last the winter.

Ruth gave a slow nod and watched the cow eat, then went outside to the chicken coop. She checked the feeding trough and put a hose in the waterer for a few minutes and walked around looking at the hens. Then she shut off the hose and went to the nest boxes and gathered eggs from the four still laying.

We'll be getting a full dozen by Christmas, she said to Bo. You wait and see.

I expect to see, he said.

She opened the door of the coop and went outside and looked around at the sky just as Hannah had taught her. Krasna nestled her head under her hand and Ruth scratched the dog's ear.

I'm going to take these inside, she said, holding up the basket of eggs. Are you home the regular time tonight?

No, he said. I've got to head up to the hill house and meet the contractor. It's getting close to done. You ought to come see it sometime.

One day, she said. I'll keep a plate of food in the oven for you.

He nodded and walked to his truck, opened the door, and turned. You around tomorrow?

She smiled. And where would I be going, Bo Konar?

Well, I'm coming over early to finish my hutch. One last coat of varnish to go. Maybe after that we could hike up to the bend and I could show you the house?

Maybe, she said. Let's see.

Bo called Krasna and the dog started, then stopped and stood by Ruth's side.

You've got to decide, he said, and the dog sat down.

All right.

He got in the truck. He had to turn it over a few times before it started, but it did finally, and he backed down the drive.

As the summer progressed, Bo began to see the house his grandfather had given him as an ongoing conversation with the old man, one in which Bo spoke to him if he had a problem, told him what he planned, and promised that he would bring some kind of order to the place. It deserved that much.

But in my own good time, Pop, he would say out loud in the truck, walking in the field, or in the barn. In my own good time.

After he had mowed the place at the end of July and they got some rain that August, the grass came back green around the house and out to the edge of the fields, and this Bo mowed every other week on Fridays after work to keep it from ranging out again.

He bought a new oil burner and put it in the basement. The plumber installed a propane tank at the back of the house and brought the gas in to a new water heater and kitchen stove. Then he roughed out and installed a sink and toilet on the third floor and brought water pipes up along the chimney. Outside, the builders tore off the old front porch to the footers and framed a new one wrapping around to the kitchen door, replaced the rotten fascia board, and put up new rain gutters.

In late August Bo found someone who wanted to lease the land and grow winter wheat, and the up-front money paid for most of the repairs. On that Friday after work, Bo met Matt Devlin and the contractor at the house, inspected the porch that had just been finished and went back over all of the plumbing, then wrote the two men checks for the final amounts due and drove over to the farm for his dinner and a beer, talking to his grandfather the whole way.

Most weekends, Bo stayed at the farm with Hannah and Ruth, disappearing into his wood shop to work on the hutch. He had assembled it back in early August, and now he took advantage of the cooler days to sand the sides and insides flat with four-hundred-grit paper, tack it clean, and brush it. The entire piece was a beautiful one. It stood even and balanced. The dovetail joints he had made for the insides fit as if they had grown that way, and the drawers opened and closed as smooth as water over a stone. He had chosen and planed his own cherry boards from the same tree and left them exposed in the tally shed to let the shade of the heartwood deepen before he went to work on them. When he did, he was surprised at the color that the wood gave off, a kind of unsettled red, like a sunrise that presages a storm.

On the morning of Labor Day he woke and had breakfast with Hannah and Ruth, then went into the wood shop to get an early start. He sanded the finish with six-hundred-grit paper for the fifth and final coat, picked up a varnish brush, and tried to put out of his mind the things that always seemed to draw him elsewhere.

It was just before noon when he finished, and his head was reeling from the fumes. He was rinsing out his brush when he heard the door rattle and he turned and saw Ruth. Her black hair had grown out and she pushed one side of it behind her ear and kept a strand from the other side in her mouth. She wore another one of Sam's flannel shirts with the sleeves rolled up, jeans, and her harness boots.

Hannah wanted me to tell you that lunch will be ready in about a half hour, she said. She had an apple in her hand and bit into it, winced, and spat the pulp into a trash can by the door. When do these things get ripe?

End of September, Bo said. How are those chickens getting along without me?

Like good girls. I was just about to round them up in the yard. They've been out there all morning. She began to walk around the shop, picking up discards of wood and putting them down until she came to the hutch and stood staring at it. That's nice work, she said.

It needs to sit for a few days, while the finish dries.

She nodded and peered around all four sides of it.

I made it for Hannah, Bo said. I thought a place to keep the letters about Sam that came back with some reply might make her feel like writing them was a lot less futile.

Ruth came over to the sink where he was standing and leaned in. He could smell her perfume, sweat, and the green apple on her breath.

It's her boy, she said. She won't stop until

they find him, one way or the other. She turned away and walked over to the lathe. So what are you going to work on next?

Table and chairs, I think, Bo said. For the house.

She nodded. My father used to talk about that place like it was the only time he was happy in life. He was going to farm it. Maybe raise some chickens, too, for all I know. I think that's why I've been dragging my feet about going up there to see what you've done.

You might not recognize it, he said.

Wouldn't have recognized it before. I've only seen it once, and that was from the front seat of a car out on the road.

Bo put his brush in a can of turps and placed it on the windowsill. I'll let you read the ledger my grandfather left for me along with that land. Then you should sit down with Father Rovnávaha. You ever hear anything about your grandfather Walter?

My father never said that name without wanting to spit. I asked him how a man could get so angry, and he said, *You asking about me or him?* I was sitting in my aunt Mary's kitchen once when the conversation turned to where she grew up, so I asked why she and Daddy didn't still have it, and she just said, *Ruth, honey, the Lord giveth*

243

and the Lord taketh away. Nothing else you need to know.

Bo said, Well, I'm not sure how much the Lord had to do with it. The men pretty much took care of the taking away themselves.

Ruth pushed some leftover wood shavings from the tool rest of the lathe onto the floor. I'll come see it one day, she said. When it's all yours and I won't recognize it for anything but a good house on a hill that a Konar fixed up and lives in now.

They heard Krasna pawing at the shop door. Ruth went over and opened it and the dog came in and lifted her head and barked.

I know, Ruth said. Bo's almost done. Then you'll get your lunch.

Krasna barked again and ran outside.

I've got no sticks to throw, girl, she said. Bo, hand me one of them scrap pieces you've got over there.

She doesn't want to play fetch, Bo said. That girl never barks. There's something going on.

He and Ruth stepped out of the wood shop and watched the dog bolt in the direction of where the chickens were left to range in the yard and orchard, and they ran after her in that direction.

They found the hens huddled around the

stone fireplace, against the side that faced away from the banana-apple tree, and even as Krasna ran toward them they stood there. The dog came up short and turned around to bark again, then raised her snout toward the tallest tree in the orchard, where Bo could see now the red-tail perched at the top.

The chickens had about twenty yards of open ground to get across from where they were hiding to the cover of the coop. The hawk was waiting for them to break for it and Bo wondered why the chickens had not, then he looked over and saw that every time the new hens tried to emerge from the shadow of the fireplace chimney, Celeste beat them back with her wings, and Krasna ran across the grass in front of them.

They're trying to get to the coop, Ruth said. I'll run with them and keep them covered.

They won't all make it, Bo said. That bird wants one, and that's what he'll get if they run. Stay here. I'll get the gun.

Ruth watched him sprint for the house and disappear through the back door. She called Krasna and the dog ran back to her, and Ruth knelt down and held her head and said, Listen, girl. When I say go, you go. I'll be right behind.

The dog broke from her and ran toward the fireplace. Ruth followed after, and when she got to the flock in the shadow of the chimney, she yelled, Go, Krasna, go! and waved her arms, and the dog and the old chicken seemed to know exactly what it was she wanted to do. Krasna leaped forward and circled back and ran forward again, and Celeste beat her wings and pushed the others, and the entire flock began as one to run toward the coop by the barn, Ruth bringing up the rear and holding out her arms and flapping them as if they were chicken wings themselves, calling, Go! Go! as they raced across the yard.

She had them more than halfway there when she thought it just might work, that she and the dog and Celeste might have done a remarkable thing by themselves on that farm, when she heard a sound behind her like a blanket on a clothesline snapping in a strong wind, and the sun above her was shadowed as the hawk swooped down like a stone toward the pullets scampering just a few steps ahead of her. She wished she could run faster. Wished she could dive on those chickens and save them, every one of them, no matter if the hawk bit her in the back of the head or tried to carry her away instead. But in the second when she felt that wind and saw the sun darken, she saw, too, the burst of feathers and the squawk of some bird, fowl or raptor she did not know, and the pullet right in front of her rose off the ground in the red-tail's claws as she reached out her hands to grab it herself, tripped and fell off balance, and went facedown into that ground.

When she tried to push herself up, she could taste the blood running from her nose into her mouth. Krasna came over and licked her ear, panting hard, and then stuck her snout under Ruth's jaw and licked her face. Ruth winced from the pain, then reached up and petted the dog's head. She tried again to stand and could not, then felt someone helping her. It was Hannah, who had grabbed her under the arms, lifted her, and held her. Ruth stood hunched over and spat blood and grass and began to cry, and Hannah said, Oh, look at you. Let's get you into the house.

They walked with their arms on each other's shoulders and hobbled like that in the direction of the back porch and passed Bo coming toward them with his rifle. Ruth pulled on Hannah and they spun around and stopped to watch as he took off his shirt and threw it over the stone edge of the fireplace, then knelt on the ground and used that edge as a barrel rest. Ruth followed his line of sight and saw the hawk roosting, the young hen unmoving in its claws, and she wondered why the hunter had not flown away. Flown somewhere it might eat its prey in peace. Unless it was not done with what it had come for. She heard the sound of the rifle safety snap and looked back at where Bo knelt, watched him pull the trigger, the report of the twenty-two no more than a thin whiplike crack, and when she turned to the trees where the hawk had landed and perched, it was no longer there.

■ ■ ■ ■ ■

PART 3
AS WE WAIT

■ ■ ■ ■ ■

CHAPTER THIRTEEN

He woke on a Sunday morning to gray light and the sound of wind as it buffeted the house from the east, crawled out of the sleeping bag he had been using on the floor of the living room, and went into the kitchen to wash and then stoke a fire in the wood-stove. He put a small pot of oatmeal on the gas range and walked outside to the barn, brought two loads of wood into the kitchen, and stacked another two loads on the porch by the door. Then he made coffee and waited for his breakfast to cook.

After he had eaten, he went into the living room and raised a fire in the fireplace, sat down in a chair that was the sole piece of furniture in the room, and opened *Sometimes a Great Notion.* Ruth had given the book to him as a moving-over-the-mountain gift (she called it), but he went through more coffee than pages and put down the book and picked up an atlas he had found in his grandfather's study and brought over when he had moved his things on Saturday morning.

It was about four hundred and fifty miles to Abas, West Virginia, he figured. A little over eight hours. If Jeff called him back today and told him the saw was still there, he would leave early in the morning and be back by midnight.

The week before, he had sat in the trailer office at the mill and clicked a pen against a legal pad and jotted down the numbers he had come up with on the adding machine. One quarter over, another about to begin. Endless Roughing could increase its output by a third into '73 if the orders he had projected held, and there was no reason to believe they would not. But that meant more men and a bigger mill if the hours returned to what they had been since June, and he had neither more men nor a bigger mill. Dardan was still rebuilding, but it was tapering fast in anticipation of winter, the bulk of the big projects already close to done. And he could see that the extra hours he was asking his men to work was taking their toll. How long before some of those men said, *All right, we did our share.* How long before all of them began to grumble and complain on break, take shortcuts, or call in, regardless of what Bo gave them or told them they had coming. There was a limit. It had been a good run.

So he told Jeff Lamoreaux to put up a notice in the break room for a meeting on the last Friday of September, and the men knocked off at three-thirty and gathered in the tally shed. Bo got up on a stack of wooden soda crates and told them how the mill had done that summer. How they had put out more lumber in those three months since the flood than they had in almost the entirety of the year before. He thanked them for their work and told them that their hours would go back to seven-thirty to four-fifteen, with a forty-five-minute lunch break at noon and coffee breaks at ten and two, effective Monday, along with a bonus of anywhere from ten to one hundred dollars in their first paycheck in October, depending on a man's seniority. Then he stepped down, and Jeff got up and told them there was beer in the back of the boss's truck and they should help themselves. Some of the younger boys hollered, and everyone made for the door until the shed was empty except for Bo and Jeff. Bo went over to the desk and opened the tally book as though he might find something in there that he did not already know, flipped a few pages, and closed it.

What's on your mind, boss? Jeff asked.

Earlier in the day, Dave Cummings had come into the office and informed Bo that one of the older ripsaws had broken down for good. Bo told Jeff this and asked him what a new one cost.

More than we should pay, Jeff said, and pulled a cigarette from a pack in his shirt pocket and tucked it behind his ear. Turns out, though, that I got a call last week from a guy I know in West Virginia who went to an auction at a mill that had gone out of business. Told me he saw a Diehl in good shape go to some guy who buys and sells those things.

Where is he? Bo asked.

Outside a town called Abas, Jeff said. About a day's drive. Daylight, that is.

Bo stared down at the cover of the tally book and did not say anything.

Heard of it? Jeff asked.

Bo nodded. Call him back.

The next day Bo moved all that he had except what was in the wood shop from the farm to the hill house. Hannah asked if she and Ruth could come up for lunch at noon on Sunday, and Bo told her he would like that.

He sat in his living room that Sunday and

watched the fire burn, glanced at his watch, and saw that it was nearly twelve already. He closed the cover of the atlas and left it on the chair, put on his coat, and went outside.

It had been a warm month, that morning the first when there might have been a frost, but there was not. Bo walked to the edge of the grass to inspect the shoots of winter wheat coming up, and he saw Hannah and Ruth coming out of the woods from the meadow and down along the field. Their arms were looped one inside the other, Ruth holding a wicker basket in her free hand. He watched them for a while from the distance, as though they would keep on along the border with the woods and pass him by, as though there might be no house there on the hill at all. But then they angled through the rows of wheat in his direction and he walked out and greeted them by the barn, took the basket of food they carried, and led them inside.

They hung their coats over the chairs at the kitchen table and put their boots in a tray by the stove. The room was light-filled and warm and smelled faintly of fresh paint and wood smoke. Bo offered them coffee, slid another log into the stove, and poured the soup they had brought into a saucepan he placed at the back of the gas range. Hannah sat and drank. Ruth stood, her hands wrapped around the coffee mug for the warmth. After a minute or two, Bo said, Let me show you what I've done with the place, and they both stood and followed him into the living room.

From the day Bo had walked into the house in May, he understood how it had been built, whom it had been built for, and he wanted to keep that spirit of the place alive, even if not one of the Youngers who lived there back in the twenties was around to see it. The old wide-board pine floors were refinished and glowing a soft shade of gold beneath the grain. The walls were painted natural linen. The window frames and fireplace mantel he had varnished to match the floors, and the slate hearth was repointed and polished so that the thin rust-colored veins and slight green hue of the stone shone like the day they were put down.

Bo, it's beautiful, Hannah said. This is — She stopped and stood at a window and did not finish her sentence.

Ruth asked him if he did all this work himself and he said no, he had hired out the carpentry, painting, and plumbing but had stripped and refinished the wood trim by himself in August.

He took them upstairs and showed them all four bedrooms, painted but bare. He said he had not picked a bedroom for himself, but he liked the one that overlooked the fields and the woods beyond.

Where do you sleep? Hannah asked.

On the floor in the living room. It's only been one night.

Goodness, Bo, she said. We've got more beds over at the farm than you can shake a stick at. And a couch, too, for that living room of yours.

I was thinking of making my own bed, he said. But a couch would be nice. Place to sit in front of the fire.

When they came back down to the kitchen, Bo moved the soup off the stove, ladled it into bowls, and took bread from the warming tray of the woodstove. Then they sat down. Hannah asked the Lord to bless the food before them and the house to which they had come, and they ate, speaking only of the weather.

After the meal, Ruth asked Bo where he was planning on going. He looked at her as if he did not understand and said, I'm not going anywhere. I'm staying right here.

She turned and glanced into the living room as if to make sure it was there. The atlas you were reading. Just brushing up on your geography?

He drank off his coffee. Sam ever talk to you about a Captain Burne Grayson? he asked.

He mentioned a Commander Grayson, she said. I didn't know he had a first name. When I landed in Honolulu and we were riding around in the taxi and catching up, nervous, I guess, Sam said morale was high in their unit because of Grayson. He let them be marines. I asked if Grayson came on R and R with him, too, and he laughed and said no, and that was the last I heard of him. Except in that letter you showed me.

Bo stood up and poured himself another cup of coffee. I was looking at how far it is to West Virginia. I'm driving there tomorrow if I hear back from Jeff before dinnertime.

What's down there? Hannah asked.

A saw I might want to buy for the yard. It's in storage outside of Abas, northern part of the state, off of 33.

That's where Captain Kraynack said Grayson's from, Hannah said.

Yep, Bo said.

Ruth leaned forward. I want to go with you.

He looked surprised and scratched his

beard. I don't know, Ruth. I mean, I don't know who or what's down there.

Why should that matter for me and not for you?

He set his coffee cup down on the table, walked over to the pile of stove wood and picked up two logs, put them into the stove, and closed the lid. It doesn't. But I'm leaving early. I need to get down and back before Tuesday morning. I can't make it a road trip.

Road trip? she said. What's that supposed to mean?

I mean it's just work.

Captain Grayson's in the saw business now?

I don't even know if I'll have time to look for Grayson. I'm going down there to buy a saw, not to listen to some vet's war stories.

Ruth shook her head, and Hannah said, It'd be nice to have the company, Bo.

I don't want any company, he said. He ran water in the sink and took dishes from the table, and Hannah and Ruth said nothing. Listen, he said, and turned to face them. I'm sorry. Let me check this out by myself first. If he's for real, Ruth, this Grayson, I'll drive back down there just for you, and we can hear what he has to tell us about Sam.

She nodded but would not look at him as she rose and got her coat and said, I'll be outside, Hannah. Take what time you need.

He woke at four in the morning and left the stove damped and walked out into the darkness, where a waning moon was in the sky to the east above the field at the top of the hill like a broken and rounded-off dinner plate. The Big Dipper hung right overhead. He stood looking up at the stars and wondered if he ever would see his brother again, then got in his truck and drove down the mountain.

The traffic lights in Dardan Center were flashing yellow, and a cop sat half asleep in his cruiser, parked nose-out by the back of the drugstore. Bo took a left at the creek and drove up the hill toward the farm and saw the light on in the kitchen. He got out and rapped on the back door, and Ruth stood and came to it. He did not wonder if she would be ready. She was dressed in her boots and a CPO jacket he remembered was Sam's, and he knew that Hannah would have said to her last night, *You'd better be waiting for him, because he's going to be here.* She had tied her hair back and tucked it underneath a green field cap that must have been Sam's as well, although Bo had never seen it.

You ready? he asked.

She nodded.

We'll get breakfast on the way.

They took 118 West, and as they approached the mill Bo slowed and rolled the pickup to a stop and sat staring in the half-light at the outlines of sheds and treetops that looked pale in the weak luminescence of the yard lights.

What's wrong? Ruth asked.

Nothing, he said. It just seems strange to drive past it and not pull in. Habit, you know? I've been doing it since I was nineteen, and I've never wanted to do anything else.

Hannah mentioned to me once that you had done a year at school, Ruth said. Place in the South.

Semester only. I didn't want to go back. Bo rolled the window down to listen to the engine idle. It sounds a little rough, he said, but it should get us there and back. He rolled the window up.

Did you love her? Ruth asked.

Love at eighteen, he said, and put the truck into gear but kept his foot on the clutch.

I was younger than that, Ruth said.

Bo turned to look at her. That's why, he said.

That's why what?

That's why I didn't go back.

They were quiet for a long time, and Ruth said, That's why I stayed.

A truck shifting out of a lower gear crested the hill behind them, and Bo looked in the rearview mirror to judge its distance, then back at the road. He let his foot off the brake and eased the clutch and drove.

From Ricketts Glen to the junction with Route 220 in Hughesville they passed farm tractors and delivery trucks and were overtaken by a '66 Camaro SS with a V-8 that Bo could hear growl as it came up and moved into the oncoming lane, the driver tense at the wheel with a cigarette in his mouth. He never turned his head as he lurched past the pickup like a traffic cone in the middle of the road. Ruth said out of nowhere, *Race car* spelled backward is still *race car.* Did you know that?

I do now, he said.

When the sun was up, they found themselves among the steady traffic of loggers, fuel tankers, and eighteen-wheelers coming in from Interstate 80. They took 80 for a stretch of about twenty miles, through the Nittany Valley of the Alleghenies, where

Bo's grandfather had told him that a lion or two were said to be hiding. (Bo remembered then the week before the old man died, the two of them sitting at the kitchen table while Jozef talked of shepherding in the old country and the big cat he had shot in the early dawn. But the next day Jozef said to him, *To bol vlk,* the man speaking in Slovak as though he had spoken this language to his grandson his entire life. Bo asked what he was talking about, and Jozef said, In the Tatras. It was a wolf, not a mountain lion. But my own father dreamed for so long of living here, in America, that even what stalked us then was part of that dream.)

They exited and stayed on 220 West for State College. At eight o'clock they pulled up to a diner that advertised twenty-five-cent coffee and free refills, and they ordered toast and bacon and eggs. Bo looked out the window and across the street, where a young woman stood in the parking lot of a building and handed out cattails to passersby, stems she took from a cardboard box brimming with them, on the side of which was a sign in blue and red Magic Marker that read, *For they shall be called the children of God.* He touched Ruth's shoulder and pointed, and the two of them watched the young woman dance from person to person, offering each one her symbol of peace. She seemed grateful to anyone who held out a hand, and undaunted by anyone who did not.

He had the old truck up to seventy on the highway outside of Bedford, Pennsylvania, hoping to make some time and listening to Ruth talk about three new hens she had introduced into the flock that weekend, when he saw the police lights behind him. He pulled over and gave the cop his license and registration and the officer took off his sunglasses and asked Bo where he was going in such a hurry.

West Virginia, Bo said.

That so?

Bo nodded. But I didn't think this thing could go that fast. I just had it rebuilt a few months ago.

The cop pretended not to care. Business or pleasure? he asked, and glanced inside at Ruth, who sat and stared straight ahead.

So Bo told him about the flood and the mill and the lead he had gotten on a good used saw and who knew what else, and that he was hoping to get down there by noon, though he had not planned on breaking any laws along the way. He said nothing about the marine captain named Burne Grayson, or his brother who was dead or alive in some jungle in Vietnam.

That so, the policeman said again. He looked to be about Hannah's age, though something in his frame and face made him look older than he ought to have been, and Bo wondered what sons, if any, he had at home.

The cop walked to the back of the truck and looked in the bed, empty but for a metal toolbox and a length of rope, then came back over to the window, handed the license and registration to Bo, and said, Make sure you drive a little slower, then, Mr. Konar, or them boys in West Virginia'll give you a ticket just for talking too much.

At the Maryland state line they pulled up to a restaurant on the outskirts of Cumberland. Bo bought a map and went to a phone booth and called the farm and told Hannah they were making good time and expected to be home by midnight if things went as planned. There was a pause on the line, and she asked how Ruth was.

You can ask her yourself, he said.

No. You two just be careful. Call me when you're headed back. I don't care what time.

It was eleven o'clock and warm in the sun when they stopped in Clarksburg for gas and to check the map for the last leg of the trip. Then they took Route 19 out of town to 33, the road winding along the edges of forests, mountainsides, the banks of creeks, and old rail lines like a live wire brought down in a storm. Ruth said she had never been this far south or west, and he asked if she saw a familiarity in the landscape of mountains and rivers that reminded him of home.

Some, she said. These hillsides, though. They're steeper here. Like everyone lives in a bit more shadow than light.

He said, I thought that, too. Just couldn't put my finger on what it was.

Jeff had given him a mile marker to look out for, and when he passed it an hour later, he slowed and peered into every cut in the trees on the side of the road that might look like a driveway, until he saw a post with two reflectors nailed to it and a patch of gravel grated from the berm into the woods. He took the turn and pulled in to what might be called a yard, were it not for the intrusion of machinery and parts of machinery that had not run or worked in any recent year and had been strewn about the grounds in a manner that told him they had been dumped and left to rust.

He parked and shut off the engine and listened to the silence of decay. A fat man in a T-shirt and overalls came out of a shed and walked toward them, looking at Bo first, then Ruth, and not taking his eyes off of Ruth.

Bo got out of the truck, extended his hand, and said, Bo Konar.

The man ignored him, reached into his pocket and took out a plug of chewing tobacco and tucked it into the back of his mouth. Here about the saw, ain't you? he drawled.

The smells of pine and morning air gave way to stale engine oil and unwashed sweat. That's right, Bo said. Let me get my tools and we can get this over with. He opened the front door of the truck and said to Ruth, Lock these doors when I go in.

He took a flashlight from behind the seat, then closed the door and reached into the truck bed for his toolbox and followed the man through the yard and into the shed.

The saw sat uncovered in a corner. Bo walked around it, then came in close, knelt down, and turned on his flashlight. It was a DL 750, built in '52 by the serial number, and he could tell that someone had taken care of it. It would need a new chain, but the lubrication unit was intact and most likely operative. He took off the spindle housing, and the air gap clearance between the rotor and the stator was fine. Then he checked the pressure roll assembly for wear and axial play, and everything looked good. Even the guide rail and the stock rail were in nice shape.

The fat man watched Bo as he worked, and when Bo lifted his head up and stepped back from the saw, the man said, Know what you're doin', don't you?

Sometimes, Bo said. He turned and looked at the man. I'll give you five hundred dollars for it.

The man scoffed. That's what I paid fer it.

No, you didn't. Five hundred, and I'll have a flatbed down here tomorrow to pick it up.

Lemme think on it.

You can think on it all you want, Bo said, and looked around at the rest of the junk jammed into that shed, which foretold what the saw would become. But that's more than you'll get leaving it here to collect cobwebs and batshit. I'm going home.

He had decided as he walked from the shed to the truck that if the man let him get inside and turn the engine over, he was going to drive away no matter what. He was tired and hungry and in no mood to bargain. Bo opened the door of the pickup and said to Ruth, Count to five for me, would you? Out loud.

When she got to four, they heard the man holler like he would never see that truck in his yard again. All right! You got yerself a saw.

Bo got out and yelled back, Good. He reached into his pocket for his wallet, peeled off four fifties, and waited for the man as he sauntered over to the truck.

Two hundred now, three hundred when my guy comes to pick it up.

Bo gave him the money. The man counted it out slow, twice, then folded the bills and put them in the chest pocket of his overalls.

I'll be here, he said.

Chapter Fourteen

By the map, Abas was five miles or so west along that same road, and Bo drove until he came to the town and pulled up to the first place he found that served food. A diner, though it had no name that he could see. He called the mill collect from the pay phone outside and told Jeff that he had bought the saw and would need a flatbed down there tomorrow.

Anything else? Jeff asked over the phone.

No, Bo said. I was lucky to get this one.

The diner was empty except for two men in garage coveralls eating at the lunch counter, and they never looked up. A woman wearing a pink and white apron over a denim dress stood at the end by the soda fountain and smoked. Her left arm was holding up her right arm at the elbow while she dragged on the cigarette and tugged at a coil of dirty-blond hair that she had pulled from around her back and over her shoulder. She had on scuffed saddle shoes and no socks, and Bo could see behind the makeup that stopped in a line underneath her jaw that she was older than she wanted to look.

He and Ruth slid into an open booth and the woman crushed out her cigarette and came over and stood next to their table. What are you havin'? she asked.

Bo tried to read the menu, but his mind was still in that shed. The woman tapped the pad with her pencil and said, You take a minute. I'll be back.

No, Ruth said. We'll have two coffees, a ham sandwich, and a hamburger.

The waitress flipped the pencil with one hand and scratched again, dropped the pad into her apron pocket, and walked toward the kitchen door.

You okay? Ruth asked Bo.

Getting there, he said. How did you know what I wanted?

I didn't. But I'm starving, and I'm guessing it's all the same around here.

The coffee came a minute later, and Bo hunched over his cup and drank and felt like he was waking up in the middle of the day. The hamburger and sandwich took some time, but they were better than expected, so Bo and Ruth each ordered a piece of the apple pie that the woman told them had been baked that morning at a bakery in Spencer with apples from an orchard in Jefferson County.

When she came back a minute later with two plates of pie and a new setting of forks, she said, So, you two here just to buy scrap off of Hollis? Or is there some other reason you drove to Abas from wherever it is you're from in Pennsylvania? Because I know you ain't here for your honeymoon.

Word travels, Bo said.

'Round here it does.

Bo pulled his plate toward him. We're looking for Morning Ridge. A man named Grayson.

Burne? she asked, and Bo said yes. She studied him for a moment. You don't look like the law.

We came here to ask him about my brother. Her fiancée. He served with Grayson in Vietnam.

The woman folded her arms against her chest and glanced over at the two men finishing their lunch. Let me take care of those boys, she said. She strolled over to the counter and put her arm around the one closest to the edge. He was wiry and nervous-looking and ate with his hat on. She spoke to them both, then moved her hand down the thin man's back and around to the inside of his thigh, and squeezed his leg. He smiled with his teeth and put a single bill on the countertop. She swept it up fast and put it in her pocket, and the two men stood, gave a little hop to settle their coveralls, and walked out the door.

When the waitress returned, she took an order pad and a pencil from inside her apron, tore a sheet off the pad, and set it down on the table. Look here, she said, and sketched a large calligraphic Z on the paper with a line running through the middle of it. That's Main Street right out there. Take a left at the service station and keep following it until the road bears left again, real sharp, like you're fallin' off the world. Then keep going until the road stops. That's the ridge. That's where you'll find him.

She pushed the drawn map toward Ruth and put the pad and pencil in her pocket. No idea why he came back to this shit hole, she said. I seen all them medals he's got. You'd think a man like that could live wherever he wants. She pulled at the hair on her shoulder. Or have whoever he wants. But he's got that house his daddy built. And a new dog since he's been home.

She stared outside and followed a car down Main Street with her eyes, then shook her head and turned back to Bo and Ruth at the table. Four dollars even, she said to Bo. For the coffee and lunch. I'll be at the register when y'all are ready.

They drove longer than Bo believed was the distance that the waitress had intended on her map, the road climbing and climbing, dense woods on one side, sheer cliff on the other, the left they were told to take nearly a mile behind them now. He slowed the truck and rolled down the window. He could hear on the crisp air the unmistakable TOK of an ax rounding into wood. He heard it again and put the truck in gear and kept going up the road a few hundred yards until they came to a bend and into a clearing. There in front of them stood the back of a two-story log cabin with a broad fieldstone chimney rising up the center, the house itself perched on a ledge that looked like it hung in the sky. The place seemed built not to take in the view so much as to take flight from whomever or whatever might climb up that mountain and find it.

Bo turned off the engine, and he and Ruth got out and listened to a breeze stir in the oak and beech in the woods behind them. There were stone steps to the side of the house, and they heard again the sharp TOK of someone splitting firewood. Someone good at it. Bo moved in that direction and Ruth followed him, but the first flat rock at the top of those steps tilted when he came down on it. Bo dropped and let out a yell.

A hound began to bay and Ruth stopped. Bo stood up fast and dusted himself off, the underside of his forearm and elbow smudged with dirt and blood. He saw a blue-tick approach the bottom step and begin to howl.

Hector! a voice shouted, and the dog stopped and sat. A man carrying an ax came into view, looked up, and said, Don't worry. He's just a puppy. We don't get many visitors.

He was a tall man with a slight paunch and a fine blond beard. A shock of that same blond fell into his eyes, and he pushed it aside as if he had just gotten used to it being long. He had on a black-and-green-checked flannel shirt with a white T-shirt underneath and double-front canvas work pants that were worn at the knee. Bo guessed that they were about the same age, but he felt humbled somehow in the man's presence, student to a master in a course unknown, and he might have bowed if they had been on level ground.

You going to stand there at the top of my

steps? Or are you going to come on down and say hello like polite folks do?

Bo and Ruth walked the rest of the steps. The dog sniffed at them and stayed by Ruth, and she petted his head.

We're looking for Captain Burne Grayson, Bo said.

Retired, Grayson said.

I'm Bo Konar, Bo said, and reached out his hand. And this is Ruth Younger.

Grayson shook Bo's hand without much of a grip. I know who you are, he said, and let go. I know, he said again. He turned and walked over to his woodpile and sank the ax into a chopping block. He whistled for the dog, and clipped him to a rope eye-bolted to the house. He turned back to Bo and Ruth and said, I was just getting ready to knock off for the day. Let's get you something for that arm.

They followed him up a wooden staircase that wound around the slab of stone on which the entire house sat and went into a living room built of glass and timber with a view of the valley so striking that Bo had to reach for the door handle as he turned and stood before it. Behind him was a fireplace large enough for a grown man to stand inside. What looked like the kitchen was an alcove with a sink, a refrigerator, and an old

Franklin stove. Nothing else. Furniture consisted of a wooden chair with an embroidered cushion, and this sat before a rabbit-eared television set (the lone evidence that this man lived in an age that could claim electricity) on top of an orange crate. There was another flight of stairs that led to a balconied hallway, and on either side of the large chimney were two doors, one open, the other closed.

Grayson rinsed a dish towel at the sink in the kitchen, wrung it out, and handed it to Bo, who spot-cleaned the blood and dirt from his arm. He handed the towel back to Grayson.

Might want to cover that up, Grayson said. He rinsed the towel again and went to Bo and wound the dressing around his elbow and tucked the two ends inside the wrap. That ought to do it. Keep it straight for now.

He went back into the kitchen, took a ceramic pot from a cupboard, doled three spoonfuls of chopped green needles from a Mason jar into the pot, then poured hot water from a kettle on the Franklin into the pot. He put a lid on it and placed three more empty Mason jars on the counter by the sink. White pine tea, he said. Good for what ails you. Let's just give it a moment to steep.

There was nowhere to sit but the lone chair, and Grayson did not offer it. So Bo stood holding his arm and Ruth slumped down on the floor by the window. Grayson poured the tea into the Mason jars and picked one up like a man picking coals from a fire and handed it to Ruth. It's hot, he said.

She pinched the mouth of the jar with her fingers and held it that way. Grayson gave the other one to Bo and took his own and motioned to the deck outside as he walked. Bo and Ruth followed.

They sat with their backs against the house and cups of tea between their legs, the sun past its equinox tilting toward the west, the trees on the other side of the valley looking in their leaves like a wash on a canvas that moved from green to yellow and orange. Near the mountaintop they were a flamelike red.

Airy this morning, Grayson said. That's how you caught me chopping wood into the afternoon. Afraid I'm behind, if this winter promises to be a bad one. They're saying by Friday there might even be a skift of snow on the ground in the elevations.

Grayson sipped his tea and stared out at

the sun as though it held some clue on how he might recollect and sift through what he ought to tell. Bo had seen that look on his grandfather's face. A look of unburdening. And he wished in the faintness and fatigue that had come over him all of a sudden that he could stand and walk away and leave the burden for Grayson himself to carry, if he was the kind to carry burdens at all. But Bo knew that Ruth would not leave until she had heard something she could take back with her, something she could place on that chest of drawers where the pictures of Sam lay, and she could say, *Now there are two things I know.*

It was a long time before Grayson said anything, so long that Bo almost got up to leave. Then Grayson swirled the green needles in his jar and took a long drink and whispered as though to himself, So you're here about old man.

He didn't say, *What do you want to know? Or Heard any more about him? Or I've heard Sam Konar talk about you two since the day I asked him what town he was from, then had to order him to quit talking.* He said, That's what we called him. Old man. Not *the* Old Man. Just old man. First his squad. Then the platoon. After a while the whole rifle company got used to it. He'd talk to himself.

Real quiet. And the guys would say, Who the hell are you talking to, Konar? and he'd say, *An old man.*

That was our grandfather, Bo said. Hard to shake him even when he's not around, so you end up talking to him instead.

Is he back in Pennsylvania?

He's dead.

Grayson nodded. Well, only Konar could get away with it. PFC then and already a kind of talisman when I was a first lieutenant. Guys in-country clung to anyone or anything for luck, as long as they believed it was going to get them out of there. Your brother found a tripwire once that didn't trip. Another ville we were checking out got attacked. Small-arms fire. A grenade rolled right between Konar and the doc, and that damn thing was a dud. Other stuff, too. All coincidence, but not when you're counting days and all you want to do is go home. Guys started to fight for who got to be next to him on patrol at night. There was a sergeant who chewed his ass out once. *Don't give me that old man bullshit, Konar.* But he stopped right quick when your brother spotted some VC setting up to ambush them. Just movement like the breeze, except there was no breeze that day, and Konar knew it.

Grayson took a sip of his tea and smiled.

Not all the Vietcong were hardened jungle warriors, he said. And as a result there were six fewer of them by that sergeant's count.

Bo watched and listened to the man, not wanting to interrupt but wanting to know when he would get around to telling them what it was they had come to hear. Grayson put his head down and stared into the dregs of pine needles that he swirled slowly in the jar.

Bo said, Captain Kraynack told us in a letter that you're the reason my brother's still listed as MIA.

Grayson looked up. That's right, he said. He unlaced his boots and pushed them to the outer edge of the deck, sat up straight, and tucked his feet under his legs in a lotus position. A gust of wind lifted his hair, and Bo could see the fresh scar tissue of a wound on the back of his head.

Kraynack tell you where I live, too?

Waitress at the diner drew us a map, Bo said.

Oh, Ashley, Grayson said and shook his head. She and I were in high school together. She was the homecoming queen, and I was a bookworm on his way to Morgantown and dreaming about what it'd be like just to talk to her. She used to torture me something fierce. Now she finds her way up here every once in a while. When she's got no one to talk to, I guess. I kinda feel sorry for her.

He stared in the direction of the valley. But we were talking about Kraynack, weren't we. He and I go back to Okinawa in '65. We were on the same C-130 that took us to Danang. And look at us. We both made it. I was even stupid enough to do a second tour. And then a third.

He raised his arms above his head and arched his back and exhaled. He turned to Ruth. How do you like that tea? he asked.

Better than Ashley's coffee.

Ain't that the truth, Grayson said, and laughed. You get a slice of pie, though?

Ruth nodded.

Hell yes, Grayson said. He turned to Bo. How's your arm feel?

Not bad, Bo said. Look, we'll finish up and leave you to your woodpile. We were just wondering, you know, if we should put up a marker for Sam and get on with it. Or keep waiting.

We? Grayson said.

Ruth and me and Sam's mother.

Grayson drew a deep and audible breath through his nose and exhaled out his mouth. You might put up a marker regardless, he said, and raised his face to the weakening sun and closed his eyes. He sat like that for a minute, and Bo looked at Ruth and motioned with his head that they ought to go. Then Grayson opened his eyes and said, I remember once on my first tour, my platoon was doing patrols with a unit of South Vietnamese soldiers, and we stopped at a village one day to talk to this old lady that the commander said he got good intel from every now and then. I couldn't believe it, but we went along. She wasn't a day under a hundred, I swear to God, and she talked, and he talked, and she talked some more. And when I asked him what she said, he said that she had seen some Vietminh soldiers come through a few days ago, and they told her that her son would be home soon, so she'd been tidying the hut and fixing up his corner of it the same way it was when he left, praying every day to her ancestors to say thank you. She means Vietcong, I said, excited now that we were getting somewhere, and the commander said no. Well, when the hell's he coming back? I asked. We ought to stake out this ville and see if the whole damn army shows. But he thanked the old lady, who smiled and bowed and said all kinds of nice things about us as we walked away. I told my men to set up on the perimeter, and the commander said that wasn't part of the orders. I told him I didn't take orders from him, and that if we knew there were VC coming back into this village, my men were going to wait and meet them. Lieutenant Grayson, the man said like I was a petulant six-year-old, that woman's son disappeared in 1954, when the Vietminh marched against the French at Dien Bien Phu. She's not seen him in eleven years. But every time I visit her, she says he is coming home tomorrow.

Grayson turned his head as if to make sure Bo was listening. Could you wait eleven years for your brother and still feel like you do today?

I don't know, Bo said.

What about you? he said to Ruth. You're young. And pretty.

Maybe I wouldn't, Ruth said.

Wouldn't what? Grayson asked.

Ever feel like I've waited too long.

You might. When you're old and alone and he's still not come. Or maybe not so old, like my friend Ashley waiting tables down there in town. You just might.

He stood and cracked his neck and went into the house. When he came back out, he held three bottles of Duquesne beer in one hand and a bar blade in the other. He popped the caps off all three bottles and said, Fridge is bare once we drink these, so you best enjoy what little hospitality I have to offer.

He handed one to Bo and one to Ruth and sat back down with his feet pulled up to him and his knees high.

I got to know that commander pretty well, he said as though there had been no break at all in the conversation. Went to French schools in Paris and still referred to his country as Indochina.

He looked over at Ruth. Do you know what Ho Chi Minh's first words were when he stood in the middle of the square in Hanoi in 1945 and addressed his people?

She shook her head.

Of course not. I didn't, either. But they went something like this, according to Captain Nguyen. *All men are created equal, endowed with certain inalienable rights. Life, liberty, and the pursuit of happiness.* He told me that and I said, You're shittin me. And he said, Lieutenant, I shit you not.

Grayson smiled, like he still held a fond memory of the man about whom he had been speaking inside his head and it pleased him to go back for that reason. He took a long swig of beer and held the bottle from the neck by his thumb and forefinger and let it dangle between his knees. Killed in a chopper crash, Captain Nguyen. Going nowhere special. R and R, I think. Just hitching a ride with the army. He always said he hated to fly.

Grayson was quiet then and seemed to remember that he had a beer, and he drank off the rest of the bottle and set the empty down right beside him. He was a believer, though. Like Corporal Konar. That's why I asked your brother to join CAP.

Ruth fidgeted where she sat, and Grayson said, Sorry. He wasn't your brother now, was he?

That's all right, Ruth said, and put her head down.

You drinkin' that beer? he asked her, and she stood and handed it to him and he held the bottle up as if to say thank you.

Ruth sat back down on the deck, and said, What's CAP? Sam mentioned that once in a letter he wrote before he left for his second tour. But then I didn't hear any more about it. And then, well, we didn't hear anything at all.

Combined Action Program, Grayson said. That's what I went back for. That's what I told Corporal Konar he'd be doing if he re-upped. I was assigned to the command structure of a Combined Action Group in Quang Tri, putting rifle squads in local villages to live and work with the Vietnamese. You know, winning hearts and minds. That sort of thing. Let them know that you're not there to call in napalm. And I wanted Konar with me. I put him in charge of one of the squads because he was in the zone for sergeant. And because he had the respect of the other men. November '71 was going to be our last month in-country.

Grayson drank from the beer Ruth had given him, and when he was done he stared out and down at the valley, then spoke in a kind of trance, not moving his eyes left or right.

He told Bo and Ruth that in the last village where Corporal Konar's squad lived, there was a local elder who knew a lot of VC. He had already given Grayson information that had saved more than a few marines' lives, and they had a good rapport, or so he thought. The day when Konar's squad was getting ready to move out, Grayson had come to the village with another CAP squad he had picked up a few miles away. He liked to collect the men when they were coming back, see how they looked and felt in the field and what they had left behind, and he could not believe the camaraderie he saw between Konar's marines and the Vietnamese locals who knew they were there to protect them.

I believed in it, too, then, the war, the program, the certain inalienable rights of those villagers, Grayson said, though he said it slowly and with a snarl so that the hair beneath his lip bristled.

They had been moving only ten minutes when they stepped into the ambush, a classic L-shape, with VC at the base in front of them and another unit at the stem to the side. They did what they always did, concentrate return fire in the direction of the attack and open fire on the stem to try to outflank the enemy. Then Grayson's lieutenant took a round in the head, and Grayson grabbed the radio from the RTO and that marine went down right next to him. He yelled for rapid fire into the brush and could see Corporal Konar out front, could hear him shouting *Tie in left!* over shouts for the corpsman. Grayson started firing, and two quick grenade blasts came from the front and the flank. *Boom. Boom.* Just like that, and he went ass over tin can, deaf as a doorpost, his head ringing like a bell. But he saw movement and told himself to get up in case it was the enemy coming out into the open. He glanced to his right and saw Corporal Konar on one knee and firing short bursts from his rifle. As if he would kneel there all day and fire at the enemy until given the command to cease. Grayson moved his gaze away for five seconds to make sure he had the arms and legs and sorry ass to get back into that fight, then came up with his sidearm, all he had, and when he looked to his right again, Corporal Konar was gone. Like some ghost who had never been there at all.

Bo was not for or against the war. When Sam enlisted in the marines on the same day the charges against him for grand theft auto were dropped, Jozef said, No one in his right mind is in favor of war. What I will never tell a man who would stand up for what he believes in is that what he believes in is not worth dying for. We've all got some reason to die.

When Sam shipped out, Bo and Hannah watched the nightly news, the body counts at the bottom of the screen like the score of a football game, ten-second footage of helicopters flattening out elephant grass and artillery firing into jungles, and then the cut to angry faces of American college kids screaming and shouting to get the hell out of Vietnam.

When Sam came home from that tour, he took the bus to Wilkes-Barre from Camp Lejeune, and he and Bo hung out just like

before, fishing in the morning on the weekends, then heading back for more in the
evening and stopping for beers at the Sunset
when it got dark. Bo never told Sam he was
wrong, and Sam never told Bo what it was
like to feel a mortar blast or to see a man
take a bullet in the neck. He spoke of the
heat and what it was like to ride close over
the jungle in a Huey. Sam's old buddies
came around sometimes, and he would talk
to them but not for long, and when Bo
asked him why one day, he shook his head
and said, I've seen better die on a tripwire.
On the weekends when Sam had leave and
did not come home, Bo knew he was with
Ruth somewhere. But they never talked
about her, and now Bo wished they had. In
August 1970 Sam came home on a week's
leave and, at the dinner table, told Hannah
and Jozef that he had reenlisted for three
more years and requested to have the length
of his rotation reduced so he could go back
to Vietnam for another tour in late September. He had made corporal.

What happened to everyone else? Bo
asked Grayson. He could feel his elbow
starting to throb, and he shifted his own
body as he felt it cramping where he sat,
and he considered the fact that although he
had waited a long time to hear what Gray-

son was telling him, he was not sure anymore if he wanted to know the details of what were likely his brother's last moments on this earth.

Well, fighting like that stops as quick as it starts, Grayson said. You want to talk about ghosts? Fucking VC. We got ourselves rounded up, got Doc working on the wounded as best he could, then looked for a clearing and secured a landing zone. Then I had some of the men who weren't walking wounded come with me to search for your brother. It had started to rain hard, and the ground, red as goddamn blood that ground was, in no time was like a quagmire inside a shit house. We couldn't find anything or anyone. No VC. No bodies. No Konar. Not a sound in that jungle except the sticks we broke on the ground and our boots when we pulled them out of the mud. For the next week I sent what search parties I could, until I just couldn't anymore. Then I wrote my report.

But you told the board he ought to remain carried in a missing status, Ruth said.

Grayson looked at her like he had seen something on her or in her that he had missed before. He took a moment to consider it, then nodded.

Why? she asked.

Whatever it was, Grayson no longer seemed interested in it. He turned his head and looked down at the deck, then back at Ruth. Because I never liked to lose any of my men, he said, sounding angry. Especially the good ones, and he drank off the rest of his beer in three long pulls.

But the board, Ruth persisted, pushing her legs out in front of her as if about to rise and go off in search of Sam herself. They've never found anything else? No reason to say he's in prison, or he was shot dead and left?

Grayson put his head down and stifled a belch. I told you, he said. We gathered the dead. Konar just disappeared.

There was a general ruckus of birds and insects in the woods below them, and the sky was turning as the sun went down. Bo closed his eyes and thought, *I could sleep right here,* and remembered he had a drive in front of him that would likely keep him up past midnight. He had drunk only half his beer, and when he opened his eyes, he saw Grayson staring at him.

Still with us? he said.

Bo nodded.

That's good. He talked about you a lot. Said you knew more than anyone he'd ever met, and he wished he'd had sense enough to stay home and learn every last bit of it from you.

I don't wish he'd stayed, Bo said. I just wish he'd come back.

I wish they all could, Grayson said, and gave the bottle in his right hand a little toss as if to test its weight, then heaved it off the deck so that it spun end over end through the air, spilling dregs of beer as it dropped down into the ravine and out of sight, where it smashed with a muffled *ooff,* and everything was quiet.

CHAPTER FIFTEEN

They drove back down the mountain in the dusk and were only a few miles outside of Abas when the truck would not accelerate, then it stalled and rolled to a stop. Bo called on the CB for a tow, and the wrecker that came took them back to the Phillips 66 station in town and left them in the lot under a lone incandescent light.

They got a room in a small motel next to the diner, and Bo called Hannah and told her the truck had likely seen its last and they would not be home until Tuesday daytime at the earliest. Hannah said she would drive down in the Dart and pick them up, but Bo said they would get a ride back with the flatbed coming the next day for the saw.

The room had two double beds. Bo turned out the overhead light and they each climbed into one with their clothes on. They lay breathing in the dark, and Ruth said,

Thanks, Bo. For bringing me down here.

For a while he just lay and listened to the intermittent traffic outside. Then he said, How did you know I'd swing by this morning?

Hannah told me you might. I was in my room feeling sorry for myself after we left your house, and she knocked on the door and said, *If you knew him like I do, you'd get yourself to bed and get up early, because I'll bet you a laying hen he'll be in that driveway before first light.* I asked her if she'd called you, and she said, *Call him on what? Those tin cans we got strung on wires that stretch through the woods? Go to sleep.* She sure is something, your mom.

She is that, Bo said, and there was another long spell of silence in the room.

It had begun to rain, and cars passed by outside with a hiss of tires that rose and fell along the same arc as the headlights that swept through the blinds and across the back wall of the room as though in search of a fugitive hidden in the dark. Bo could tell in that light she had not closed her eyes.

I wish I could give him back to you, Ruth, he said. Trade places somehow and let you two live out the life you should have had.

She said nothing, but he could hear her breathe, a soft stuttering heave as she tried to regain control of her voice.

We had the life we should have had, she said. I was just thinking — where would I be if you and Hannah hadn't wanted to help me?

Never occurred to us not to, he said.

I can't believe that.

Why?

Because your grandfather took my grandfather's land. And my father shot and killed your father. Any one of those would be a good reason for a family to feud. And I don't remember ever being invited up to your house for a Thanksgiving dinner.

Bo sat up in his bed. Your grandfather sold that land to my grandfather. I'll show you the book that proves it. And I don't believe my father died for any reason other than bad luck. Your father told me himself that he never meant to hurt the man and was sorry his whole life for the way things turned out.

Your mother never once told Sam to stay away from me? she asked, and he could hear the fatigue in her voice.

I don't know what they talked about, Bo said. I know my brother loved you. And my mother knows why now. Seems like, after the summer we just had, none of that past should matter anymore.

He waited for a while, waited for her to say something about that past and the one person left from it who might come back to her, but when he looked over at her bed in another spray of headlights, he saw she was asleep.

In the morning, Bo told the garage mechanic he thought it was the cylinder heads, and the man nodded and went into the service bay and disappeared under the hood of the truck. An hour later he came into the office, where Bo was standing next to a soda machine, and said, You drive that thing from Pennsylvania? Bo said yes, and the man said, Far north?

Around Wilkes-Barre.

The man shook his head. You're lucky you made it to the Maryland state line.

Is it what I said? Bo asked.

Warped sure enough, the man said.

Bo ran his hand through his hair. He glanced outside and could see Ruth tossing stones into the creek water at one end of the bridge.

Can anyone around here shave it down? Bo asked.

The man smiled and let go a stream of tobacco juice out the open office door. Got to send it to Charlestown. Take you some time.

What's the alternative?

Isn't one, if you want to drive it.

What'll you give me for it? Bo asked.

Now, that's an interesting proposition, the man said, and turned his head to look at the truck inside the service bay. What d'ya got in mind?

Five hundred.

Shoot, the man said, and laughed.

Four.

I'll give you two-fifty right now. And a lift to Hollis's, where there's supposed to be a flatbed pickin' up a saw sometime today. Ain't there?

Bo could smell the same stench of stale engine oil and sweat in the garage office. He eyed the man and nodded, then went back outside to see Ruth and tell her what had happened with the truck. She reached down and picked up a stone the size and shape of a large egg, with orange lines of rust running along its circumference, and threw it into a pool at the deep center of the creek.

I'd be sorry to see that truck go, all you've been through with it, she said, and leaned back against the stone parapet of the bridge. I can wait here with you until they fix it. If that's what you want to do.

I don't think it can be fixed anymore. His head was down and he stared at the road. All of this for a saw, he said, when I could have stayed home and done just fine.

She kicked his foot and took his hand. You got more than that, she said. Grayson gave us something. Enough for me, anyhow. She tugged on his arm. Come on, Konar boy. Let's go get your stuff out of that Dodge. I didn't think it was going to make it down here when I got in it back at the farm.

Then why'd you come?

I figured you knew something I didn't.

The man at the garage gave Bo an empty Pennzoil box for his tools and rope and whatnot, then peeled off two hundred and fifty dollars in cash. Bo held it in his hand for a minute, letting his mind go over the possibility of waiting for the parts and coming back to pick up the truck and taking it home to the barn. *Where what?* he thought. *It'll sit and rust and I'll have to buy a new one anyway?* He put the money in his wallet and walked around the truck with his hand brushing against the side of it. He opened and closed the tailgate just to hear the sound of it and looked through the back cab window, then went around to the driver's side and opened that and checked behind the seat and inhaled the smell of the cab as though he might smell the years. Then he closed the door and said, All right. Let's get a bill of sale signed and she's yours.

Bo and Ruth walked back over to the diner and sat down for breakfast and coffee. Ashley came out of the kitchen and pretended not to notice them. Bo called her over to the booth where they sat, and he thanked her for the directions she had given them and told her they had had a good long talk with Grayson.

I know it, she said. Heard about your truck.

Someone from the kitchen yelled, Order up, Ash!, and she nodded and walked off.

She came back a few minutes later with eggs and bacon and coffee, and when they were finished and Bo asked for the check, she said, This one's on Burne. You're all set.

It was just after ten when the tow truck from the garage dropped them off at Hollis's yard. Bo was wondering how they would pass the time on those grounds when the flatbed from the mill pulled in. A kid Bo had hired in the summer was behind the wheel, and Bo asked him how he got down there so fast.

I left last night, he said. Mr. Lamoreaux gave me directions and the keys to the truck, so I just got in and drove. I'd have been here sooner, but I stopped at a rest stop when I started weaving at about four.

Bo cursed under his breath. All right, he said. Let's get that saw loaded and tied down, then. You can sleep on the way home.

They used a pallet jack and ramp to move the saw and got it onto the truck. Hollis helped, but not much. The kid tied it down and covered it with a tarp and secured the corners, and Bo gave Hollis the balance he owed him. Then all three got in the front seat of the flatbed, and Bo pulled out onto the road heading east.

They called Hannah from the mill at seven o'clock that evening, and she drove over in the Dart and took them back to the farm. She had supper for them, and they sat down and ate. Afterward, Bo seemed to cast about for some way of recounting what he had found down there. He told his mother about the fat man and the saw he bought for the mill, the diner, and the way his truck sounded when he tried to turn it over after it had stalled out on the side of the road.

Bo, she said, her tone short. Don't give me the goddamn background stories. I want to know what the captain told you about Sam.

She listened without a word as he told her what Grayson had said about the ambush when they left the village in Quang Tri. Nothing else. He took no more than a few minutes, and when he was done, Hannah turned to look at Ruth as if to check whether Bo had left anything out, but Ruth stared down at the table and said nothing.

Is that it? Hannah asked.

You wanted to know what happened, Bo said. That's what the man getting shot at said happened.

But he saw him? she said. Grayson saw Sam.

Yes.

I don't mean earlier in the morning or when they set out. Or at a distance on the ground.

She said this with some excitement. Not like she was trying to assuage her grief but like she was making a good argument, as if to herself. I mean that the last he knew, Sam was alive. Fighting.

Yes, Bo said again.

Hannah took a sip of her tea and looked disappointed that it had gone cold. She put it down and called Krasna, and when the dog came, she petted her head and said, Let's go outside, girl. Then she stood and turned and went out the front door with the dog.

Bo could hear the slats of the chair creak as she sat down, and he listened for the rumble of the rocker against the wood of the porch, but it never came.

Will she be all right? Ruth asked.

She won't talk to us for a while, Bo said. Don't take it personal. It's just the way she works these things out.

Days?

Maybe. Is that going to bother you?

No.

Bo stood and put on his coat and reached into his pocket. Damn, he said.

What's wrong?

I need to get home and to work in the morning, and I don't have a truck anymore.

Hop in the car, Ruth said. I'll drive you.

That's all right. I can walk. It'll be a nice night for a hike over the mountain. But if you could come by in the morning, I'd appreciate a lift to the mill.

I'll be there bright and early, she said, then leaned in and kissed him on the cheek. That's for yesterday. And today.

He put his head down and said to the floor, I was glad you came. When he looked up again, she was smiling, and he smiled back.

Good night, Bo, she said.

He nodded and put on his hat.

There was no moon up, so it was dark, but he never used a flashlight in the woods because of what it shut out of his peripheral vision. He walked and waited for his eyes to adjust. The smell of rotting apples in the orchard gave way to leaves as he picked up the path and moved away from the reach of the lights on in the kitchen of the house.

He loved the woods in autumn. Decay like a fulcrum on which the seasons sat at level, there seemed more life somehow as the balance began to tilt toward the stillness of winter, and all that lived in those woods knew it. As he began to climb, he thought not of his father but of Sam, how his brother had come to him one day when he was twelve and Bo had already been working at the mill for a few years. Sam asked if he could go with him into the woods the next day, a Saturday. Sam had something he wanted to show his brother. Bo said sure, and they were up early on this same path to this same place when Sam veered away from the rocks and detoured in a half-circle around the base of the ridge and they came into a grove of beech and mountain laurel invisible to anyone walking along the path that went up the mountain.

I want to build a cabin here, he said to Bo. And I need you to help me cut and lift the logs.

It was part fascination with the history of the westward expansion he was learning at school in his sixth-grade class with Mr. Bennett, and part desire to have a fort, a hideout of his own, he told his brother.

You mean a log cabin? Bo asked, and Sam said yes. He figured it could be no harder than building with the Lincoln Logs he used to stack as a boy, but they would be too big to lift by himself once the walls got waist-high. He needed two more strong hands and a chain saw.

No chain saw, Bo told him. Pop'll hear us. Axes and a two-man crosscut.

It was September when they started, the week before Thanksgiving when they were done. It was a nine-by-nine log hut with a door and one window built into one side wall, and they had pitched the roof so there was headroom as they came through the door, though Bo had to stoop some at the back. Every log was cut and notched in the surrounding forest and hauled to the fort and stacked. And when their grandfather wanted to know what the two of them were doing on their Saturdays, Bo said he was helping Sam with a lean-to. A lean-to? Jozef said. You can do better than that, can't you?

The Saturday in November when they nailed the last of the tarpaper shingles to the roof, Bo looked down to see the old man standing in the clearing with his hands behind his back and a leather firewood pouch slung over his shoulder. What's going on in my woods? he asked, and Sam whispered, Oh, shit. Jozef came toward the cabin and inspected the walls, ran his hand along the door that Bo had fashioned and framed at the mill (along with a table that stood inside by the back window and on which they put their lunches and some tools). Then Jozef went through the door and, after a minute, called out, You boys better get in here.

He had put a candle on the table and lit it, then pulled a bottle of Hires root beer out of the pouch along with three highball glasses. We toast babies and new houses, he said to Sam. He pointed to the candle on the table and said, Figured it would be dark in here. Looks like I figured right.

Bo stood in the clearing that night and could just make out what was left of the cabin. Three walls stacked two high. It had remained intact for some years, Bo remembered, until Sam started playing football and then learned to drive, and Jozef took down the log walls with a chain saw one fall, carried the wood by himself back to the farm, and burned it all in the stove over the course of the winter. Bo could see the shadow of leaves piled like drifted snow into the corners of those logs, the hideouts now of mice and smoky shrews. Why his grandfather left those six, Bo never knew.

He heard the whimper of a porcupine somewhere off in the dark, and he walked back out to the path that went to the top of the ridge, where he stopped again and listened to the night. He turned to look over his shoulder as though he might still see the kitchen light on at the farm, see Ruth in the window washing up before she went to sleep, hoping that Hannah would come out of her melancholy sooner rather than later and be grateful for what she had, until he realized he was no better than she was, and he walked on.

At the top of the field, the sky opened to a blanket of stars, and Bo's eyes followed it down to the porch light he had left on. He stood in the wind on the hill for a moment and imagined what it would be like to wake in that house, his house, and see his brother standing where Bo was now, alive and home and coming to greet him, and he set off down the hill.

He went in the door by the kitchen and lifted a lid on the stove. Cold. He took off his coat and rocked the ash in the fire grate and stuffed the box with papers and kindling and lit them. He put a kettle on the gas range, filled the percolator basket with coffee for the morning, and took a mug from the cupboard and some peppermint tea and placed these on the counter. Then he put a log on top of the blaze inside the stove and sat down to wait for the water to boil on the range. He touched his cheek where Ruth had kissed him, then put his elbows on the table and his head in his hands.

When he heard the kettle whistle, he stood to put two more logs in the stove, then took the kettle off the gas fire and poured the water over the tea in the mug and sat down at the table. He needed sleep, and he needed to get back on a routine at the mill.

Good for what ails you, he said out loud, and sipped his tea.

And when he was done, he piled some oak logs into the stove so that it would be warm in the morning when she came. He slid the draft closed and went upstairs to his room, leaving the porch light on and the side door open.

Chapter Sixteen

She measured time now like a whittled stick. The years, months, weeks, and days carved down to a point that she could hold not just in her hand but in two fingers and wonder from where had the knife come that bared this point and the sharpness that could not be made round and dull again. And so it was the hours that she reached for and clung to, the ordinary time, the counting down, the waiting. This she filled with the work of her morning (food, animals, gardens, the house), and in the afternoons she retreated to her room and the Underwood typewriter on her desk.

Years ago — her father and Bo at the mill, Sam in school — Hannah prepared translations from Slovak of an inventor priest named Murgaš for Sister Peter Claver, who was writing a biography of the man. But when the nun was made mother superior of the convent at the college and put aside her studies, Hannah put aside that work, too. Then Sam left for boot camp, and the only letters she wrote were addressed to him. Parris Island. Camp Lejeune. The fleet post office number that found him no matter what jungle he had come out of in the highlands. The ones from Vietnam were the ones for which she waited with fear and then relief, the envelope with FREE written in the right-hand corner. She would take the letter upstairs before Jozef or Bo could see that she had received one, read how much or how little he had been able to write to her (*I am just back from patrol and stealing a minute before the sun's too hot*), see his sweat stains in the ink, rub the paper between her thumb and two fingers so as to touch the dirt he had touched and left hiding in the folds, then sit down at the typewriter again and write back with news that was important to no one save that it came from her. *Chýbaš mi, Sam,* she wrote, because she had taught him what that meant, and it was true. She missed him. Then her closing, like a prayer, the only one she ever wanted answered. *Come home.* Until they told her that he was not coming home, not until they found him, and the letters she wrote after that were to men who sat at desks and typewriters of their own, not a trace of dirt or smudge of sweat on anything they sealed up and sent to her.

The day after Bo and Ruth returned from West Virginia, Hannah came down to breakfast and found eggs and bacon in the warming tray. She ate, and as she was finishing, Ruth pulled up in the Dart and came into the kitchen by the back door.

Bo needed a ride to work, she said, a little out of breath as she hung up her coat.

Hannah nodded. I figured that's where you were. Thanks for making breakfast.

Ruth sat down and poured coffee and asked Hannah if she was all right after yesterday. Hannah said she was and would just need time to let what Bo had told her sink in.

I thought about it all night, she said, shook her head, and rubbed sleep from her eye. Can't you tell?

You look fine, Ruth said.

Well, I don't feel fine. I feel like the first day they told me he went missing. Like I didn't know which was worse. Knowing that I'd get my son back with a flag draped over him? Or not knowing and holding on to some hope that he might still be alive.

She spoke in a level voice bereft of what emotion might be there, and Ruth reached across the table and took her hand and held it. It's only time, Hannah. Everyone tells us it'll all work out in time, but whose time? Bo asked Grayson if we should stop waiting, put up a marker and get on with our lives, and Grayson told us a story about some old Vietnamese woman who waited for her son for eleven years, even when everyone knew he was dead. I don't even know if it was true. But I remember thinking, *You were there and you still can't tell us anything.* I wanted to throw something at him.

Ruth shook her head. She had raised a fire in the Pittston before she left to take Bo to work that morning, and it was getting colder in the room, so she stood and put a log in the stove and then sat down.

When did you stop believing? Hannah asked from across the table, and Ruth looked up, surprised by the question. I mean, Hannah said, when did you decide that he wasn't going to come back?

Ruth shifted in her chair. It was never a matter of belief for me, she said, and turned to look out the window as though she were alone in that room, talking to herself, figuring things out. Nothing any of us believes in would have changed what happened over there.

Her gaze swept down to the floor, where

312

she hoped she would find Krasna and the dog would come to her and nudge her hand, and with that simple touch Ruth Younger could tell Hannah Konar what it was she would have to say one day.

It was always a matter of waiting, Ruth said, and looked up so that their eyes met. And I don't want to wait anymore, Hannah.

Hannah watched the girl and thought of herself sitting there at that age, a mother and a wife whose husband had gone to war, not knowing if or when he would ever return, and she thought, *We are so nearly the same,* and she looked away. I knew something had changed in you when we were on the dock out at the lake, she said. You didn't just sound tired.

Before that, Ruth said. It used to be every corner of Dardan conjured him for me when he left. Not a memory of him but *him,* and I thought that would be how I would keep him with me. But when he came home after his first tour, he had changed. He spoke of wanting to move to California. San Diego, I guess, and I told him I didn't want to live in California. He was a little distant, too. I figured that was the training and the war.

Ruth tilted back her coffee cup and looked

at Hannah and said, Did you know he told you and his grandfather he had reupped before he told me?

It was right here at this table, Hannah said. And when I asked him if anyone else knew, he shook his head. He understood I meant you.

Ruth nodded. My father said he was doing the right thing. But when he left again, I didn't see him where I used to see him. I didn't miss him anymore. I kept writing him letters, same words from the same girl who had the same crush on him, but I could count on one hand the number of letters he wrote back to me. Then he called me in August to see whether I could meet him in Honolulu if he got the leave. Sent me the plane fare and everything. And when I got there, he talked about how things were going to be different, it was clear to him now, and when I asked him what things, he said, *You'll see.* Then he took out a ring, told me he loved me, and asked me to marry him. And it was like he had rematerialized right there. The man I had missed for so long. And just as I was late in October and wondering, *Am I going to have a baby?* the casualty assistance officer and a priest were pulling into the driveway of this house.

Krasna came into the kitchen then, and

the two women watched as she walked over to her bed by the stove and lay down.

I cried for two days straight after Bo came and gave me the news, Ruth said. I stayed in my room and my father brought me food and water and called the hardware store to tell them I had the flu, until I woke up one morning and walked out into the kitchen and he said, *I heard.* I told him I was pregnant, too, and he held me like he would fall down if he let me go. *The Lord gives,* was all he said.

Hannah listened to the clock and thought of her own father's words in those days when she cried for Sam, and she looked at Ruth's hand and said, You don't wear it anymore. The ring.

I lost it in the accident, Ruth said. It was the first thing I reached for when I woke up in the hospital. And when I didn't feel it, that's when I knew.

On a warm Friday afternoon in October, Bo called Father Rovnávaha from the mill and asked if he would like to come fishing at the bend in the morning.

What's the occasion? Rovnávaha asked.

No occasion, Father. I haven't seen you since August, and things are finally settling down for me. I thought I'd do a little fishing one last time this year, in this warm weather, and wondered if you might like to come along. For the old man, let's say.

For the old man, Rovnávaha said. I'd like that, Bo.

Bo was up at five o'clock the next morning, and the priest's Scout pulled into the drive not long after. They sat at the table in the kitchen and had a cup of coffee and Bo poured the rest of the pot into a thermos. Then they walked outside, hiked across the field and into the woods, and had their lines in the water by six.

They split up on the stream. Bo took the faster water up top and fished with a muddler minnow. Father Rovnávaha worked a black ant in a lower pool where brookies were rising to terrestrials. In all this time, from house to stream, they had said no more than five words to each other.

When they knocked off at eleven and sat down on the log near the creek side and drank the rest of the coffee from the thermos, Rovnávaha broke the silence and asked Bo how he had been doing since August, when he and the priest had driven Ruth across the valley back to Dardan.

Bo told him that aside from his trip down to West Virginia, it was all work all the time. And that's not a bad thing, Father, as far as

I'm concerned.

I heard about your truck, the priest said. I like the new one.

I stuck with Dodge, Bo said. It's a stripped-down D100. No radio. No bumper, even. Just a spare tire. I wrote a check for twenty-three hundred dollars and drove it off the lot.

The priest pulled one of his cheroots from his vest pocket and lit it. That's the old man in you.

Some things he taught me stuck, Bo said.

From what I hear of it, the house up there is another one. Hannah tells me it's a beaut now that you're done.

It was a good house from the start, Bo said. The Youngers knew how to do things right in their time, didn't they?

It's what they say, Rovnávaha said, and puffed on his cigar and watched the smoke carry away on the breeze. So what's on your mind, Bo?

Bo looked upstream away from the priest, then back to him. I went down to West Virginia hoping I might hear something about Sam that was more than what's in those letters Hannah gets from a bunch of pencil pushers. I don't know. Something like, *I saw him crawl away,* or *VC carried him off,* or *He's in a prison somewhere and only the locals know about it.* But his commanding officer didn't tell us any of those things. He told Ruth and me that Sam just disappeared. He called him a ghost. No more to go on than that.

Bo stood and walked over to the water and crouched down at the edge. He picked up a mayfly from a stone and came back and held it out to the priest.

Nice little olive, Rovnávaha said. Seems I was using the wrong fly.

Bo launched the ephemera into the air and sat back down on the log beside the priest. How long do we wait for my brother, Padre, before someone says he's dead and we can let him go?

Rovnávaha smoked like a chieftain and considered the question placed before him by this man of whom he was so fond.

That's not for me to tell, Bo. We can press the Navy Department, but they have protocol. I thought this Grayson fellow was part of why Sam's status is still missing.

Bo shook his head. It doesn't matter to him anymore. He's out.

Have you talked to your mother? Rovnávaha asked. She's the one who writes to them every other week.

She'll just keep on writing. What does she get if they type a letter that says, *Corporal*

318

Samuel B. Konar, killed in action, seventh of October 1971? There's no body. No casket. Nothing to tell her she's got her son back.

The priest rubbed his silver goatee and adjusted the tin cloth hat he wore on his head. What do you get out of it? he asked.

Bo kicked at the stones beneath his feet and turned to the priest. It's not for me. It's for Ruth.

I see, Rovnávaha said. That is a conundrum. Only for Ruth Younger? You don't have any interest in the matter whatsoever?

I wouldn't say that.

Well, what would you say, then?

Is this confession?

Not unless you need it.

All right. I want to be with her.

Like man and wife?

Let's not rush it, Padre.

How long have you known?

I don't know. Weeks? Months? The first time I saw her walking down that hill toward my house I knew.

Rovnávaha nodded and stubbed his cigar out on the bark of the log and dropped it on the ground. Bo got up and walked back to the creek side as though he needed some distance.

Listen, Bo, Rovnávaha said. I'm not surprised at all by this, and I doubt Hannah is,

319

either. Your mother and I have watched the two of you all summer, wondering when you'd come around. But just take your time. I say that not as a priest but as your friend. You promise me?

Bo stood by the water, staring into it as though some answer might be floating below the surface. Then he turned and said, All right, Padre.

They broke down their rods and wrapped them in cloths, and Rovnávaha said, It's nice to see Ruth in church with Hannah.

Is that your doing? Bo asked.

I am a man who does the Lord's work, Bo. Not my own.

They go to the cemetery afterward, you know.

They have a lot in common out there, the priest said.

They forded the creek and walked back up the hill through the field, Bo out in front so that he had to stop and look back every twenty yards or so, to make sure Rovnávaha was not tiring, and to show him he was listening as they spoke of the town and the church. Of those who no longer graced the doors of St. Michael the Archangel. Those of another generation who had passed on. And those of this generation who had not found in the church the same peace and meaning their parents had found. Yet the priest said that he would deny there was no longer faith to be found among those whom the devout called fallen away. Grace was given, but faith was an act, and who was to say that God did not have some larger plan for all actions, by young and old, devout and questioning?

At the top of the hill they watched a small herd of deer walk through the clearing and disappear back into the woods. Rovnávaha said, It's beautiful land you've got here, Bo. *The heaven of heaven is the Lord's. But the earth He has given to the children of men.*

One week later, the first Friday of November, Hannah cooked dinner for Ruth and Bo at the farm, and when Bo got up to drive back home, Ruth walked him out to his truck.

When am I going to see you again? she asked him.

Whenever you'd like. Let's go out to Ricketts Glen tomorrow and hike the falls trail. Probably be the last chance to get out there before the winter.

Can't, Ruth said. Hannah's going to teach me how to can red beets.

Why don't you come up for dinner, then? Bring some of those beets.

She said she would and took his hand in both of hers and held it. When he began to pull her in to him, she smiled and let go and watched him as he got into the truck and rolled down the window.

I left you something in your room, he said. To read.

Good night, Bo, she said, and waved, and he backed down the drive.

Before dinner, Hannah had raised the embers in the living room fireplace back to a fire and was sitting down and reading the paper when Ruth came in.

I'll see you in the morning, Hannah, Ruth said.

Is everything all right?

Everything's just fine, she said.

The leather-bound ledger was leaning against the door to her room. She picked it up and found a note inside the front cover that read, *There is no more to it than this. Bo.* The faint smell of wood smoke came up the stairs from the fireplace, and she sat down in a chair she kept by the window, turned on the light, and began to read.

She had been poring over the pages for half an hour, slowly going back and forth over entries, searching Jozef Vinich's spare notes for some clues about her own family, when she came to a bookmark that she knew Bo had put in there. It was the map that Ashley the waitress had drawn of the road up the mountain to Grayson's house. It was placed by the entry that recorded the purchase in 1930 of the house and land at the top of the hill that Jozef Vinich had left to Bo, and she understood now why her father had spoken so rarely and with such disdain for his own father.

She read on through the ledger without stopping. Of the afternoon Becks Konar came to the farm. Of the night Helen Vinich died. Of the day her grandfather went from this world and a family's last hold on their land was lost, Paul Younger's own words recorded there and telling her why she had grown up in a house on the Flats. *I'll be no sharecropper, Vinich.*

At the entry dated March 20, 1951, she read words that she could not decipher. *Bexhet, Boh t'a miluje.* She did not know what they meant, but they sat on the page alone enough for her to believe that the one who had written them was no longer simply recording the externals of his world within the boundaries of lined paper. After that, there were two whole pages left blank, and she thought this a strange sort of emptiness, if not waste, from someone so meticulous about his holdings. Nineteen fifty-nine began at the top of a new page with a string of entries noting that Bo was going off to college in the fall. Sam had shot his first turkey in the open of the meadow. And in December, *Driving to Wilkes-Barre to pick the scholar up at the bus station.* Then, January 1960, *Bo working at the mill.*

She closed the book and placed it on the chest of drawers and lay down on the bed. *No more than this.* But it had told her nothing in the end. So why? For that reason alone? That there was no feud. Not anymore. Not among anyone alive. And that they should get on with their lives. With their life.

And so Bo was not surprised to see her at his door on Saturday.

I thought you were with Hannah all day, he said.

She stood on the porch in her coat and he could tell she had walked there.

I asked her if we could do it another day, Ruth said. There was somewhere I needed to be.

Bo asked her if she wanted to come in, and she said, No, I want to stay out here. I want you to stay out here with me.

They sat on the porch facing the hill, the sun in the late-morning sky, and she took his hand in hers and looked out at the small shoots of wheat.

We have to go slow, she said finally.

We'll take what time we need, he said.

And they sat there on the porch and spoke of what they would do together, where they might travel, but always coming back to the house they knew now belonged to both of them. There were long stretches of time when they sat and said nothing, just watched the sun track across the sky until it looked as though it had perched at the top of the hill, the days shorter, daylight saving time over, and that same herd of deer drifted across it in silhouette.

They went inside and he put a pot of water and a fry pan on the gas range, then gathered up some peppers, onions, and mushrooms and chopped and scraped them into the pan on the stove. He took a leftover pot roast out of the refrigerator and cubed the meat and stirred that into the pan and let the contents simmer. He began poking through a spice rack built into a cubby in the pantry, found what he was looking for, and shook the contents of the entire container into the mix. Then he reached for a bottle of sweet wine, poured a glassful over everything in the pan, and put a lid over it. The water had come to a boil, and he emptied a bag of noodles into it, gave it a stir, and said, A poor man's goulash. The paprika is the secret. We'll be ready in ten.

After supper they sat on the couch Bo had brought over from the house and talked into the evening in front of the fireplace, then said nothing at all for a long stretch when they watched the flames consume the logs, listened to them crack and burn and settle into their bed of embers, until there was nothing but dark outside and Bo asked if Hannah would wonder where she was and if she needed to get back to the farm.

Ruth was quiet and he thought that she might have fallen asleep in the silence, but when he turned to look, she was staring into the embers over which flames flicked intermittent and low, and she leaned back and pulled the blanket they had brought down from the upstairs room around her shoulders.

Hannah knows where I am, she said.

CHAPTER SEVENTEEN

The kitchen smelled of fresh thyme and turkey stew made from the bird Bo had shot at the top of the field two days before Thanksgiving. He had asked Hannah and Ruth if they could come to his house early on the day to help with the meal he was to prepare, and the two women arrived in the Dart at nine o'clock in the morning with baked bread and pumpkin pie, and Krasna in the backseat.

They had coffee together. Bo told his mother that Father Rovnávaha would be over after he said Mass, and Jeff and Angie Lamoreaux would arrive at noon. Then Ruth stood and began cleaning up and putting away dishes and ingredients that Bo had left out. Hannah watched her. She knew where everything went. When Bo stood and walked over to the stove, Hannah could see that the two had a way of moving so as not to hinder the other, yet they never remained at a distance for long, swinging back to each other's side as if some center pulled at them. And perhaps it did.

What can I do, Ruth? Hannah said.

Ruth showed her where there were plates and silver and water glasses on a sideboard, and Hannah set a table in the living room for six. When she was done, she came back into the kitchen and refilled the percolator and watched Krasna pace back and forth in front of the door.

The two of you don't know what to do with yourselves when you're not at the farm, do you? Bo said.

I'll take her for a walk, Hannah said. We'll be back. She put on her coat and boots and called the dog and said, All right, girl, let's go. It's too nice a morning for us to be in here.

Outside, Krasna bolted for the barn and sniffed along the edge of the doors where she knew there would be mice looking for a way into the warmth. Hannah lifted her coat collar and gazed up at the sky. She reached into her pocket for gloves and clicked her tongue twice. Krasna, *pod'me,* she said, and the dog came to her side. The two of them walked through the wet grass to the edge of the field and set off in the direction of the woods.

The sun was getting higher and melting the ground frost so that the earth was soft and slowed Hannah down as she sank into it. The wind made a sound across the field like a distant and constant wave, and she raised her hands and let her palms brush the young wheat as the heads bent away from her. She kept her eye on the back of the old dog, who had seemed more spry to her these past months, more game to get up and move, which Hannah attributed to the attention Ruth had paid the Lab all of August and into the fall.

They reached the edge of the woods and moved into the trees that made up the border and toward the brush that grew along the edge of the creek. The water was low, and she crossed in her Wellingtons along exposed stones near the rapids and came out on the opposite bank, where the old log rested in the gravel and leaves and limbs that had washed up on the high water in the spring.

The wind had not been blocked entirely, but it was quieter in the cover of the woods. The trees stripped bare this late into fall stood like sentries in the mottled silver and greenish-black armor of their bark, and she thought of how she used to walk here in the middle of winter with her father, the two of them on birch snowshoes, and he would stop and make her listen to the sound of those trees in the cold, the pops and groans that punctuated the frozen stillness as they swayed. Loud and startling for the thinness of the air. Then silence. Until the next crack.

When she was a girl, before Becks had come from the old country and stayed, her father took her to the top of Rock Mountain, wanting to show her all of their land. She could see into Dardan and through the pass, so vast had the clear-cutting been of trees for the railroads and the mines. This will be yours, he said to her as they sat on an outcropping of stone like newcomers in an old world. By the time she and Becks walked the same path years later, the land had changed, the forests growing, mountainsides of timber slowly reclaimed. And now when she walked those woods alone or with Krasna, all around it was the forest again, not as tall or as dense as the trees had grown generations before but a forest nevertheless. *It has been that long,* she would think, then stop to look up at the leafless tops of oak and maple and beech, and down at the path she was on, the same path she had always walked on. Although now some sections were overgrown or changed altogether beneath the many years of leaf fall, so that, as she kept on, she had to slow in places and reorient herself before moving in the direction of the creek. When she came to the end of the ridge and hiked down the escarpment at its farthest point, she would move toward the sound of the water, where she would sit alone on the log. She did that again this day.

The sun came down through the bare trees and she left her collar up but opened her coat for the warmth, closed her eyes, and raised her head and felt it on her face. She sat like that until she heard the rustle of brush on the far side of the stream, and when she looked, she saw a bear pawing at the inside of a rotten stump. She stood and the bear sat back on its haunches and sniffed the air. It was black with a brown nose and a white crescent shape on its chest. Hannah sat down again slowly (the water the only thing between them) and looked around to see if there were any signs of cubs wanting to help with a den, or something else that would make a mother less tolerant of another's presence, but the bear was alone, and Hannah thought it likely a traveling male, so she sat as still as she could and waited. The bear turned back to the log and poked its nose at what ants or grubs it found there, licked its paws and snorted, then lumbered away up the hill along the edge of the forest.

Hannah called for Krasna and could see the dog had wandered down into the large stand of white and red pines that grew below the bend, beyond the cattails of the upper creek. Krasna was sniffing around at the floor of needles. Hannah called out to her and again told her to come. The dog kicked up a spray of dirt with a hind paw, turned, and trotted back to Hannah, who was walking in the direction of the escarpment, away from the field. The wind was coming down the hill, so the bear would not have gotten the scent of the dog. And the bear seemed unconcerned enough, so she pointed Krasna toward the cliff side and said, That way, girl.

The rocks at the base of the drop, which held remnants of their orogenic past in the outlines of ancient and fossilized fauna, had been sheared off by time and weather and were larger and harder to walk on in her boots. She looked up at the steep side of the cliff, which had a switchbacked trail cut into it for as long as she could remember, and (for the sake of the dog) decided not to climb but to take the path along the bottom, in the direction of the old hardwood grove, farther away from the bear.

As she walked, she could hear what she imagined was a world of mice and chipmunks and tiny rodents living beneath the leaf fall, and she knew that this was the result of the warm autumn. Out of habit, she looked up for any birds of prey but saw none. The creek and the pines were a good distance behind her, neither one audible any longer. She hiked farther into the section of Vinich land that pushed into the state lands, and she finally reached the grove, a swath of old forest with towering oak and beech that looked primeval in stature and face.

She came to a stop. There was little ground cover but for some crow's-foot and wintergreen, and the area took on a quality of seeming enchantment for her, no different in her middle age than it had when she was a child. The enchantment of some ancient world, unlike the one that surrounded it. An untouched world. She stood looking up at the council of trees among which she was present. Trees so old and independent and in command of what land lay about them that they might have been summoned for advice on what to do with anything that time had placed beyond the grasp of mere humans.

Her father had seen the beauty of these few acres of forest and insisted that if someone before him had preserved them for a reason, he would do the same. Hannah (unlike her father) had never surveyed entirely and on foot the land that now belonged to her. She knew on paper where the boundaries were, and she knew her father had driven iron rods into the ground at various points of intersection with the border, or made distinguishable marks on boundary stones, but she had not gone out and kicked those rods or stood on those stones. *When would I have done that this past year?* she wondered, although the walk itself might have done her good, and she decided that in the spring she would go. Before the snakes came out. Take a day and walk her property alone. Until she did that, she would not know what the men before her had known about this land.

She walked up to a beech and touched its bark and saw what she had placed there years ago with Becks and his knife, below a smooth and nearly indiscernible JV+HP. The initials BK+HV. And she saw the line of all those who had come to that spot, her boys, to record whom they loved in the smooth silver of the majestic beech. BK+AD and SK+RY. Each one clearer, more visceral, in its presence on the tree's skin. Her fingers probed the last of these etchings, wondering when it would heal and grow over and lighten like the rest. Then she stepped away from the tree and let the quiet of the woods engulf her like an absence.

She looked around for the dog and thought she heard a noise. She walked out into a large round patch of moss and stood listening to the air.

Krasna, she called into the stillness.

She saw the black coat flash for a moment in the distance of the grove, the dog's head down, the nose no doubt after something.

Krasna, she yelled louder, and began walking at a trot. But the dog was moving away, and Hannah thought, *She can't hear me. She's found something she won't let go of.*

It unfolded then as though she were a lone spectator before an outdoor stage. The dirt floor beneath. The lack of brush and low-growing trees. The late-morning light. And the way that sound carried on a breeze. She saw the swatch of orange first, saw it rising in the distance like a paper cutout lifted up to take its part in the play. She turned and willed her dog to bark or move, to come back in her direction, but the black coat froze by the log beneath which it had stopped to sniff and paw. The orange cutout lifted its stick and she saw the hunter pushed back hard by the butt of the rifle before she heard the blast, and then the black fur as it jumped and rolled and lay still in the dirt as the report reached her.

She ran waving and shouting toward Krasna and fell to her knees beside the dog. The eyes were glassy, the mouth open so that teeth and gums showed, the shoulder a bloody mass of fur. She heard branches break behind her, the sound of someone bounding with fear and excitement through woods, and she stood up fast and turned.

It was not a boy but nor was it a man, such as she would call a man. He was decked out in hunter's orange from his hat to the vinyl chaps on his trousers, and his face bore patches of unshaved fuzz around white sores of acne across his neck and chin. He held his gun to his chest and stared wide-eyed at Hannah.

You shot my dog! she screamed. What are you doing hunting on this land!

His mouth was open too wide even if he had wanted to speak, and Hannah yelled again at him across the open forest floor that separated them, What are you doing hunting on this land!

She was shaking now, grief and rage growing, and the boy looked at her and down at the lifeless black dog on the ground, and began to walk backward, then turned and ran.

No, you don't, Hannah said. She reached for a stone as he moved faster through the brush, and threw it at him, but it fell short of where he had stood. What faintness of orange she could make out through the trees in the direction of the logging road became a blur through her tears, and she slumped back down on the ground next to the old Lab.

The others who had gathered at Bo's house for Thanksgiving were all before the fire in the living room drinking brandy when Ruth stood and pointed out the window.

Bo. It's Hannah. Something's wrong with Krasna.

Bo stood and saw his mother laboring to carry the dog as she trod from the dirt field onto the grass and stumbled. He bolted through the kitchen and out the door to meet her, took the Lab from her arms and felt the stiff heaviness of the animal, saw the wet and red cheeks of his mother, who had wept the whole way back through the woods without being able to wipe her eyes and face, and said, I've got her, Mom. I've got her now.

Ruth came out of the house right behind

him and held Hannah up so that she would not fall. Bo turned and laid Krasna in Ruth's arms and told her to put the dog on his workbench in the barn, then he walked Hannah into the house and sat her down at the kitchen table in front of the stove.

After camomile tea with a shot of brandy in it, Hannah told them what had happened among the old hardwoods, Krasna running ahead of her, which she was happy the dog was doing now, and then that flash of the hunter, the rifle crack, and the dog dead before Hannah even got to her.

You got a look at him? Bo asked.

I don't know. He ran when he saw what he'd done. I'm so sorry, she said, and put her head down and began to cry again.

Bo looked at Rovnávaha and the priest said, Hannah, let me help you upstairs. You should lie down. Bo is going to talk to the police.

Hannah shook her head. I want to see her again, she said.

Ruth had come back in the house and was standing by the door. She's in the barn, Hannah. I'll take you.

Ruth led her out of the kitchen door, and they walked together across the grass and into the barn, and there lay Krasna on a blanket spread out over the top of Bo's workbench. Hannah stood at a distance at first and stared at the dog so as to take in the entire length of her, then walked toward her and touched her fur, petting her gently, as though unsure it was the right thing to do. She touched the blood at the bullet hole below the shoulder that she knew had gone right through the dog's heart, then she scratched the ears as she had so often in the past.

She turned to see if Ruth was still there.

Sam wanted a dog when Bo went off to college, she said. We'd had a Lab named Duna, but she died the spring before. I asked him who was going to take care of the dog if we got one, and he said, *I will.* Guess who took care of her?

Ruth said, He talked about her all the time. The first letter he ever sent me from boot camp, he wrote, *I miss you more than my dog,* and I thought, *How could he say something like that?* Then that morning I came to your house? The first thing I thought when I got out of the car and she licked my hand was, *This is the dog Sam missed.* And I knew everything was going to be all right.

Hannah stepped back and wiped her eyes. I wish they could have seen each other again.

Ruth nodded but said nothing.

The police came, and Hannah gave what description she could of the hunter and made a statement that his rifle was raised and at his chest when she confronted him. They went into the barn and looked at the dog. Bo guessed it was a thirty-thirty that had killed her, and one of the officers said it could have been anyone within a hundred miles.

The police asked Hannah if she would be available to come down to the station if they called her to identify anyone, and she said she would. An officer who had come in another car and walked into the woods to canvass the grove came back up the hill. He held out an empty shell casing and handed it to one of the cops who had shown up first at the house. Thirty-thirty, he said, and looked at Bo.

You don't post that land, Mrs. Konar? the other policeman asked.

No, we've never put up signs. Never had to.

Well, you might have to now, if you don't want those woods to become the local playground.

They won't, Bo said. Not while I'm living here.

All right, Mr. Konar. But you call us first.

You hear?

I hear you, Bo said.

When Bo and Hannah went back into the house, the others were sitting at the table and passing around the bread Hannah and Ruth had brought.

Bo said, I'm sorry, everyone. It hasn't been much of a Thanksgiving.

Don't worry about us, Rovnávaha said. What do you and Hannah need right now?

Bo did not have to look at his mother to know what she wanted done. We have to bury her, he said. Back at the farm.

In the orchard, Hannah said.

Then that's what we'll do, Rovnávaha said. There's plenty of daylight still, and we have the hands. We can eat afterward.

It was getting dark when Bo threw the last shovelful of dirt onto the mounded grave that he and Jeff and the priest had dug beneath a crabapple tree at the far edge of the orchard, and into which Hannah and Ruth had lowered Krasna with a bedsheet. Rovnávaha said a blessing for the animals and asked Saint Francis to pray for all living things, and then they walked in a line across the orchard and went inside Hannah's house. Ruth heated the stew she had brought back in a pot from Bo's. Angie Lamoreaux sliced another loaf of bread, and

341

Jeff opened the bottles of Rovnávaha's wine and filled the glasses set around the table in the kitchen.

And they sat there, eating, drinking, and talking, all six of them, each with stories about his or her first encounter with the black Lab they called *Beautiful* in Slovak, then with memories of all the animals that had lived on that farm. Duna years ago. Goats that once roamed the grounds. Horses they kept when Becks was alive, especially Pushkin, his favorite. The chickens Hannah bought from Virgil each year and raised. Ruth sat next to Bo, her hand folded into his beneath the table. And when the chimes for eleven echoed down the hall from the clock in the living room, there was a long silence during which it seemed time had become once again a reminder that there were days ahead of them, and each one stood and said goodbye until the kitchen was empty of all but Hannah, Bo, and Ruth, and they sat until the dark settled and the stove burned down, and not one of them moved, too tired were they even for sleep.

CHAPTER EIGHTEEN

Christmas eve fell on a Sunday that year. Bo and Ruth woke early and took a saw and a hatchet from the barn and went across the field and into the woods in search of a tree for Hannah. The temperature, warm all month, dropped below freezing that night and there was the smell of coming snow in the air. They hiked in wool field jackets and wore gloves for the work. They found a balsam fir that Bo said he had been eyeing for some time, and he notched the tree trunk on the side he wanted it to drop, then he put the saw to it and the fir leaned and fell in a soft hush onto the ground. He took the hatchet from a holster around his waist and gave the base of the tree a *thwap,* and it separated from the stump.

Timber, he said.

Ruth shook some dead twigs and a few needles out of the top, and Bo wrapped a plastic bag around the trunk end where the sap was running and made a loop with a small piece of rope that he slid over the bag and used as a handle to carry the tree. Ruth took the front, and they walked out of the woods back up the hill with the fir, cinched it down into the bed of the truck, and drove over to the farm.

Hannah was waiting in the kitchen with coffee, and after Bo and Ruth had placed the tree in a stand and stood it in the living room across from the fireplace, they sat down and talked about the weather and the storm that was forecast. Bo wondered out loud if folks would make it for dinner that night, and Hannah said, It's never stopped anyone in the fifty years I've been alive.

She spoke about the news she had heard on television the night before, the bombings that had been going on in North Vietnam, and she said it was a shame Nixon had to do that on Christmas.

The whole damn thing's a shame, Mom, Bo said, and knelt down to lay a fire in the fireplace.

It was nine-forty-five by the clock on the wall, and Hannah stood and said, Well, I'm going to church. I'll leave you two to decorate this tree. There's plenty of food and coffee in the kitchen.

She walked over to her son and put her

hand on his shoulder and said, It's nice to see you not running off to the mill for a change. Then she went into the foyer and took her coat from the rack.

Take my truck, Mom, Bo said. He tossed her the keys and she went out by the front door.

When she had driven away, Bo and Ruth rummaged through boxes on the floor for lights and strung those on the tree from top to bottom. Bo rested an alabaster angel at the tip of the tree around the first three lights, and when he plugged them in, the angel glowed with a soft nimbus. Ruth opened boxes of ornaments, some that had been made by the boys years ago in school or with their grandfather out of pinecones, wood scraps, rounded-down glass, and tree bark dipped in shellac, so that she studied them and tried to attach the boy and the age before asking Bo if she had gotten it right, and she often had. Then she placed them on the tree, and when it looked something close to decorated, Bo stepped back and looked at the clock. I need your help with something, he said.

They walked outside and through the orchard, the air damp and colder now, though it was late morning.

Bo said, It's really supposed to come down

tonight. A foot, maybe.

Finally some winter, Ruth said.

When they got to the shop, Bo turned on the light and he and Ruth went to the back, where he pulled off the bedsheet that covered the hutch he had made in the summer. Hannah's Christmas present, he said.

Ruth approached and ran her fingertips across the hard sheen of varnish. It's beautiful, she said.

I hope she likes it.

She'll love it. You sure we can carry it out of here?

Bo pointed to a corner of the shop, and said, I brought that hand truck over from the mill. That'll get us to the front porch. If we take the drawers out when we get there, we should be able to lift it up the stairs. Ruth made a muscle with her fist and arm like a strongman at a fair. Bo squeezed her bicep between his thumb and fingers, and said, Yep, that'll do.

He padded the hutch with cardboard at the exposed surfaces and corner points, then rocked the nose of the truck under and wheeled it through the door of the shop and down the drive to the front of the house. They took the drawers out and put them on the porch, then lifted the hutch up the steps. Inside, they set it in a corner of the foyer where Bo had measured it to fit when he first drew up his plans. They took the padding off and put the drawers back in, and Bo dusted the top and sides with a soft cloth. Then he opened one of the drawers and placed inside a white card that read, *To Hannah — Veselé Vianoce!* and left the drawer open.

Ruth stepped back and eyed the piece from every side. It looks like it's always been there, she said.

Bo nodded. It does, if I do say so.

She crossed her arms at her chest and glanced outside through the glass door. Starting to snow, she said.

Feels like it. Let's keep that fire going. For Hannah.

They went into the living room, and Ruth walked over to the fireplace and moved the screen and placed a log on the embers, then knelt down on the stone in front of the hearth. Bo sat in the chair across from her and said, I see you do that, and take care of those chickens, and move around next to Hannah like the two of you are sisters, and I think the same thing. *It's like she's always been here.*

Ruth gave a small laugh. You make it sound like I do more than the two of you.

As much, Bo said. That's what I mean.

She stared back into the fire. Mr. Lavendusky asked me if I wanted to come back to work at the hardware store in the New Year.

What did you tell him?

That I would.

Good. You ought to.

She took an iron poker from the fireset and pushed apart two logs that were close and smoldering, watched them catch, and remained kneeling on the floor.

Wait there for a second, Bo said. I've got something for you, too. I was going to give it to you tomorrow but — Well, hang on.

He went into the foyer where his coat hung on the rack, and he took a long thin box from the pocket and walked back into the living room. She stood and turned to face him, and he handed her the box.

You had this on you while we were cutting down that tree? she asked.

I kept trying not to move funny so that you wouldn't see it. Go ahead. Open it.

She lifted the lid and unfolded a piece of red flannel. Inside was a small polished silver spoon.

I found it behind the sink in the old kitchen, he said.

She cradled the spoon in her hand, then turned it over and paused on the silver mark. BK was Bartley Kelleher, she said.

My great-great-grandfather.

I know. Rovnávaha told me. The day we brought you here.

She pressed her thumb into the mark and studied the impression, then pressed her thumb into it again, as though it were only a matter of time before the letters disappeared. She shook her head, wrapped the spoon back up in the flannel, and said, Thank you, Bo. I used to think the hardest thing about last summer was coming out of that flood with nothing left. But I don't feel that so much anymore.

Well, I hope this helps, he said.

It helps.

She leaned into him and buried her face in his shirt. He pulled her in closer and felt her breathe. She raised her hands to his shoulders and lifted her head up, as though there was something more she wanted to say, but she just gazed at him, a sadness in her eyes (it seemed to Bo) like so much of the sadness to which she could already lay claim. He stroked the hair that fell down the back of her neck and smelled his shampoo in it from her morning bath, and he stared down into the flames of the fire in the fireplace behind her and watched them burn.

■ ■ ■ ■

They gathered for the *velija* feast that evening at six o'clock in a slow parade to the door. First Rovnávaha, who brought wine and brandy and said he would have to leave early to prepare for the vigil Mass at midnight (though he always stayed to the end, so that midnight Mass at St. Michael the Archangel began each Christmas Eve at five minutes after twelve), then Jeff Lamoreaux and his wife, Angie, who carried the black-forest cake she baked every year. They brushed snow from their coats and came inside, and Hannah greeted them as though expecting more. Six seemed like too little to her, and she wondered if there was anyone she had forgotten, someone who might be alone on this night, someone she might offer a seat at her table, but she knew there was no one. Even Aunt Sue had wanted to stay in Brookside with the Posols now that Jozef was gone, and as she said to Hannah, You don't need an old lady underfoot. Hannah thought she felt Krasna push past her, and her hand moved to pet the dog's head, but it touched nothing. It was just the wind against her pant leg. She closed the door.

They sat down at a table set with a white

tablecloth, under which there rested lumps of straw in the middle, with one candle burning and seven place settings, the empty one at the head. Dinner began with grace and the blessing of the *oplatky* wafers, which everyone ate with honey, and a toast of white wine that the priest gave, after a blessing of the food and a moment of silence to remember all those who had gone before them that year.

Though they were few, Hannah made it a feast nevertheless. She served sour mushroom soup, potatoes, cabbage rolls stuffed with rice, prune *pirohy,* and trout broiled whole and stuffed with lemon and sage. She apologized for not having the traditional twelve courses, but said anyone wanting to make that up in brandy after the meal was more than welcome. Father Rovnávaha said, Amen. And drank off his wine. Then everyone around the table tucked in to the feast.

The conversations that arose did not range widely. They avoided talk about the flood and the war and instead asked Ruth about her chickens and Bo about the direction of the mill in the New Year. Hannah said little and watched and listened to her guests. The gregarious priest. The shy and thoughtful mill supervisor who seemed downright blushing in the presence of his wife of fifteen years who still did not look a day over twenty. Bo, who sat closest to the empty place setting that they had put out last year, too, and who kept moving his arm to touch the side of the plate as he talked with Angie and Father Rovnávaha about Nixon's victory over McGovern, how he had never liked the president much, though he could not say why. It was Ruth, though, who seemed to Hannah the youngest and the oldest one there. Ruth, who had lost in one day that year more than anyone at the table would lose in a lifetime. And yet there was a radiance to her face (her hair tied back to reveal eyes moss-colored and wet, as though she had just come back from a place where she had been crying), and Hannah wished in her heart that she would not be left alone there in the house in the New Year. But she saw now the way Ruth and Bo looked at each other, and thought, *Why shouldn't they?* There was more life left in the two of them yet. She was lucky — blessed, Father Rovnávaha would say — to be able to see one of her sons with this beautiful young woman whom the Lord in some mysterious way had taken by the hand and led through loss in order to sit at this table on this day. It was the *velija* feast. The last moments of Advent. The waiting nearly over. And here there was beauty, still, in those who remained in these hours with her.

It was eleven-thirty by the time the meal was over. Father Rovnávaha had gone to the church, and Jeff and Angie lingered on the porch in the light and spoke romantically of the snow. How they had missed it until now and hoped that it was the harbinger of a good winter.

Good snow year is a good spring year, Jeff said, and tapped a cigarette from a pack and lit it. Bo thanked him for checking on the mill earlier in the day, and Jeff blew a stream of smoke into the porch light and said, All tucked away. That new saw's working out pretty good. We're going to need a new kiln, though.

Bo agreed and pointed at Jeff's cigarette. Still trying to quit those things?

He can't, Angie said. Promised me he'd get down to two a day, and this is his third that I know of.

Ah, hell, Jeff said. So I had one over at the mill. I was just sitting there on the edge of the woods, thinking about how much I like it here, Bo. How lucky I feel to have found your grandpa and this place.

He took Bo's hand to shake it, and Bo said, Don't go getting all misty on me now, partner. There's a lot more we got to do over there.

They said their goodbyes for the night and Bo went back inside, where Ruth and Hannah stood in the foyer with their overcoats on. Hannah handed Bo his coat and they walked out onto the porch, down the steps, and climbed into the cab of the truck, Ruth next to Bo and Hannah by the passenger window.

He took his time driving down the hill in the snow and made the right turn at the feed mill by the old railroad bed that led into Dardan Center. Hannah spoke of a Christmas Eve past when she was a girl and nearly two feet of snow fell between the time Father Blok arrived for dinner and when he got up to leave. And that snow was on top of another twelve inches that had fallen during the day.

She said, Papa picked Blok up at the rectory in a Ford he had back then and told him not to worry about getting to Mass. He could get through anything with that truck. But when the time came, they couldn't even get down the drive. Papa backed out of the barn and the truck wouldn't budge, the snow was so deep. I called the rectory but there was no answer, and old Blok kept insisting he had to get back to St. Michael's for Mass and he would walk if he had to. So Papa said, *Look here, Father,* and gave him a pair of wooden skis he had bought from a man in Dingmans Ferry, and that priest set off down the mountain like he had known how to ski all his life, and he might have. Midnight Mass started at twelve-fifteen that year, but Father Blok was there for the fifty or so people in Dardan who got themselves to church that night.

Ruth laughed at the story and put her head on Bo's shoulder, then lifted it off. He closed his eyes and opened them and thought, *I'd go to church every Sunday and Christmas Day, too, if she asked me.*

At the lights, where Center Street rose up the hill to the other side of town, Bo saw red flashers in his rearview mirror and heard a siren begin its low wail, then build until it was high and clear. He steered toward the snow berm the plows had made and slowed to let the fire truck pass. He saw a Dardan police car and another fire truck following the first one, so he pulled over and stopped.

Of all the nights, Hannah said.

Bo just sat there and looked out at the road and the snow. He did not know why, but he thought of his grandfather all of a sudden, the two of them in the kitchen by the stove, the old man telling Bo about his trek as a soldier almost a lifetime ago through mountains that lured and threatened him like an enemy exacting and ready to forgive in equal measure. Falling, Bo said, as though to himself.

Ruth and Hannah both turned. What's that? Hannah asked and bent forward in the cab.

The snow, he said. It's really falling. We'll be buried by tomorrow.

Well, we're almost there, Hannah said. Father Rovnávaha will be wondering where we are.

I know, Bo said. And he put the truck in gear.

At two o'clock on Christmas morning he pulled into the driveway of his house, walked through the snow that had drifted onto the porch, and went inside by the kitchen door. The stove was still warm, and he slid the vents open for a draft and placed kindling and some smaller logs on the embers and let them catch, then he went over to the thermostat on the wall and turned up the heat so that his bedroom would not be so cold. He sat down at the kitchen table while the house warmed and looked out into the early-morning dark, where only snowflakes against the windowpanes were visible. He could use some tea, he thought, and he could also get to sleep. He stood and placed another log in the stove, watched the flames and adjusted the draft, and sat back down. He slipped off his boots and kicked them in the direction of the door and thought again of tea, then he put his head down on his arms and fell asleep.

He was on the porch with Ruth, the two of them sitting next to each other, the sun bright above them, the day warm, the field green with high wheat. They did not speak. He was surveying the hill, gazing out at a vastness that seemed to stretch farther than he remembered. Or was he looking for something? Waiting. The same herd of deer he had always seen moved across the top of the field, and he was wondering why they were out and not bedded down in the cool of the cattails when he saw the figure of a man standing alone against the horizon line. Tall and distinct, in spite of the distance between them. Fear rose in him, but he thought, *No.* He waved to the man, who raised his arm slowly and waved back. Bo turned to Ruth in the chair and said, We have to go to him. And he stood. He looked to see that she had not moved or even spoken, and he said, Ruth? We have to go to him. And still she did not move. He turned away from her and began to walk across the grass, past the barn, and into the field, along the rows of wheat that were so tall they reached past his shoulders and he could not see any farther than one row of stalks in front of him. But he kept walking, feeling the rise of the hill as he did, the sun above, the ground (plowed and fertile) loose at his feet, knowing it was Sam at the top of that hill, his brother, and he was going out to meet him.

ACKNOWLEDGMENTS

This is a work of fiction. Any resemblance of characters or settings in this novel to actual persons or places is purely coincidental. Nevertheless, the author would like to thank the following for their generous help with many of the details that have shaped this novel: Thomas C. Alexander; Florentien and Tomas Bok; Dr. Samuel M. Brown, MD; Ánh Cao; Warren C. Cook; Amelia Dunlop; Mrs. Genevieve Harenza; Stuart D. Hirsch; John T. Krivák; Martin Krivák; Matthew M. Krivák; Thomas P. Krivák; David C. McCallum, S.J.; Carla Krivák Meister; Tom Murray at Rex Lumber in Acton, Massachusetts; Harvey O'Dell; Reverend Leonard O'Malley; Michael Pitre; Mokie Pratt Porter of the Vietnam Veterans of America; Rockler Woodworking in Cambridge, Massachusetts; Natalie Silitch; and Jeffrey Stachnick.

A number of books were consulted for

historical background. Among them were Philip Caputo's *A Rumor of War;* Frances FitzGerald's *Fire in the Lake;* Charles Glass's *The Deserters: A Hidden History of World War II;* Michael Herr's *Dispatches;* Frank Kelly's *Private Kelly;* Fredrik Logevall's *Embers of War: The Fall of an Empire and the Making of America's Vietnam;* Jan Yoors's *Crossing: A Journal of Survival and Resistance in World War II* and *The Gypsies.* The author must also acknowledge use of the Library of Congress's extensive electronic collection of correspondences between service branches and the families of servicemen who were missing or killed in action during the conflict in Vietnam.

Finally, the author is grateful to Kathy Belden and Betsy Lerner for their wise counsel, and, above all, patience.

ABOUT THE AUTHOR

Andrew Krivák is the author of the National Book Award finalist *The Sojourn,* which also won the Dayton Literary Peace Prize and the Chautauqua Prize. He lives with his wife and three children in Somerville, Massachusetts.